THE GIANT'S SEAT

ALSO BY DAVE BUTLER

The Kidnap Plot: Book 1 in The Extraordinary Journeys of Clockwork Charlie

2

THE EXTRAORDINARY JOURNEYS OF CLOCKWORK CHARLIE

THE GIANT'S SEAT

DAVE BUTLER

ALFRED A. KNOPF
NEW YORK

THIS IS A BORZOI BOOK PUBLISHED BY ALFRED A. KNOPF

Visit us on the Web! randomhousekids.com

Educators and librarians, for a variety of teaching tools, visit us at RHTeachersLibrarians.com

Library of Congress Cataloging-in-Publication Data is available upon request.
ISBN 978-0-553-51299-1 (trade) — ISBN 978-0-553-51301-1 (ebook)

The text of this book is set in 11.5-point Maxime.

Printed in the United States of America
June 2017
10 9 8 7 6 5 4 3 2 1

First Edition

FOR MY PARENTS, DIANE AND DICK BUTLER,
WHOSE LOVE HAS NEVER BEEN IN ANY DOUBT

The Royal Magical Society simply *cannot* engage in more frequent weather manipulation than it already does. The problem is not the society's lack of power, but the fact that after every arcane action to reduce local humidity, or "cloud squeezing," as you call it, there is an equal reaction of dramatic precipitation and winds. Storms, sir. Sudden and violent storms.

—from a speech by Thaumaturge Hugh Rifflestop, Member for Oxfordshire, regarding the Weather Improvement Bill

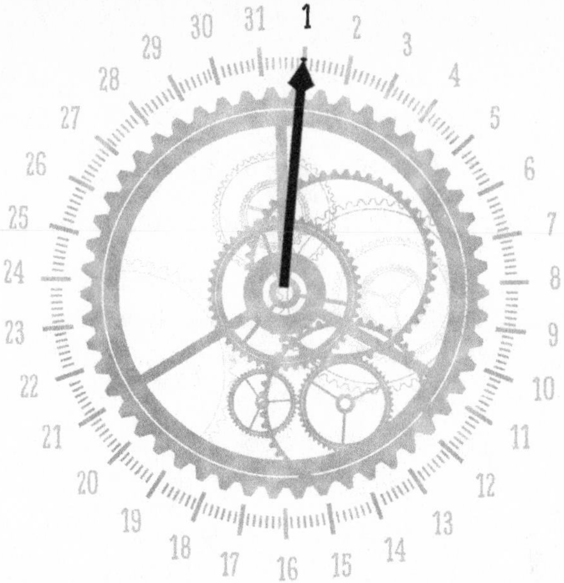

"That cloud's not making me very 'appy," Heaven-Bound Bob said.

"Nor me," added Natalie de Minimis. She flapped her green wings furiously against a sudden gust. The wind rocked the flyer, but Natalie—Gnat—was a pixie and stood only as tall as Charlie's waist. Her wings were strong indeed to keep her in place against the blast of air.

Charlie looked up. All day, their second day out of London, he had watched the bright fields and the dark patches of forest alternate, several hundred feet beneath his shoes. This afternoon, he had seen fewer and fewer fields, and more and more trees.

Bob operated her flyer. It was a pair of wings she had built, stabilized by a belt of clockwork devices called the Articulated Gyroscopes, which fastened across the wings' upper sides. Charlie's father had made the gyroscopes, and the sight of them filled Charlie with both warmth and sorrow.

Had it only been two days since his father had been murdered?

It seemed longer.

Charlie stuck his hand into his coat pocket to touch the two halves of his bap's pipe. The same events that had killed his bap had snapped his bap's smoking pipe in two.

The broken pieces nestled in a tangle of bills. Charlie had taken the money from his father's shop before leaving London, but if he had to choose between the broken pipe and the banknotes, the pipe seemed the greater inheritance.

Bob piloted the flyer and Charlie rode in front. They were each strapped underneath the wings with a leather harness. Ollie hung coiled around Charlie's neck in the form of a smallish yellow-green constrictor. Ollie could be various kinds of snakes, all of which were yellow or yellow-green in color. When he was in his boy form, Ollie had bright red hair and a habitual scowl.

Charlie looked up and saw the cloud. It roiled from horizon to horizon, black, and lightning crackled in its underside. This was bad news for the flyer, but even worse news for Gnat—water would damage her butterfly-like wings.

"Where did that come from?" Charlie could have sworn the horizon had been clear only a minute earlier.

"An' 'ow did it get 'ere so fast?"

"Can we fly over it?" Charlie asked.

"Not likely, my china." Bob was already leaning the nose of the flyer down, beginning to descend. "If you was alone, maybe, but there ain't enough air up top of those clouds for blokes like me an' Ollie to breathe."

"Nor for me." Gnat flew closer in to Charlie, sheltering under the wing of the flyer.

Charlie was careful not to laugh when Bob said *blokes.* Bob talked and dressed and acted like a boy, but she wasn't one, and she had sworn him to secrecy about that fact. Even Ollie didn't know, she'd said.

A spatter of moisture struck Charlie in his face, and the afternoon sun disappeared behind the edge of the cloud. "Maybe we'd better land."

"Indomitably." Bob pushed the flyer into a steeper descent.

Charlie laughed. "Do you mean 'indubitably'?"

Before Bob could answer, the sprinkle of rain turned into a hard hammer of wind. It swelled from below and knocked the flyer nearly straight up. Gnat yelped and clung to Charlie's coat. Ollie squeezed Charlie's neck tight—which would have strangled Bob, but only made Charlie uncomfortable.

Charlie didn't need to breathe. The man he'd known as his bap—his father—was really his inventor, a fact Charlie had only learned in recent days. Charlie's friend Bob, also an inventor and engineer as well as an aeronaut, had taken a small box of spare parts for Charlie from Mr. Pondicherry's shelves before she, Charlie, and the others had left London. That precious cargo hung strapped to the flyer's undercarriage.

“ ’Ang on!” Bob held the loops that controlled the flyer, and Charlie heard her twisting and pulling at both the straps. For a moment, the thundercloud looked as if it were going to spin underneath the craft and become a carpet for their feet, and then the flyer leveled out.

“That’s it, Bob!” Charlie cheered on his friend. “Now bring us down!” The fields had disappeared, and the ground below was one dark tangle of trees.

“Can’t!” Bob grunted. “The flyer’s not answering!”

Charlie twisted around in his straps to look back at the aeronaut. Her face was red and her cheeks puffed out. She grinned when she caught Charlie’s eye, though.

“Is it broken?” Charlie shouted to be heard over the storm, which was getting louder by the second.

“Wind! I reckon we could ’ave Ollie turn back into a lad. The weight would bring us down quick enough!”

Charlie laughed. “May I help?” he said, but it wasn’t really a question. Before Bob could answer, he turned around. Then he unbuckled himself out of the harness and backed up against her so he could grab the straps, too.

Ollie took the occasion to slither off Charlie’s shoulders and onto Bob, disappearing inside the sleeve of her peacoat. Gnat flapped her wings, snapping off droplets of water.

How much rain would it take to damage her wings, and what would happen to Gnat then?

Bob was the aeronaut, but Charlie was the strongest. He was the fastest, too, although feats of speed and strength wound his springs down faster, and if his springs wound all the way down, he would pass out.

"Help me know what to do," he said, and then he followed Bob's motions. Where Bob pulled with her left hand, Charlie pulled with his—only with more strength. Where she squeezed the straps tight, he squeezed them tighter.

The wind was a stampeding bull. Gritting their teeth and putting all their might into it, Charlie and Bob both ground the straps back, pulling down the smaller flaps that made the flyer rise and fall.

"That's it!" Bob cried.

A gigantic column of white lightning, which seemed almost within arm's reach, slammed down past the four friends and shattered trees. Charlie saw a fire spring up, but only out of the corner of his eye, because the wind, stronger from moment to moment, whisked them past.

"Bring us down now," Bob suggested. "Over on that 'ill."

The little bluff was a good choice of landmark, because everything else was just knotted forest, each acre identical as far as Charlie could see. Charlie pulled on the straps and angled down toward the hill.

A clearing marked one side of the hill, like a man going bald only in front. Charlie aimed right for the bare forehead. It showed gray clumps, probably outcroppings of rock, but there was plenty of green, too. He steered for the green, hoping it was a meadow of soft grass. Even with a little luck, it was going to be a rough landing.

The ground came closer. Lightning flashed again; in the white light the rocks on the hill looked like teeth. Gnat gripped Charlie's coat more tightly.

The tops of the trees were only a few yards beneath

Charlie's and Bob's feet, and Charlie guided the flyer, aiming to just drift over the top of the last trees and drop into what he could now see was a wide green meadow with a brook running across it.

Wind shoved the flyer down without warning—

Charlie dipped, and a thick-boled pine loomed in front of him.

"Up!" he yelled. "Higher!"

He and Bob both pulled, and the flyer's nose veered skyward again.

Charlie banged into the tree trunk, let go, and fell.

The collision knocked Gnat free, and Charlie lost track of her. He had one brief glimpse of Bob's dangling feet as she pulled the flyer away from and over the top of the pine tree. She cleared the highest branches, and then the wind wrenched her out of Charlie's sight, too.

He hit the ground hard.

"Bob!" he yelled, but she was gone.

Charlie lay in the mud and grass for only a few seconds, rain splashing into his face, before he scrambled to his feet. He looked at the hill around him, guessed which direction Bob might have gone, and ran.

Charlie moved with a limp because, under Waterloo Station, Bob had pulled a pin from his inner mechanism to use as a lockpick, and since she'd put it back, he had not been quite the same. But the limp didn't slow Charlie down.

The rain sloshed on Charlie's head. He missed his father's John Bull hat, which had been shot off Charlie's head in a milking parlor in London. The water poured through his jacket, and Charlie felt the cold like needles.

He ran to the center of the meadow, where he could see the most sky. Standing on the bank of the little stream, he threw back his head and scanned the clouds and the woods for any sign of Bob, Ollie, and Gnat.

Lightning flashes and distant fire, but not a glimpse of his friends.

"Bob!" he yelled. "Boooooooooob! Gnat!"

Still no sign.

He ran again. He slipped and fell more as the soft black earth turned into soup, and he made up for each fall by pushing himself faster. Down the hill, across a ravine, up another hill to the top of a high chalk cliff with a wide view of a wooded valley below.

No indication of his friends. No flyer in the sky.

He was alone.

But there—a light. Not the orange curtain of a forest on fire, but something smaller and more tidy.

Charlie slid down the face of the chalk, coating himself with the thick, white, claylike earth. At the bottom he rolled, and tumbled through a bramble of thorns.

Jumping to his feet, he found a path. It was wide, rutted by wheels and churned by animals' hooves, and although it wound one direction and then the other, it seemed to go generally toward the light Charlie could still see in the forest.

He resumed running. When the path turned too far to one side, he left it, shattering branches with his face and forearms as he plunged through the woods, only to find himself again on the path as it turned back the other direction.

The first time his leg jerked, Charlie skewed sideways in a slick carpet of pine needles and collided with a tree.

Lying on the ground, he considered his plight. The leg twitch was a sign that his mainspring was nearly unwound. When it unwound completely, Charlie would lose consciousness. Passing out would not be a problem if he were with his friends, who could roll him over onto his belly and wind him up again.

Alone, in a forest, in the middle of nowhere . . . if he lost consciousness, Charlie might never wake up.

Charlie rose, found the faint glimmer again, and walked.

He stepped deliberately. He didn't turn his head, trying to conserve energy. He stuck his hands in his pockets to avoid swinging his arms.

And he found that the bowl of his bap's pipe was missing. He curled his fingers around the lonely stem.

Could he leave Bap's pipe behind?

He had no choice. Stepping carefully, he continued his march.

A second twitch brought Charlie to his knees. He rose to his feet and kept going.

Emerging from a last thin veil of saplings, he found himself at the edge of a small clearing. The road ran along one end of it, and at the other stood three crimson wagons, circled around a small fire pit containing a merry flame.

The wagons had oversized wheels, and even in the darkness

Charlie could see that their trim was all gold-painted. He'd seen such wagons before, in London.

Dwarfs.

He stepped out of the woods and into the center of a circle of dwarf wagons.

The third twitch dropped Charlie face-first into the mud.

Darkness took him.

Dwarf names are reputedly serial numbers, each dwarf in an extended family receiving the number next in order as his personal name. It is unknown whether dwarfs have separate family names or whether each dwarf's number includes a series of digits identifying the dwarf's lineage. Even personal names may be difficult to learn, as dwarfs are reluctant to speak one another's names to outsiders.

—from Reginald St. John Smythson, *Almanack of the Elder Folk and Arcana of Britain and Northern Ireland*, 2nd ed., "Dwarf"

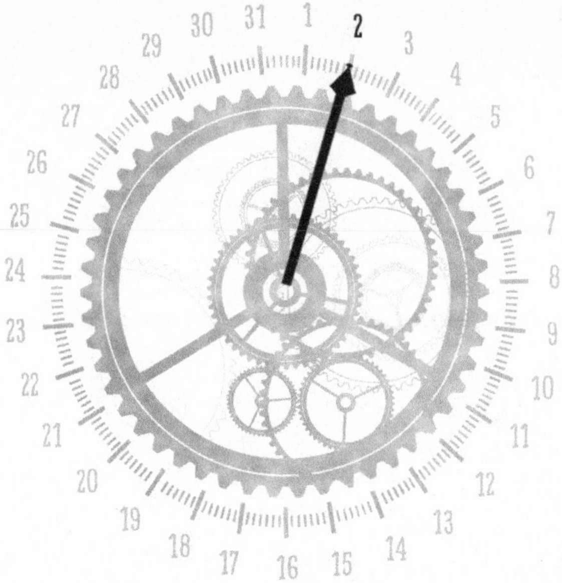

Charlie sat on a stool beside a large stone fireplace, its fire burned down to an orange heap of coals. The coals weren't bright enough to light the entire room, so all Charlie saw was the packed-earth floor in front of the fire, a rocking chair, and a person sitting in the chair.

Charlie's father.

"Bap!" Charlie tried to stand, but he couldn't rise off the stool.

Bap smiled. He had the twinkling eyes Charlie knew, but to Charlie's surprise he wore a red-checked dress and a kitchen apron. "Listen to me, boy." It wasn't Bap's voice. It was a woman's voice, cheerful and twangy, with something metallic in it. Charlie didn't recognize it. "Listen to me."

"I'm here," Charlie said.

"Come to the mountain," lady-voiced Bap said.

"What mountain?" Charlie asked.

Bap pointed into the coals. "I have something I must show you." Bap started wrapping his hands in his apron, and as he did, Charlie noticed the backs of both hands were covered in fur.

"What is it?"

"It's something important, Charlie. Something very important you should know about yourself."

What could that be?

His hands completely wrapped in the apron now, Bap reached toward the coals.

* * *

Charlie opened his eyes.

Had he been *dreaming*? Charlie had never dreamed. Before he could think about it, though, he realized he wasn't alone.

There was a dwarf.

The dwarf was Charlie's height, but thicker. His beard was black and braided in three thick strands down his chest. The braids were interwoven with thin gold wire. Beneath his beard the dwarf wore a sleeveless leather jacket with multiple pockets, and on his head he had a bright crimson scarf. He wore red-and-white-striped trousers tucked into sturdy boots laced up just above his ankles.

The dwarf sat on a boulder and squinted at Charlie. "Praise earth and sky, it's not broken." He was talking to someone behind him, rather than to Charlie.

"Hello," Charlie said. "What's not broken?"

"*You're* not."

"I'm not an *it*."

The dwarf frowned. "Mechanical devices are *its*."

Charlie cringed a little. "My name's Charlie."

"I shall call you Donkey."

"What?"

"My other donkeys have names." The dwarf jerked his thumb over his shoulder, and Charlie saw a little herd of the beasts grazing in the meadow. "There are Bill, Mary, Bess, Jim, Victoria, and Bad Luck John."

It took Charlie a moment to recognize the names, but when he did, he laughed. "You named your donkeys after kings and queens of England?" William, Mary, Elizabeth, James, Victoria, and John, who had been Prince John in the Robin Hood ballads. He had been such a bad king that no king of England since had ever been named John.

"I did." The dwarf nodded. "And someday, if you pull your load without complaint, I may call you Harry."

"But my name's Charlie. And there have been two King Charleses."

"Your name's Donkey. Don't you forget it."

Charlie looked down at himself. He was still filthy with mud and chalk, and he had pine needles, grass, and small branches stuck to his jacket. "Thank you for . . . waking me up."

"I didn't wake you up." The dwarf's stare was cold. "You're not awake. I wound your spring."

"Thank you." Charlie stood. He brushed off the biggest clumps of needles from his coat and the seat of his trousers.

"Can you tell me which way is the road for Cader Idris?" Cader Idris was a mountain in Wales, which was somewhere west of London. Charlie's bap had a friend named Caradog Pritchard who lived on Cader Idris. The Iron Cog, the evil organization that had killed Charlie's father, also wanted revenge on Pritchard. Charlie and his friends had left London to warn the man.

Could Cader Idris also be the mountain that the lady-voiced Bap had been talking about in Charlie's dream?

The dwarf sucked his teeth. "You one of the Old Man's?"

Charlie shook his head. "I beg your pardon?"

The dwarf spat. "You belong to me now, then. You'll get to Cader Idris if and when I take you there, Donkey."

Charlie turned and started to walk away.

"You won't get far," the dwarf called.

Charlie snorted and broke into a run.

He left the three gold-trimmed wagons behind, and the herd of donkeys, and the meadow. With each step he pushed himself faster, and because he knew Wales was somewhere to the west, he ran away from the rising sun. The ground was moist, but the worst of the mud had solidified and the sky overhead was clear.

He had only run a mile when his legs began to twitch.

No!

He ran faster.

"Gnat! Bob! Ollie!" he yelled.

His body stopped working and he pitched forward into unconsciousness again.

* * *

Charlie opened his eyes again and saw the same dwarf. The dwarf was grinning now and chewing on the stem of a long blade of grass. He stood over Charlie, who lay on his back in the path.

"I didn't wind you very much, you see," the dwarf said. "Donkey. And I'm not *going* to wind you very much. I suggest you stay close to the wagons and do exactly as I tell you at all times."

"You're wicked!"

The dwarf folded his arms over his chest. "I found a valuable tool lying on the ground in the forest. That doesn't make me wicked; it makes me lucky."

"I'm a boy."

"You're my donkey. And I'm not in the habit of arguing with donkeys. Now get up."

Charlie stood. He was where he had fallen after running away. The three wagons were lined up in the road, each pulled by two of the donkeys. On the high seat at the front of the first wagon, holding the reins, sat a dwarf who looked very much like the dwarf Charlie was talking to, only his beard was done into two braids and Charlie didn't see any gold wire in it.

"What's your name?" Charlie balled his hands into fists. He wanted to push the dwarf down and run, but he knew he would only stop working again and be caught. He would have to bite his tongue and bide his time. He'd get to a town or his friends would find him.

"You'll address me as Master."

Charlie tightened his fists. "I see."

"You see . . . *what,* Donkey?"

"I see, *Master.*"

"If you must refer to me when speaking to others, you may call me *a certain dwarf.*"

"A . . . certain dwarf?"

The dwarf nodded. "Correct."

Charlie shook his head. "Which dwarf?"

"A *certain* dwarf. Do you hear? If you speak to any other dwarf here, I am *a certain dwarf.*"

"I don't understand."

"You don't have to understand." The dwarf's eyebrows crowded together over a fierce glare. "You just have to do as I tell you."

Charlie shrugged. "*A certain dwarf,* it is."

"Good. Now, we're going to need firewood. I suggest you stay ahead of us and close to the lane. That way, if your spring unwinds, I'll find you easily. If you get stuck out in the middle of the forest and out of sight, it might not be worth my trouble to come after you."

The dwarf stuck two fingers in his mouth and whistled three sharp blasts. The driver of the first wagon snapped his reins, and his donkeys trundled forward. As the wagon moved past, Charlie saw that its back wall consisted of two doors, now latched open. Inside sat a beardless dwarf on a small stool—a woman. Her hair was tied in a long braid down her back, and instead of a leather jacket, she wore a padded doublet, dyed red. She held a knife, and she was carving a forked stick. As she passed, she eyed Charlie from head to toe, but her face showed no expression.

Beside her reclined a tassel-eared cat. It stared at Charlie just as impassively as she did.

The driver's seat of the second wagon held two dwarfs, both with long white hair. The woman drove the team of donkeys and paid Charlie no mind, but the man, who had a short beard and cheeks that shone so red they might have been polished, looked Charlie's way with twinkling eyes and smiled.

The dwarf who wanted to be called Master climbed up into the seat of the third wagon and took the reins. "You'll put the wood you collect in the back of my wagon," he told Charlie. "A certain dwarf will open it for you if you knock."

"I thought *you* were a certain dwarf." Charlie's confusion added to his sense of being alone, lost and trapped.

The dwarf chuckled, a hard sound that made Charlie feel small. "I'm a certain dwarf who can get things done."

He shook the reins, and the last two donkeys shuffled forward, putting the entire caravan on the move.

Charlie stood still for a moment, watching the wagons pull off ahead of him down the track. They were beautiful, all lacquered a matching crimson—the same color as the dwarf's head scarf—and trimmed in gold. There were curious markings, like letters, painted in vertical gold columns up the wagons' corners. The beds of the wagons were long and narrow, but the shingled and arched roofs were wider, so the side walls curved up and out to end in eaves under the rooftops.

From before or behind, the wagons appeared wedge-shaped. Each wagon had multiple shuttered windows and a little iron chimney.

"Clock off," Charlie muttered.

But because he had no choice, he started. He had to trot a little to get ahead of the three wagons, and then he began to forage for wood.

Charlie quickly found that he got the best results by locating large evergreen trees not far from the path. They usually had lower branches that were dead, dry, and easy to snap off. He gathered his first armful of wood and jogged to the back of the caravan. The dwarf who insisted on being addressed as Master nodded as he passed, but didn't say anything.

A certain dwarf? Charlie was baffled.

Charlie knocked on the double doors at the rear of the wagon, and one of them opened. A lady dwarf nodded at him. She had red hair, and although the interior of the cabin was a little dark, Charlie thought she had it done into three braids.

"A certain dwarf told me you'd be knocking," she said.

"A certain dwarf? Do you mean the certain dwarf who can get things done? The . . . master?" Charlie felt humiliated. He didn't want to call anybody his master.

"Give that here." The dwarf leaned forward and took the armload of pine branches from Charlie. Beside her, Charlie saw an iron stove and a wooden box; she stacked the branches neatly into the box. "If you see any dandelion by the side of the path, pull it up and bring it here. Be sure to get the root, mind. A certain dwarf has an upset stomach."

"A certain dwarf?" Charlie hesitated and almost stopped walking. "Do you mean . . . Wait—who has an upset stomach?"

"A certain dwarf who is quite a bit younger than your master." This time she nodded beside her into the darkness of the wagon as she said it.

Charlie peered in and saw a baby.

The baby sat in a frame of leather and springs hanging from the ceiling, so as the wagon rolled, the baby bounced around slightly. The contraption reminded Charlie of the harnesses hanging beneath Bob's flyer, and he tried not to think of his missing friends. The baby wasn't particularly tiny, but it did have fine reddish fuzz on its cheeks and jaws, a baby beard. As Charlie looked, the baby's stomach emitted a loud gurgle.

Charlie didn't really know what to say to a parent, and especially not to a dwarf parent. "He's a sturdy little fellow."

"She's a girl," the dwarf lady told him. "That one's a boy." She nodded again, and deeper in the wagon Charlie saw a small dwarf in short leather trousers and short sleeves. He lay in one of several hammocks that stretched across the broad upper part of the wagon, reading by the light that came in through the slats of a shuttered window. Charlie craned his neck but couldn't see what was printed on the pages.

Below the hammock dozed another tassel-eared cat.

"Oh." Charlie felt awkward.

"Donkey!" called the dwarf who could get things done, and Charlie was grateful for the excuse to withdraw. He jogged around to the front of the wagon. "Get up here a moment," the dwarf said. "Let me give you a half turn."

Charlie climbed onto the high seat and turned his back. His master wound Charlie's mainspring, but only a little bit, and then Charlie hopped down and looked for dandelion.

He found a patch in a sunny little glade just off the track and carefully pulled as much of it as he could before the wagons passed him. The moistness of the earth from the storm helped. Then he trotted back to the rear wagon and knocked again.

Charlie handed the red-haired dwarf the roots. "*The Collins Herbarium* suggests cutting the root into small pieces and roasting it before brewing it into tea."

She cocked her head and looked at him curiously. "*The Collins Herbarium*?"

"It's a book." Charlie shrugged. "I've read a lot of books."

"Thank you." She moved to shut the door again and then stopped. "My name is Yellario," she said. "And the certain dwarf with an upset stomach is Yezi. She would tell you herself, if she could speak."

"I'm Charlie. I mean . . . my master calls me . . . that is, a certain dwarf calls me Donkey. He says that maybe in the future he'll call me Harry. But my bap called me Charlie."

Yellario laughed, a sound like a song. "Thank you." She shut the door.

Charlie nodded at the back of the wagon. Then he jogged around to look for more wood.

*A Recipe for a Certain Pie**
(served in all the best dwarf camps)

12 mice, cooked and shredded
1 handful mushrooms, poisonous
1 pint donkey's milk
1 onion, stolen
salt and pepper, heaps
much monotonous whining about the days of yore

Jostle all ingredients in a wagon until pompous.
Garnish with additional whining and cat dander.

*Cognoscenti of the relevant lore inform us that this questionable delicacy is also called "Tedious Torte."

—*Punch*, Christmas Number, 1886

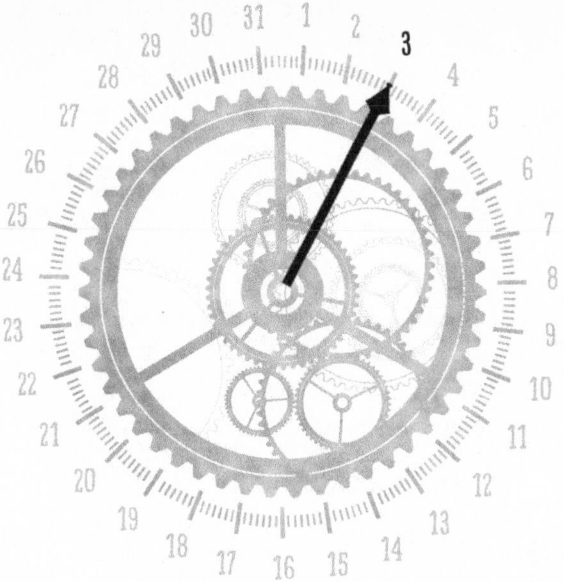

If Charlie stayed ahead of the wagons, the dwarfs would be able to find him in the event his mainspring wound down. The trees immediately beside the track had already been stripped of the best branches, so he turned and walked a few paces into the woods.

Those steps took him out of sight of the dwarfs' wagons, and suddenly he saw a person. The stranger sat on a fallen log, hunched forward, face hidden by a broad black hat. He or she seemed to be writing in a blank book with a fountain pen.

Charlie stopped.

Of course he had known that people wrote books. Someone—Robert Louis Stevenson, one of the Brontë sisters, or Sir Walter Scott, for example—had to sit down and actually write words on a page before a book could come into existence.

And he'd seen his bap writing in ledgers many times, keeping track of work done and amounts billed to clients.

Still, to come across a person in the forest, alone, writing words in an open book . . . it was a magical moment. Charlie felt as if he were in the presence of a creature of fable.

"Hello," he said.

The person looked up; it was a man. He was neither particularly old nor particularly young. Under his broad hat he had a pale face and longish hair that stuck out in all directions. His clothing consisted of a high-collared black jacket, trousers, and boots, not unlike what Charlie himself was wearing. His eyes rolled around, and when they came to rest, they weren't pointing in exactly the same direction. One eye looked at Charlie, but the other aimed off to the side and behind him.

"Hello," said the man. "Shoe duck he?"

Charlie hesitated. Had the man just spoken gibberish? Was he insane? "I beg your pardon?"

"Ah," the man said, shutting his book. "Key see sice. You're English. Well then, how do you do?"

"I don't think I *am* English," Charlie said. "Not *really*. And I'm not doing very well." Had he said too much?

The man smiled. "I'm not English either. I'm come row, a Welshman."

"Come . . . come row?"

The Welshman chuckled. "Spelled *C-Y-M-R-O*. Not an Englishman, not a sice, spelled *S-A-I-S*."

"That's Welsh." Charlie didn't know any languages other than English, but he knew Welsh was the language people spoke in Wales. He also had the vague idea that those same people all herded sheep and ate a lot of cheese.

"I am. Although we don't actually call it that, you know. *Welsh* is an Old English word that means 'foreigner.'"

Charlie's heart lifted. Of course a Welsh person could be anywhere, just as an English person or a Punjabi could, but meeting this Welshman, however odd he was, made Charlie feel that maybe he was close to Wales and the object of his quest.

For the moment, he forgot about firewood.

But he wasn't entirely sure what to say to the man. Should he ask the mysterious writer to wind his mainspring? But in the first place, Charlie wasn't entirely sure *how* to wind his mainspring, since he'd never seen it himself, and in the second, the thought of telling a stranger that he was a device and how he could be wound filled Charlie with dread.

Couldn't this Welshman imprison Charlie just as easily as the dwarfs had? Was Charlie any better off trading one master for another? "I'm sort of a foreigner, too."

The Welshman laughed. "There's a story in there—excellent! Stories are powerful things."

Charlie knew he should be gathering wood and didn't want to anger the dwarfs, but he couldn't help himself. He pointed at the book. "Are you writing a story?"

"A song. Naturally, every song is a story. But I need a song specifically."

"You *need* a song?" Charlie didn't know what to make of that.

The Welshman pointed at a pile of sticks near his feet. The sticks were arranged in layers that alternated directions and left room inside for wadded paper and wood shavings. Charlie knew exactly what such a stack was for because he'd read how to start campfires in one of his bap's books, *A Rambler's Guide to the Lake Country.*

"You see, I know a song," the Welshman said, "and it even has a line that seems as if it ought to work for me: 'Oyer eeoor tea heb dan un a gaia'—which means 'Cold is the house without a fire in winter,' you know. Only I'm singing the line and it doesn't work. So I'm trying to write my own song about lighting a fire instead. A song personal to *me* to light *my* fires."

"Oh." Charlie remembered something he'd read in Smythson's *Almanack.* "Does that mean you're a dewin?" The *Almanack* said that Welsh wizards were called dewins and performed their magic by singing.

"I've given myself away."

"I'm sorry. I don't always have the best manners."

The Welshman grinned. "I'm *trying* to be a dewin." Charlie had pronounced the word *DOO-in,* but apparently it was supposed to be *DAY-win.* "I have some talent on me, but I'm not sure how much. And I know some songs, but I'm not very good at controlling them, or getting them to do a lot."

"Oh." Charlie could have said something similar about himself. He was able to do things, unusual things, but he wasn't really sure how far he could push himself, and he definitely didn't feel in control at the moment.

"But I keep trying because it seems as if . . . well, it seems as if this is my special talent, so I ought to use it, oughtn't I? And oughtn't I to use it to, you know, help others?"

Charlie thought of his bap, who had been kidnapped and whom Charlie had failed to rescue. He nodded.

"You say you're a foreigner, but you sound English enough." He squinted at Charlie. "Indeed, though, you're a bit distinctive-looking. Some kind of elder folk, are you? Gnome, kobold? Maybe you're from Egypt or the Indies? Too tall to be a pixie, no?"

Charlie straightened up. His bap had always slathered him with skin creams when he went outside, to mask the fact that Charlie didn't look quite like a flesh-and-blood boy. The chalk and mud on his skin must have been having the same effect. "Have you seen other pixies? I mean, have you seen a pixie in these woods?"

The dewin shook his head. "Tell me this story of yours, boyo." He opened his book to a new page.

Charlie considered his words carefully. "My name is Charlie Pondicherry. My bap was from the Punjab." And his name, Charlie thought with a pang, was really Singh.

"India!" the Welshman cried. "Land of the treasure-hiding yaksha and the half-bird kinnari."

Charlie nodded. "We lived in London, in Whitechapel, only now . . ." The fact that this wobbly-eyed stranger seemed to know some of the same stories as Bap made the broken pipe stem in Charlie's pocket heavier. "I'm looking for some friends. Two London lads. One of them is named Ollie and wears a bowler hat. He's a ginger. Bob wears a bomber cap.

And they're probably in these woods somewhere." The storm could have blown them a hundred miles away. "Also a fairy, a pixie. Her name is Natalie de Minimis, and she'll be the Baroness of Underthames one day, once she . . . well, the barony was her mother's, but Gnat has to earn the right to take it back. But she will. She's fierce."

As Charlie told the Welshman about himself and his friends, the dewin took notes. He wrote in a fast hand that was large and hard to read. Even granted that Charlie was seeing the words upside down, they all looked like straight lines to him. Was the dewin really writing words at all? And was it Charlie's imagination, or were his eyes rolling in his head as he wrote?

Charlie didn't mention that he was a machine.

"My name is Lloyd Shankin," said the dewin when Charlie had finished. "And I come from a magical spot, which is to say a place of poetry and madness. It's a mountain, a rocky hill called Cader Idris. *Cader* means 'chair,' so that's 'the seat of Idris' in Welsh, you see, Idris being a giant and needing a whole mountain to rest his backside upon. I come from Cader Idris, and I'm on my journey home now. But I haven't seen a bowler hat or a bomber cap in weeks, and I've never in my life seen a pixie. It's said there were pixies once on the Cader, but they've been gone a long time."

Cader Idris! Cader Idris was where Charlie was supposed to find Caradog Pritchard, his bap's friend, and warn him. Did he dare ask about Pritchard? When his bap had repeated to him the name in a tunnel under Waterloo Station, he had accidentally told the man's location to the Iron Cog, the organization from which Raj Pondicherry and Caradog Pritchard had both been on the run. "Did you write in your book about me?"

"Yes, because I can't resist a good story." The dewin sighed. "Though it may be no use. You see, I think what I need are songs that are tied to *me* somehow. To me or to my folk. I suppose, in a way, that's what a folk is: a group of people tied together by stories and songs. So if I sing 'My gen ee thavad thee,' I can sometimes get a spark out of it and make it do something for me, like, say, pacify an agitated ewe, but 'Farewell and adieu to you, Spanish ladies' leaves me cold."

"Because that's an English song."

"That's what I think, boyo. So if you were a dewin, the songs that would probably work best for you would be Punjabi songs. Or maybe songs about London—are Londoners your folk?"

"I don't know," Charlie said. "I'm not sure I have a folk."

The dewin pursed his lips and blew through them softly. "That's a sad thing. If you don't have a folk, you're alone in this world. But don't rush to think it about yourself. Maybe you do have one and you just don't know it. You simply haven't figured out who they are."

"I had my bap," Charlie said. "He . . . he's gone. And there's the queen."

"The queen?" The dewin's face lit up. "Queen Victoria, you mean? Well, that's a grand folk, isn't it, if it includes a queen?" His hand shot across the page, scrawling out more words Charlie couldn't read.

Charlie nodded. "And my friends. They make a strange kind of folk, though. A pixie and two trolls and two chimney sweeps." The trees seemed to have doubled in height, and he felt alone.

"I'll keep an eye out for your friends," Lloyd Shankin said. "Are there hulders with them, then?"

Charlie shook his head. "The hulders stayed in London. Grim Grumblesson—he's one of them—is afraid of heights, so even if he weren't too big for the flyer, he couldn't have come with us. Also, he had business in London. And he and Ingrid, I think they're going to get married."

The dewin laughed as he wrote. "Charlie of Whitechapel, you've lived enough life for three songs, at least. And who knows? Perhaps you and I shall become great friends, and then songs about Charlie Pondicherry will become personal to me, and songs of power."

Charlie decided to take a risk. "Do you know a man named Caradog Pritchard?"

"Caradog Pritchard, is it?" The dewin dropped his pen into the crack of the book and stared at Charlie with a curious expression, craning his neck like a bird. His eyes drifted together, focused on Charlie, and then kept going, until he looked cross-eyed.

It was too late to take the name back, but Charlie did his best to look casual. "He's a friend of my bap. I'm going to see him."

"Is he, then?" The dewin laughed. "Well, boyo, your bap knows some interesting people. Caradog Pritchard is mad."

"Oh." Charlie's shoulders slumped.

"It's the Cader, you see. There are three stories about the Cader. Old stories. Gerald of Wales knew them, and he wrote, what, a thousand years ago."

"Gerald?"

"Indeed. He was a churchman, old Gerald. Wrote one of the first books about Wales, and he said, first of all, the fish swimming in the streams and lakes of the Cader have eyes only on one side of their heads. One eye each, Cader fish. And he also said there's an island in a lake in the high valleys of the Cader that shows up in a different place on every map. That one at least is true." He chuckled. "Mind you, only the English even try putting it on maps anymore. The Welsh know better because we know the island moves."

Cader Idris was beginning to sound like a very odd place. "You said three stories?"

Lloyd Shankin nodded. "The third story is this: you sleep a night on the Cader, and either it makes you mad or it makes you a poet." He leaned forward slowly and winked at Charlie. "Or both."

"Have you . . . slept on the Cader?"

The dewin Lloyd Shankin set his book down and stood. "Caradog Pritchard, that's a name to conjure with. I first heard of him, oh, a decade since, maybe. I suppose he must have come from somewhere else, down from the north, I wager. They're strange up there. Too Welsh, if you know what I mean." Shankin grinned a crooked grin, and his shoulders hunched up around his ears. "Mind you, in the south they're not Welsh enough. I never heard of Pritchard as a boy. But a few years ago, folks around Machine-Town began to talk of the madman Pritchard, who lived alone with the birds up on the top of Cader Idris."

A madman? Charlie's bap wanted him to find and talk to a madman?

Could Shankin be insane? His eyes bulged and spun when he talked about the mountain.

Charlie took a small step back. "Machine-Town?"

"Well, that's what the Sais, the English, call it. It's the town where I lived as a child." The dewin wrung his hands and frowned. "Sad, really. That's time, though. It changes everything, and there's nothing can stop it." He leaned forward. "But listen, Charlie, you're on a journey into Wales, and you've met me in a lonely place. You know what that makes me, don't you?"

Charlie shook his head and stepped back farther. He avoided the dewin's gaze.

"I'm the curious old man at the crossroads, boyo. I'm the toad at the well. I'm the crow perched on the fence, warning you of what's on the other side."

"I don't understand." The dewin was sounding more mad with every sentence, but there was also something convincing about his voice. Charlie half expected to see one-eyed fish swim through the air between the trees around him.

"I mark the beginning of your journey. I point the way forward into your adventure, in which you'll gain great treasures of knowledge." Lloyd Shankin crept forward a step with each phrase, forcing Charlie into a slow retreat. Then, suddenly, the Welshman backed away and grinned, his eyes returning to their usual slightly unfocused stare. "Anyhow, that's the way a storyteller would have it."

"Really?" Charlie asked. "How can you be sure it isn't the other way around?"

"Pardon?"

Charlie felt a little bit pushed, and he wanted to push in turn. He stepped forward, forcing the dewin to back up a pace. "How can you be sure *I* don't mark the beginning of *your* journey? Maybe I point the way for you to go to have an adventure and learn treasures of knowledge."

Lloyd Shankin cocked his head to one side and opened his mouth, but he said nothing.

Charlie heard the dwarf's whistle, a long, sharp blast.

Should he tell Lloyd Shankin he was a prisoner?

But what if the Welshman was mad?

"I'm sorry," he said to the magician. "I've got to go."

For all their visibility on the highways and in the markets of Great Britain, British dwarfs are tight-lipped and clannish. They do not take easily to outsiders. As far as history records, no Englishman has ever managed to learn to speak Dwarfish.

—Smythson, *Almanack*, "Dwarf"

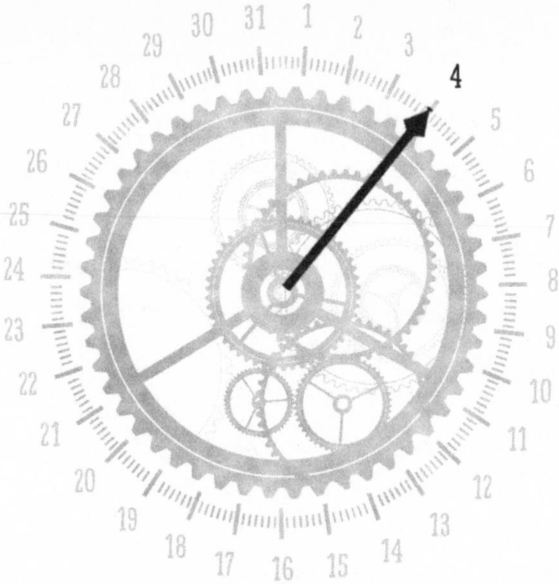

When Charlie came back to the wagons with his third armload of wood, they were stopped. The first wagon was mired in a muddy trough formed where a stream flowed into the track and, rather than flowing over it and continuing on, filled it for several wagon lengths with thick black mud.

The driver of the first wagon was heaving dirt from the forest in front of the wagon wheels with a shovel. The forest soil was only somewhat drier than the mud of the path, so it wasn't helping very much.

The dwarf who could get things done stood in front of the team of donkeys, holding them by their bridles and pulling. He threw his whole back into it and shouted guttural words Charlie didn't understand, with the donkeys' names in the middle of the nonsense. "Chakhta rukho Mary sham! Bill khuffatum yacha!"

The donkeys didn't move. They tried, but the mud sucked at their hooves and at the wagon's wheels, and they made no progress.

The dwarf saw Charlie. "Toss your sticks under the front wheels!" he shouted.

Charlie did as he was told. Then he stepped back and crossed his arms over his chest.

"Go collect more branches, Donkey." The dwarf threw his back again into pulling at the donkey team.

The donkeys all had slightly different coloration, so Charlie knew them by name. Mary and Bill didn't budge. Mary put her head down and seemed to ignore the dwarf pulling her bridle. Bill reared back and made noises that sounded like whimpering.

"I can pull the wagon out of the mud," Charlie said.

"No, you can't."

"I can." Charlie wasn't sure why he was offering to help. After all, this dwarf was his captor.

Only he wasn't really offering to help. In his heart, he wanted to show the dwarfs he was stronger than they were.

Charlie's master stopped pulling and looked at Charlie through narrowed eyes. "You can, can you?"

"You'll have to move the donkeys. And wind me a little more."

The dwarf snorted, but then rubbed his chin thoughtfully. "Not much, though. Another quarter turn."

"Fine." Charlie didn't really know how much that was, because he couldn't wind his own mainspring, which was in the middle of his back. All his life, his bap had wound it while pretending to give Charlie back rubs. Since his bap's death, he'd had his friend Bob to help instead.

Maybe someday he'd get a tool that would let him reach the center of his back. Maybe Bob could help him with that.

Detached from the wagon, the donkeys managed to slosh their way through the mud and out onto the track, though Mary never looked up and Bill didn't stop whimpering until he was on firm footing. Charlie took his shoes and socks off and set them aside, then stepped into the wet spot. Mud squelched between his toes, and mosquitoes buzzed around him.

Charlie grabbed the pole Mary and Bill had been yoked to. It had a crossbar with metal eyes in it, and each donkey got yoked under one side of the bar. "Wind me."

Muttering under his breath, the dwarf sloshed through the mud. He reached under Charlie's coat and wound Charlie a bit. As his mainspring tightened, Charlie felt more energy in his chest and limbs.

"Thank you," he said.

The dwarf frowned.

The dwarf with the shovel stepped back and leaned on his tool. "You sure you're not going to break your new toy, Syz?"

Charlie's master shrugged. "If it breaks, I'll scrounge all the parts. Maybe the Old Man will want them."

Charlie rested the crossbar across his shoulders. The long

pole pressed against his neck and pointed forward. Could he really do it?

He pulled. The wagon inched forward, but not much, and he heard the sucking sound of the mud as it pulled back.

Charlie leaned forward and grunted. He felt his body hum with the effort, and he kicked back against the ground, trying to dislodge the stuck wagon.

The dwarf who could get things done chuckled.

Charlie pushed with all his might. "Pondicherry's of Whitechapel!" he roared, and the wagon rocked free.

The two dwarfs shouted and jumped aside as mud splattered up onto their leather and silk. Charlie staggered forward—and slightly to one side, because of his limp—and the wagon came with him.

He kept roaring as he charged up onto the drier ground and for a dozen steps beyond that, and he was still roaring when he fell facedown onto the dirt. The donkeys' pole fell on top of him and he lost consciousness.

* * *

Charlie opened his eyes with his face in wet dirt. The dwarf who could get things done stepped away from him. He must have been winding Charlie's mainspring.

Charlie dragged himself out from under the pole and climbed to his feet.

Charlie's master looked at him and frowned. "I expect I have to call you Harry now."

"Thank you," Charlie said. He didn't feel grateful, but being called Harry was much better than being called Donkey.

"My name is Syzigon." Syzigon stroked his triple-plaited beard.

The other dwarf laughed. "I'll move the donkeys out of the way so Harry here can pull across the other wagons." He touched two fingers to the silk scarf wrapped around his head. "Atzick."

That sounded like a name, too. Charlie didn't want to introduce himself as Harry, so he just nodded.

Atzick started unhitching Bess and Jim from the second wagon. Bess leaned to her left and bit Jim every chance she had, and Jim brayed constantly. The two older dwarfs sitting in the front of the second wagon waved at Charlie.

"Well, Syzigon," Charlie said. "Better wind me a little more."

"You still call me Master," Syzigon said, but he reached up under Charlie's coat to tighten his mainspring.

Syzigon unhitched his donkeys and led them across. Bad Luck John tried to run away as soon as he was unhitched, but Syzigon had a tight grip on the donkey's bridle, and the escape attempt ended immediately. Victoria seemed to be sleeping until Syzigon tugged her bridle to move her.

Charlie pulled the remaining wagons across more easily because he got a running start on the dry ground before hitting the mud. The other dwarfs said nothing to him as he performed the task, though afterward, when they were again traveling west on the forest track, the old woman sat with Syzigon for a long time on the last wagon. Huddled close together in discussion, they looked up at Charlie as they talked, and Charlie wondered what they were saying.

Charlie gathered firewood.

He saw no more trace of the wild-eyed storytelling dewin Lloyd Shankin. When Charlie had filled the wooden boxes in all three wagons, the sun was low to the horizon before them, and Syzigon blew three sharp whistle blasts to call the wagons to a halt.

As the wagons rolled into a tight circle, every adult sprang into action at once. Astonished by the sudden motion, Charlie sat on a fallen log and watched. Atzick unhitched the donkeys and retethered them to pegs in a thick patch of grass a couple of paces from the wagon. Atzick also hobbled Bad Luck John with a short leather strap around both his front legs, just above the hooves, and he tethered Bess away from the other donkeys. Atzick whistled and laughed as he worked.

The two elders then rearranged the wagon poles, together lifting and attaching each pole to a ring on the side of the wagon before it, to turn the space around the fire into a little blockaded shelter. One seemed to know what the other was about to do before it was done, and the dwarfs touched hands and shoulders often as they worked.

Syzigon took sticks from the wooden box in his wagon, piled them in a careful wigwam within a ring of blackened stones, and lit a fire. Charlie thought of Lloyd Shankin and his efforts to sing a fire into existence. Was the dewin mad? And if he was, had his words about Caradog Pritchard been true? Or had everything he'd said been nonsense? Syzigon's fire building involved no music, just short, efficient actions, and when he struck flint and steel together, he seemed to be *commanding* sparks to come into being.

Yellario emerged from her wagon with two sacks that turned out to contain metal rods. Baby Yezi rode in a sling on her chest. Yellario quickly constructed a spit from the rods, and by the time yellow tongues of flame danced up from Syzigon's fire, a row of birds hung over them, waiting to be roasted. Yellario's arrangement of the birds was beautiful: they were evenly spaced, facing the same direction, and wrapped and stuffed with rosemary and other herbs.

The little boy jumped out of the back of his wagon with a tassel-eared cat, which he led over to the donkeys before unleashing it. He then let a second and a third cat out, one from each wagon. All three cats circled the donkeys slowly, sniffing at the air, and then disappeared into the trees.

The woman dwarf from Atzick's wagon took a small box from her pocket and began walking in circles around the camp, including the space where the donkeys were picketed. Her first circle was walked at a normal pace, but after that she began to shuffle in an irregular, dancing gait. She moved like a bird, ducking her head forward and then throwing it back, and she sang words Charlie couldn't understand. He thought she took pinches of dust from the little box and scattered them every few steps.

He was afraid to ask her what she was doing and even more afraid when she caught him looking and pierced him with a green stare.

"I can stand watch," Charlie offered Syzigon when the smell of roasting bird filled the air and the dwarfs began to sit.

Syzigon chuckled. "You mean I should wind you all the way

so you can stay up all night and keep us safe from harm? And you promise you won't run away, don't you, Harry?"

Charlie hung his head.

"I won't be winding you any more tonight," Syzigon said. "I suggest you lie under my wagon. You'll be safe there, and I'll know where to find you in the morning. You wander off somewhere and shut down, there's no guarantee we don't leave you."

Charlie crawled under the wagon. It was cold, but he could stand it, and besides, he knew he would lose consciousness before long.

"You want some chicken?" a tiny voice at his ear said.

Charlie turned his head and saw the young dwarf boy from that morning. He was squatting, his head barely beneath the bed of the wagon, and holding a roasted bird's leg in his hands.

"Hello, I'm Charlie."

"A certain dwarf who is my father says you're Harry," the little boy said. "But you can be Charlie to me. I'm Aldrix. And a certain dwarf who is my mother says I can offer you a little chicken if you like. She doesn't think it will hurt you."

Charlie shook his head. "I don't need to eat. But thank you."

Aldrix shrugged and sank his own teeth into the chicken. "That's a good trick, Charlie," he said between mouthfuls. "I need to eat a lot."

"I'm . . . I'm different," Charlie said.

"You're a machine," Aldrix said. "That's good. We're going to Machine-Town. Maybe you can meet other machines there."

Wasn't that where the dewin had said he had lived as a child? "Is that where the Old Man is?"

Aldrix shook his head. "Close, though. The Old Man lives in a maze. I've been there."

That didn't clarify anything. "Who's the Old Man, then? Is he a dwarf like you?"

Aldrix considered. "I don't think a certain dwarf who is my father wants me to say too much to you. You're not one of us."

"I'm not?" It was a silly question.

"No, you're more like a tool, or a helper. Like one of the donkeys. Like the Old Man, maybe."

"Why do you talk like that, anyway? I mean, are you not allowed to say your father's name?"

"That's not the right way to do things, saying too many names, is it?" Aldrix licked his fingers. "It might tell somebody outside too much, and that's no good. A dwarf keeps his head down."

Keeping his head down sounded pretty good to Charlie. "And . . . a certain dwarf who is . . . uh, married, I guess, to a certain dwarf man who is . . . uh, not your father . . ."

Aldrix nodded. "A certain dwarf who is my mother's sister."

"Yes. What was she doing? You know, dancing around the wagons."

Aldrix threw the bone into the trees. "You're not one of us, Charlie. But I do like you."

Then he crawled out from under the wagon and joined his family at the fire.

The dwarfs ate mostly in silence, and when they spoke, it

was in the guttural language Charlie didn't understand. They were a folk, weren't they? Not only was Charlie not part of their folk, but he was a tool. A beast of burden.

He watched the dwarfs and the light glinting off their cats' eyes in the forest until he started to twitch.

"O where are you going, my glint-eyed child,
With paws all a-hushing and tail out behind?"
"It's never a mouse I have heavy in mind,
Softly, softly, and wild."

—Francis James Child, *The English and Scottish Popular Ballads, Including Certain Lyrics of Britain's Ancient Folk,* No. 53

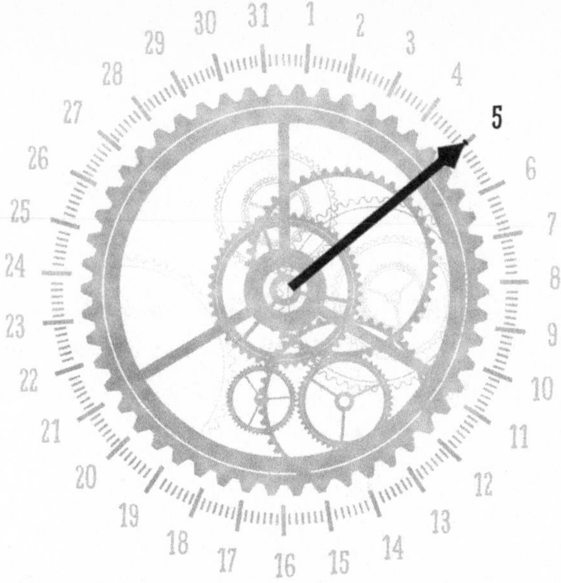

Charlie opened his eyes in the morning to find that he was no longer underneath Syzigon's wagon. All three wagons had been pulled forward and now waited in a line, ready to depart.

Charlie stood.

"A decision has been made," Syzigon announced. "We're taking you to the Old Man."

Charlie nodded. He didn't want to go see the Old Man. He didn't want to find out who the Old Man was. He wanted to stop being used like a pack animal. He wished he had asked Lloyd Shankin for help, mad though the man might have been. He wanted to find his friends and escape.

"Have you seen a flyer in the last two days?" he asked.

"A glider, just big enough for a couple of lads? With a pixie, maybe?"

Syzigon shot Charlie a hard stare.

Charlie shrugged and backed down. It had been worth an attempt. He had spent an awful lot of time unconscious. How else could he know what he'd missed?

"I've wound you a little more than I did yesterday," Syzigon growled. "Don't fool yourself into thinking anything of it. I got tired of winding you so much, and the forest is too big for you to get anywhere on your own."

Atzick jerked a thumb at his own chest and winked at Charlie. "He does the same thing to me, too, Harry."

Being called Harry slightly spoiled what was otherwise a pretty good joke.

At that moment, Charlie heard a loud grinding sound. It came from behind them, the east. Then a whistle blew—*too-whoo*—and a machine rolled into view.

It barreled up the track on enormous India rubber tyres, and it was wide enough to flatten trees on both sides of the track. From its front rose a boxy room with glass windows on all sides. Behind the room stretched a flat deck like the deck of a ship.

Too-whoo!

A man stood inside the boxy room. He appeared to have his hands on a ship's wheel, and as he came into sight, he turned the wheel and pulled a lever down.

The machine shuddered slowly to a halt, ten feet from Syzigon and Charlie. The donkeys brayed, snorted, and scooted sideways to try to get a few feet farther from the vehicle. Bill wept like a baby, and Bad Luck John yanked out his tether and hobbled into the trees.

The man behind the ship's wheel emerged. He was tall and rotund, and he was dressed in a top hat, a frock coat, and high boots, all a dark, glossy green that made him look a little like a fly. He had muttonchop side-whiskers and long hair, and when he removed his top hat to wave it in salute, his hair fluttered in the breeze.

"Hallooooo!" He stepped to the edge of his machine, onto a piece of the deck that jutted out from its main body, and there he threw a long switch. Steam jetted out from around the piece of deck on which he stood, and then it began to descend. Standing and waving his hat, the man rode this small platform down a chain to within six inches of ground level. When his platform stopped moving, he stepped to the ground.

"Hello." Pulling his hat firmly over his ears, he made a beeline for Syzigon. "I'm looking for the dwarf who can get things done."

"This isn't your first time," Syzigon answered. It sounded sort of like a question.

"I know the cat friends." The man eyed the wagons, including the six dwarf faces staring coolly back at him. "My name is William T. Bowen. I'm looking for investors."

Syzigon snorted. "Speculator."

Bowen shook his head. "Incorporator."

"Is there a difference?"

"You injure me. I want to talk to dwarfs, and specifically to dwarfs. Why? Because I think a dwarf is best positioned to understand the value of my invention. A dwarf is best able to know how my customer thinks, which means a dwarf is best suited for making a hefty profit by investing in my company on the ground floor."

Syzigon snorted again. "You've got us wrong. It's kobolds you want."

And then Charlie saw the pin.

There it was, right in broad daylight, on the lapel of the man's frock coat: a pin shaped like a cog. Just like the one the Sinister Man had worn in London—the symbol of the Iron Cog.

Charlie swallowed. At least he was still covered in layers of mud, chalk, and twigs. Hopefully he looked to this man like a really dirty dwarf. Trying not to attract any attention, he casually turned and walked away from Bowen, toward the wagons.

"Aren't you tired of feeding and grooming those donkeys, though?" William T. Bowen pointed at Bad Luck John, who was attempting to hide behind a thick evergreen. Syzigon laughed, and Charlie wondered if he was thinking about feeding and grooming Charlie. "You'll be able to walk away from all that. Live cleaner, travel cheaper, move faster. Thanks to the power of steam."

"What's the *T* stand for?" Syzigon asked. *"Thick?"*

Charlie had the hindmost wagon between him and the Iron Cog man, and he turned and leaned against its wooden side.

"Terrific!" Bowen shot back. "And *thoughtful*! And *timely*!"

"You have an accommodating mother."

"I chose the name myself." Bowen laughed. "As I chose my

line of business, and my partners, and my future! I tell you, it's a bright road ahead, my friend. Dwarfs leaving their donkeys behind and joining the nineteenth century . . . maybe even leading us into the twentieth. You and that cute little certain dwarf of yours riding in style around the countryside in a conveyance capable of maintaining speeds of twenty miles per hour! More than that, you won't need bridges anymore, because, thanks to the Bowen Buoyancy System—patent pending—you'll float right across any river too deep to drive through."

Syzigon snorted.

"As a shareholder, you'll be able to take your dividend in kind. That's right, you'll be able to have a steam-truck yourself, right off the line, as merely the first fruits of your shrewd investment in Bowen Steam and Power." Charlie couldn't see Bowen anymore, but he could hear his voice getting higher and higher pitched as he worked himself toward the climax of his appeal. "And the best part is, because you're getting in now, you'll buy at an astonishingly low share price."

"I was waiting for this part." Syzigon hooked his thumbs into his belt and stood with his feet planted apart. He looked as if a galloping horse couldn't knock him over.

"Five pounds sterling, my friend. Five pounds sterling per share is all ownership of Bowen Steam and Power will cost you, with a minimum investment of one hundred shares."

Charlie expected another snort, or for Syzigon to say something dismissive, but instead there was a long silence.

"I'd like to see inside," Syzigon said.

"Step right this way."

"Harry!"

Charlie hesitated. The Iron Cog had killed his father, murdered him right in front of Charlie only a few days ago, and now Syzigon was demanding Charlie accompany him aboard this steam-truck piloted by an Iron Cog man.

"Harry!"

Charlie had no choice. If he didn't do what Syzigon wanted, the dwarf would simply refuse to wind his mainspring and leave Charlie alone in the forest. Charlie didn't know whether he would rust or rot, but if no one ever saw him again, it didn't really make a difference.

He jammed his hands into the pockets of his trousers, looked down at his shoes, and shuffled out from behind the wagon. He felt tight, from the top of his head to the tips of his toes, ready to punch someone or run away.

"There he is," Syzigon muttered. "Harry, stay with the wagons."

Charlie almost fell over in relief.

Syzigon whistled, and the three tassel-eared cats emerged from the forest. Syzigon followed William T. Bowen to the platform at the edge of the steam-truck. It wasn't large enough to accommodate both men and the cats, so Bowen worked a lever at the bottom to send Syzigon and the cats up first. He squinted suspiciously at Charlie as he did it.

Charlie resisted an urge to run over and strike William T. Bowen in his big stomach. Had the speculator realized Charlie wasn't a dwarf? Did his squinting mean that he recognized

Charlie? But Bowen sent himself up the little elevating platform, and he and Syzigon disappeared.

The doors to the hindmost wagon opened, and Yellario stuck her head out. She looked around as if searching for something else, and then her gaze fell on Charlie. “Where is a certain dwarf?”

Charlie pointed at Bowen’s steam-truck. “A certain dwarf who is your husband is on that steam-truck. I think he’s considering whether he wants one.”

Yellario shook her head. “A certain other dwarf who is my son.”

“Oh!” Charlie looked around. “I don’t know. Is he not in the wagon?”

Yellario said something guttural and violent. “Would I ask you where he is if he were in the wagon, Donkey? He was playing with the sheyala! The cats!”

In the forest, then.

Charlie trotted a few steps into the woods. He was a little nervous as he did so, because he wasn’t sure how much his mainspring was wound. He saw no sign of the boy Aldrix.

He wished he were a tracker. Like the hunter Allan Quatermain in *King Solomon’s Mines,* which he’d read three times. If he were Allan Quatermain, he’d look at the ground and see clear signs of where Aldrix had gone and who he was with and exactly what the boy had eaten that day.

Instead he was Charlie Pondicherry. He looked at the ground and saw scuffed leaves and pine needles, and they told him exactly nothing.

He ventured deeper, trying to follow the scuff marks as far as they went into the forest and then come back. That was sort of like tracking, he thought. If he could cover the maximum possible area into which Aldrix might have gone, surely he'd find the boy.

But he didn't.

And when he had covered the entire area in the woods in which the earth was disturbed, Charlie came back to the track and saw Syzigon and the three cats. The cats lay in a rough circle around the dwarf, licking the backs of their paws.

"So I've seen your steam-truck, Mr. Bowen," Syzigon was saying, "and I understand why you like it. But let me tell you about three more *T*s you may not have considered."

Bowen's smile continued to dominate his face, though the knuckles of his hands, holding his hat before him, were white. "Yes?"

"Tired," Syzigon started. "As in, tired of the constant change. And *tried.* As in, I know my ways and I know they work, because not only are they my ways, they're the ways of my father and his father and his father before him. This steam-truck"—he gestured vaguely—"it'll be gone tomorrow, replaced by something else."

"My dear sir—" Bowen tried to object.

"And lastly, *trust.* As in, I don't trust your device and I don't really trust you. I do business with friends and, earth and sky help me, if I were ever to buy shares in a joint-stock company"—Syzigon snorted—"it would be in the company of a friend. Not a stranger. Not you."

Bowen opened his mouth, but Syzigon silenced him with an upraised hand.

"I see." William T. Bowen quietly put his hat back on his head, nodded, turned, and left.

As the would-be incorporator put his steam-truck into gear and it rumbled forward, Yellario emerged again from the wagon. "Did you find the boy?" She looked at Charlie.

"No," he admitted.

Syzigon's head snapped up. "A certain dwarf my son?" He whistled sharply, and the cats sprang into action. They sniffed about in the forest where Charlie had been. . . .

But they quickly left that patch of trees and circled around to where the steam-truck had idled. When they reached the spot, they stopped and mewed.

Charlie and the two dwarfs looked at the steam-truck vanishing into the trees ahead just in time to see the ladder up to its deck.

Syzigon gasped. "He's on the steam-truck!"

The name Wales does not come from that of a leader called Walo, or from a queen called Gwendolen, as we are wrongly told in Geoffrey of Monmouth's fabulous *History*. . . . It is derived from one of the barbarous words brought in by the Saxons when they seized the kingdom of Britain. In their language the Saxons apply the adjective "vealh" to anything foreign, and, since the Welsh were certainly a people foreign to them, that is what the Saxons called them.

—Gerald of Wales, *The Description of Wales*, Book I, Chapter 7

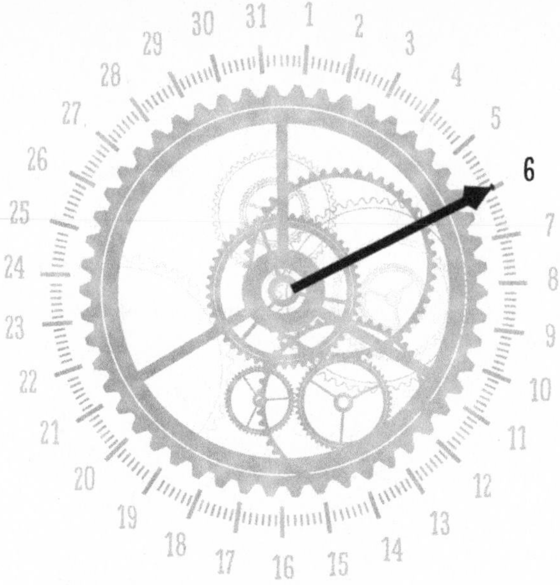

Charlie sprinted after the steam-truck.

Only seconds later, he regretted it. Shouldn't he have waited and asked Syzigon to wind his mainspring? At the best of times, he had no way of knowing how far he could go or how fast. Now he had to assume his mainspring was almost unwound.

So he ran efficiently. No turning his head to look back, no looking to either side—he just willed speed into his legs and rocketed after the retreating incorporator.

It must be a mistake. An accident. Aldrix had climbed into the back of the steam-truck by himself because the big, growling machine was exciting. If nothing criminal had happened, shouldn't Mr. Bowen be happy to return the little boy?

The track grew narrower and twisted a little. Charlie expected Bowen to slow down so he could better negotiate the turns. Instead the man in the top hat accelerated. The steam-truck tore trees from the earth on either side of the track. It bounced several feet off the ground as it ran over the largest of the logs or caromed off the top of boulders too close to the path.

Bowen wasn't slowing down. He knew he had the boy.

He *wanted* to have the boy.

Charlie came within reach, so he jumped. He grabbed the ladder, but the jump was a little more energetic than he'd intended, and he banged against the back of the truck.

He held very still, hoping no one had noticed.

After a few long seconds, he climbed the ladder. At the top, he peered over the deck to scout out the vehicle.

He saw the flat deck itself, which was a crosshatched brass sheet. Two pipes stuck out from it, angling away from the front of the steam-truck, one jetting out black smoke and the other steam. There were several large reach-in crates, apparently built into the surface, and the little house on the front, with its spoked and handled wheel. William T. Bowen stood at the wheel and steered, his bottle-green back turned to Charlie.

But no sign of Aldrix.

An open hatch in the surface of the deck suggested there were chambers inside the steam-truck's body. Just as Charlie pulled himself up onto the deck to sneak toward the hatch, a head came out of it.

A head he knew.

The mustachioed, sneering head of the Sinister Man.

Charlie froze. He only knew a few things about the Sinister Man. He was French. He had been the leader of a group of thugs who had kidnapped Charlie's bap for the Iron Cog. And Charlie's bap had died fighting the Sinister Man in a carriage of the London Eye, an enormous leisure wheel, shot by another of the Frenchman's thugs.

Bap had been shot, and then he'd fallen a great distance onto pavement.

The steam-truck hit a large rock, launching it several feet into the air. Bowen flexed his knees and rode out the bounce; the Sinister Man smacked his face against the deck and cursed.

Charlie fell.

He grabbed for the ladder. His fingers hurt as he stubbed them against metal, and again as the rungs rattled through his grip one after the other. He thought he was about to be left behind, but he caught the last rung in both hands.

His body slammed to the ground.

He wanted to cry out and he wanted to let go. He did neither but held on to the ladder, gritted his teeth, and began the slow process of dragging himself back up. Rocks scraped him, sticks poked his skin, and dirt poured into his pockets by the shovelful. It felt like an hour before he managed to get hands and feet firmly on the ladder.

Now what?

He was unarmed. He was alone. And he might start to twitch at any second.

But Aldrix was unarmed and alone, too, and he was just a

little boy, taken from his parents. He must be terrified, and he was almost certainly in danger.

Charlie climbed the ladder. At the top, he peered over and saw the Sinister Man and William T. Bowen standing in the wheelhouse, looking ahead. From behind, Bowen was a broad green wall and the Frenchman was a thin tower wrapped in a black cape. Charlie wasted no time. With a heave of his arms, he dragged himself onto the deck. He rolled as quietly as he could to his feet, crept forward, and dropped down the hatch.

"It's true, they may not be carrying supplies. But if not, we can always use another litter of the mouse eaters in our service," he heard Bowen say. "Better still if we don't even have to pay these ones." The words made no sense to Charlie, so he kept going.

He tumbled quickly down the stairs and found himself in a short hall with several doors. Light came from globes set into the walls that looked a little like gas sconces, but when Charlie squinted at one, he saw a tiny humanoid figure inside, winged and glowing. The little being burst into a flurry of activity and hummed faintly until Charlie backed away.

"Aldrix!" Charlie counted on the growling of the steamtruck itself and the sound of the countryside being churned into toothpicks and dust to cover his noise.

What was he doing? He had a mission, to get to Cader Idris and warn Caradog Pritchard that the Iron Cog was coming for him. Instead he was now sneaking aboard a vessel that appeared to belong to the Cog, to rescue one of the people who had been holding him prisoner.

He told himself that he was doing it because he had to. If

he didn't rescue the boy, Syzigon would let Charlie wind down and abandon him in the forest. But he knew in his heart it wasn't true, even as he formulated the thought.

He was doing it for the boy.

The boy had brought him chicken and called him Charlie.

And Charlie knew what it was to be alone and afraid.

"Aldrix!" he called again.

This time he was rewarded with a "Murmph!" from underneath the stairs. Charlie peered into the deep shadow there and found the little dwarf boy, tied hand and foot and silenced by a gag in his mouth.

Aldrix definitely hadn't stowed away by accident. He'd been kidnapped.

Charlie hated kidnappers.

"Shut your mouth down there!" The voice came from the deck, and Charlie recognized the French tones of the Sinister Man.

Charlie pressed himself against the wall in a shadowed corner and held still. Peering up the stairwell, he saw the Frenchman's sneer and his eyes searching into the dimmer space belowdecks.

Then the Sinister Man cringed as if he'd been poked. He turned and looked aft, toward the back of the steam-truck, and a stone struck him in the forehead.

"Let my son go!"

Charlie heard the voice and knew it instantly, too: it was the harsh bellow of Syzigon. The Sinister Man staggered back as another stone struck him.

Charlie wondered whether Syzigon was just throwing the

rocks or if he had a sling. And was he riding one of the donkeys? He only wondered for a moment, though, because the Frenchman pulled his long pistol from his belt and stalked toward the back of the steam-truck with murder in his eyes.

Bang!

As the shooting started, Charlie grabbed Aldrix and yanked the gag off the boy's mouth. "Let's get out of here," he whispered. Carefully, so as not to hurt the boy, he ripped the ropes from his wrists and ankles and then set him on his feet. "Is there any door other than that one?"

"No." The little boy's cheeks puffed up and he bit his lower lip.

The truck ran on steam, which meant it burned *something.* "Is there a coal room?" If coal came *in* through some sort of passage, maybe Charlie could take that same passage *out.*

Aldrix only whimpered.

With the boy in tow, Charlie searched. He found a galley, with dishes and food. He found a bunk room, with six beds that folded down from the walls. He found a captain's cabin, with a single bed, shelves, and a desk.

He found the boiler room, with a glowing furnace surrounded by a maze of pipes, some of them red-hot. And there, in a corner, was a big bin full of coal. And above the bin was a trapdoor in the wall. That had to be the way the steam-truck received coal.

Charlie climbed up and pushed the trapdoor. It didn't budge.

He punched it. Nothing.

Scrambling around the room, he found a shovel.

He swung the shovel against the trapdoor with all his might.

Bang!

The inside of the boiler room rang like a bell. The trapdoor still held.

The sound of shooting from above continued.

"Is that man shooting a certain dwarf?" A single tear crept down Aldrix's cheek.

Charlie managed not to laugh at the strange wording. "No," he said. "He's only shooting *at* your father. And he's still shooting because he hasn't hit him yet."

And also because he hadn't heard Charlie's efforts to break out. Or he'd heard the noises and assumed they were caused by something else . . . such as maybe William T. Bowen driving the steam-truck over boulders.

There had to be another exit.

He pushed open the last two doors. The first opened into a storage room, with shelves on all four walls stacked deep with tinned food.

Behind the other was a tiny washroom. The entire room was brass and glass, and there was a drain in the floor. Against the right wall were a washbasin and mirror; sprouting from high in the back wall was a nozzle that Charlie guessed must be for standing under and washing the body; against the left wall was a small metal flush toilet.

At that moment, Charlie's legs both twitched, throwing him to his knees.

"No." He gritted his teeth and pushed himself back onto his feet, mostly leaning on the shovel he still held. "Step away," he warned Aldrix.

The little boy barely had time to scoot back before Charlie swung the shovel against the toilet.

Gong!

He had no time to listen to learn whether he'd been detected. The toilet had budged an inch from the wall, and water was gushing from it. Charlie wedged his shovel between the toilet bowl and the wall as tightly as he could. His legs shook violently as he braced himself, threw his back into it, and yanked.

Sprong-ng-ng!

The toilet leaped from the wall and smashed into the mirror. Glass shards flew across the washroom, and as the toilet fell, it ripped the washbasin from its place, too. Water spouted up from the floor.

Where the toilet had been, Charlie saw daylight. A hole, big enough for both of them.

Charlie trembled. He dropped the shovel and scooped Aldrix up into his arms. "Don't worry. You'll be safe."

He wrapped his arms and legs around the boy, shaping himself into a ball as much as he could. Then he threw himself into the hole, just as his vision went black.

Dwarf magic is the magic of secrecy. Consequently, this author finds himself unable to tell his readers very much about it.

—Smythson, *Almanack*, "Dwarf"

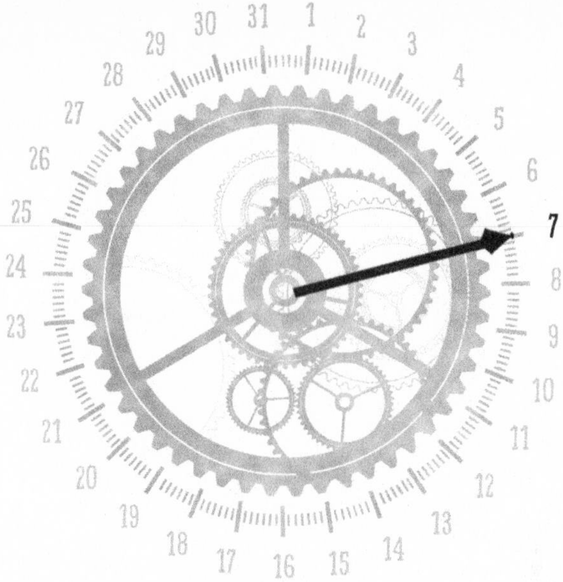

The skin of Charlie's face stung. His arms and legs ached.

He opened his eyes.

He lay on his back under trees. The dwarf wagons stood lined up in the corner of his vision, and Syzigon sat by his side. The other dwarfs waited around the wagons; they looked off into the distance through the trees.

"The first thing I need to tell you," Syzigon said slowly, "is that I've wound you up all the way."

It was true. Aside from the many pains in various parts of his body, Charlie was well. Alive. His body hummed, and he felt within himself that he could again run fast, jump far, and perform feats of strength. He nodded.

"So when you want to leave," the dwarf continued, "you may do so. And I will give you whatever aid I can, and the last thing I will do before you depart is wind your springs to their maximum tension again."

Charlie sat up. They were off the road, and he couldn't tell how far. He wasn't even sure how the wagons could have gotten into forest as deep as this. They were narrow, but not *that* narrow. Maybe the oversized wheels let them roll over smaller bushes and shrubs? The trees were other species here, too. Older, it seemed. Less pine and more oak. The forest smelled different.

He nodded again.

"The second thing I need to tell you is that I owe you a debt. Thank you for saving my son."

"You're welcome," Charlie said. "Anybody else in the same situation would have done the same thing."

A smile cracked the dwarf's face and he laughed. "Earth and sky, no, I'm much too old to believe that nonsense. And even among those people who *would* have helped me, precious few could have done anything *useful*."

"Maybe." Charlie tried not to look the dwarf in the eye. He wasn't sure quite where the conversation was going.

"And the third thing is this: I'm sorry. I apologize for mistreating you . . . Charlie."

A flood of strong feeling washed over Charlie, and he lay back down. He wasn't lying on pine needles, but on something softer and cooler. Moss.

"Pondicherry," he said. "My name is Charlie Pondicherry."

"Thank you, Charlie Pondicherry. My friend. I hope you will call me by my name: Syzigon."

"Is Al—is a certain dwarf well?"

Syzigon patted Charlie's shoulder. "A certain dwarf my son was terrified. He doesn't know why those men snatched him, and I don't really know what to say to explain it. But thanks to you, he's safe now, and not injured, and with a certain dwarf my wife."

Charlie still wanted to know why the dwarfs talked about each other that way, but this didn't seem to be the right moment to ask.

He sat up again. "What about those men? Bowen and the Frenchman?"

"The Frenchman?"

"The one who shot at you."

Syzigon nodded. "They've passed us several times on the track, looking. They haven't seen us, and they won't." He grinned again. Each time he did it, his smile was more natural, warmer. "We're very good at hiding."

"That's dwarf magic, isn't it?" Charlie thought back to the night before. "That's what a certain dwarf who is . . ." He tried to remember what Aldrix had said. "Your wife's sister . . . was doing last night."

Syzigon nodded. "With the Dust of Distraction. That's a warding, a dwarfish spell that pulls the eyes of enemies away from a dwarf. Or a dwarf's friend." He smiled again. "You can't move much when you're warded with the Dust, but as long as you can stay still, it becomes very difficult to see you."

"What about when you're moving?" Charlie asked.

"You have many questions. Are you planning to take up dwarf magic?"

They both laughed.

"I like to know things," Charlie explained. "I've read a lot of books, but I'm learning lately that books don't have all the answers."

"The wagons themselves are protected by a different spell." Syzigon pointed at the column of runes painted on the wagon nearest to them. "It's not as effective, but if you keep the wagon doors shut and move slowly, it discourages inexperienced eyes."

"The Iron—that is, Bowen saw you."

Syzigon nodded. "He's a stranger to me, but that man has known dwarfs."

"Why do you want to stay hidden so badly?"

Syzigon's face became very serious. "We have a long history. And few friends."

"Hiding magic must come in useful."

"That's not quite it."

Charlie stared at him, not understanding.

"Dwarf magic isn't hiding magic," Syzigon said.

"What is dwarf magic, then?"

Syzigon hesitated. "You must understand, Charlie. I'm talking to you as I would to a brother."

"Thank you," Charlie said.

"Dwarf magic isn't hiding magic. It's magic of finding and not-finding. We call our magicians *dowsers* for their gift in locating objects that are lost or hidden. The same gift that lets them locate things—or people—allows them to make things and people difficult to find."

Charlie let that settle in.

"So if we're to part ways now, Charlie, we'll try our hardest to see that you remain unfound. Those men may be angry with you because you rescued a certain dwarf."

Charlie thought it best not to complicate Syzigon's life by mentioning the Iron Cog, so he just nodded.

"A certain dwarf who has the gift will ward you as well as she can. Paint runes on your clothes, maybe. Fill your pockets with the Dust of Distraction. She will know what's best; she's the dowser."

"Thank you," Charlie said. "I believe there will be a parting of the ways. A certain dwarf your son mentioned you're going to Machine-Town, and I must go to Cader Idris." He thought of the Welshman Lloyd Shankin and wondered again whether the dewin was mad. "I have friends to find, and I must . . . well, it's a long story, but there's a man there, and I must warn him that his enemies are coming for him."

As Charlie spoke, Syzigon smiled broader and broader, and as Charlie finished, he broke into a full chuckle. "Charlie, this is good fortune indeed. We're going to the same place."

Charlie shrugged. "Are we?"

"Machine-Town is a nickname. The real name of the town we're going to is Machynlleth." Charlie had a hard time catching the town name that Syzigon shared; it sounded a bit like *ma-HUN-heth.*

In any case, he didn't know the town, so he shrugged again.

"I'm sorry. I don't know the country at all. In fact, until a few days ago, I had never left a single tiny alley in London."

"Machynlleth is the town at the foot of your mountain. Cader Idris. It's spelled a bit like the English word *machine,* and it . . . well, you'll see, but it has more than its share of mechanical devices."

Charlie straightened out of his shrug. "Oh, very good," he said, relieved. Now that Syzigon was his friend, he'd be traveling with someone who could share his dangers and wind his mainspring when he needed it. Then a thought occurred to him. "Why did Bowen want a certain dwarf who is your son?"

Syzigon's face, which had progressively lightened as their conversation continued, grew suddenly dark. "Bowen didn't want me to buy shares in his joint-stock company. He asked about the Old Man, and I think that's what he was really after. If I hadn't had the sheyala with me, he'd have kidnapped *me* instead. Maybe tortured me."

"Sheyala? Oh, the cats."

"More than cats, Charlie. We and the sheyala are the same folk."

Charlie nodded, though what Syzigon said made no sense.

"And because I *did* have the sheyala with me, he kidnapped a certain dwarf my son instead. Or his associate, this Frenchman of yours, did. Again, I am in your debt."

"Does a certain dwarf who is your son know about the Old Man?"

"Not the kind of information Bowen was asking for. So

maybe Bowen would have held a certain dwarf as a hostage and demanded my cooperation."

The thought made Charlie angry. He wanted to mutter something suitably dark, but he couldn't think of any words that would really express his feelings and ended up just growling.

Then he had an idea. "Wait . . . the Old Man . . . is his name Caradog Pritchard?"

Syzigon's eyes opened wide, and Charlie knew that his hunch was correct.

"Be careful with names, Charlie," the dwarf said. "Even a false name, worn long enough, acquires something of the essence of the thing it names. A name identifies a person and can grant power over him."

"I see." Charlie nodded. "So I know what the answer is. And I need to go see the Old Man, too." He sighed. "In fact, I didn't want to tell you this because . . . because it just becomes more complicated, but I need to warn him about the people who attacked us today."

"William T. Bowen?"

"Not only him." Charlie tried to think how he could condense what he knew. "I think he's part of a . . . of a group. They call themselves the Iron Cog. They killed my father, and I think they plan to kill the Old Man, too."

Syzigon stroked all three braids of his beard. "Why would they do that?"

"I don't really know. I think my bap and the Old Man used to be part of the Iron Cog, but then they left it. And when they left, they took secrets with them, and that interferes with the Cog's plans." Charlie didn't mention that he himself was the secret technology his bap had taken from the Iron Cog. "I think maybe they want to rule the world."

"Then, Charlie," Syzigon said, "we need to get as quickly as we can to Machine-Town, and we need to do it without being seen."

"Agreed." Mentally Charlie added: *And find Bob and Ollie and Gnat.* "But how do we do that?"

Syzigon grinned his biggest grin yet. "That's easy. We ask the alfar to help us."

The two older dwarfs chose that moment to approach Charlie and Syzigon. In the background, the rest of the dwarfs were climbing into their wagons and preparing to leave.

Syzigon and Charlie stood up.

Syzigon nodded his head so deeply to his elders that it was almost a bow. "A certain friend who rescued a certain dwarf is also bound for Machine-Town, I have learned. I have invited a certain friend to sleep in our wagons. I hope that my invitation may meet the approval of those who decide."

The old woman and man looked at each other and clasped hands. They didn't say anything, but their eyes met, and they seemed to be communicating through the pure power of gaze. Finally they broke eye contact with each other, still holding hands, and they looked at Syzigon.

"The invitation is a valid one," the old woman said. She turned to face Charlie. "My name is Patali. You have saved the life of a certain dwarf who is my grandson. You are welcome to our wagons."

The old man looked at him, too. “We have decided. I am Calphor. Welcome to our wagons.”

Syzigon nodded, satisfaction visible in his face. “Thank you,” he said to his elders. Then he grasped Charlie by the elbow, a wild gleam in his eye. “Tell me—what do you know of the elves?”

Acutauris dendrophilus (common names: alfar, elf, fey)—Britain's alfar are largely responsible for the massive reforestation of the island in this century. This has been driven by their dietary needs: alfar only eat fruit.

—Smythson, *Almanack*, "Alfar"

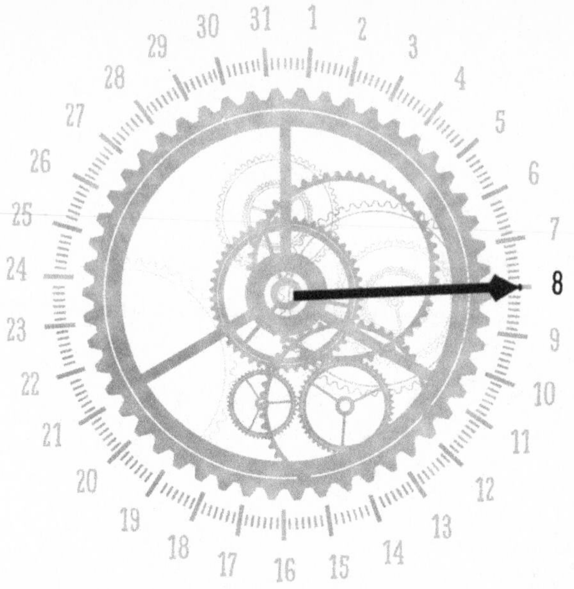

"I am Thassia." Thassia was Atzick's wife, the last dwarf of the caravan whose name Charlie learned. She was the one he had seen dancing with the Dust of Distraction around the dwarf wagons.

She was a dowser.

She stood in front of the foremost wagon; the donkeys were hitched to their poles, and the wagons were ready to roll at her instruction.

Thassia held a forked stick, two feet long. Straightening her back, she gripped the stick with both hands by the fork and closed her eyes.

"What kind of wood is it?" Charlie asked.

Thassia opened her eyes and laughed. "A certain friend is even more curious than you said!" she called back to Syzigon.

"I'm sorry," Charlie said.

"For what? If you never ask questions, you'll never know anything. It depends on what I'm dowsing for. For instance, if I wish to find water, hazel is best."

"This one's oak, isn't it?" Charlie had seen her cut and trim the branch, humming and chanting as she did so. Her melodies seemed aimless and her rhymes sounded like nonsense, but of course they couldn't be.

She nodded. "Oak for dowsing stone."

"I thought we wanted to find the alfar. Do they live in stone houses?"

Thassia chuckled, closed her eyes, and didn't answer.

Slowly, she rotated to her left. She held the stick pointed out in front of her and angled slightly down. When she had turned about a third of a complete circle, the tip of the stick dipped sharply.

She rotated back the other way, and at the same point of orientation the stick dipped again. She opened her eyes and walked forward when it did.

The wagons followed. Warned to stay close, Charlie walked at the side of Atzick and Thassia's wagon. He was careful not to get trapped under the big wheels, but his eyes were fixed on Thassia. She continued to swing her dowsing rod in front of her as she walked, and she adjusted her course to move in the direction indicated by the dipping of the forked oak stick.

"The road," Atzick called.

Thassia slowed as the caravan approached a track. It looked

to Charlie like the same track they'd traveled before, but he couldn't be sure. They all peered left and right down the road and then rumbled across as quickly as they could.

The trees on either side of the track were scraped, smashed, and uprooted, and in the still-damp earth Charlie saw deep imprints of knobby India rubber tyres. He shuddered, scooted into the trees on the other side, and tried to stay focused on Thassia.

"A certain dwarf isn't looking for the alfar themselves," Atzick murmured to Charlie. He chuckled. "That would be impolite, and besides, I think it would require a dowsing rod of some exotic wood she doesn't have. She's looking for a good menhir."

Charlie knew what that was. "A standing stone."

"Yes. It isn't always true anymore, but the standing stones used to be the place to contact any of the elder folk. Ancient crossroads, they are. Your pixies and kobolds and hulders and djinns and alfar all kept watch on the standing stones near their homes. If you went to those stones, you had their attention."

"Dwarfs, too?"

Atzick shook his head. "We've never had a home. At least, we haven't had one for thousands of years."

"You said it isn't always true anymore. That the stones *used to be* the place of meeting. So you mean that even if we find a standing stone, the alfar might not be paying attention to it?"

Atzick looked about. Thick pine boles and spreading oak

branches formed a gigantic canopy over and around them. "This deep in their forests? The alfar will be paying attention, all right. It's as if I walked right into your home, stood by the fireplace, and knocked on your chimney. Besides, we've got something they'll want."

Charlie walked for a minute, lost in his own thoughts. "What's it like, not to have a home?"

Atzick was slow to answer. "You miss it. You talk about the home you used to have, a long time ago. Your family becomes very important. Your folk. And your traditions."

Charlie's traditions had mostly been the small ceremonies he'd shared with his bap: teatime, dinner, a back rub during which Bap would wind Charlie's mainspring, reading in the attic while Bap worked. Charlie no longer had a home, and his traditions had been destroyed.

And what was Charlie's folk? Did he have one?

"Where was your home a long time ago?"

Atzick laughed. "That's a good question, isn't it?"

"That's why I asked it."

Atzick said nothing.

Abruptly the trees cleared, and on Thassia's heels Charlie entered a small meadow. In the center, on a knob of earth surrounded by a trickle of water too small to call a stream, stood two upright stones. They leaned against each other like gray teeth in a mouth that had seen many years, with yellow-green lichen creeping up one side of their pitted surfaces.

Thassia snapped her dowsing rod over her knee and threw it aside. As she passed Charlie, he saw her face; she looked very tired. She opened the back doors of her wagon, crawled in, and shut them behind her again.

Syzigon stepped forward.

He didn't look into the trees around the clearing, or at the sky, or at the brook. Just as if he were stepping up to someone's front door and knocking on it, he rapped his knuckles on the stone. "I wish to speak with the people of the woods!"

Then he took one step back and folded his hands in front of him.

Within a minute, two people emerged from the trees on the other side of the clearing.

Charlie had never seen alfar before, and neither the line drawings in the *Almanack* nor the mosaics inside Waterloo Station did them justice. They were tall and slender, and their features were elongated and angular. Wide eyes shaped like almonds, with piercing green-and-brown irises, dominated their faces. Their mouths were almost lipless, and they constantly smiled. Their ears swept up and came nearly to a point. Their hair climbed even farther and fanned out in a way that reminded Charlie of . . . well, of leaves. And their skin was barklike: one had silvery skin with spots and streaks of black that made him look like an aspen or a beech, and the other had skin a dark grayish-brown color. Their clothing was simple: long green tunics of a material that resembled velvet.

As the alfar reached the stones, Charlie took a step back. Then he screwed up his courage and took three steps forward so he was standing right at Syzigon's shoulder.

"Greetings, dwarf," said the gray-brown alfar. "How fares the search?"

"The search never ends," Syzigon said. "Always we are parting. How grow the saplings of your nursery?"

"They are many," said the silvery elf. "But never enough. Men fell them for fuel, and to make room to till the earth. Always we are planting."

Syzigon nodded. "I bring your people gifts."

Both the alfar smiled, showing tiny teeth. "Seeds?" asked the gray-brown one.

"Ah, you know us too well."

The alfar laughed. "No, dwarf, it is you who know us. Tell us of these seeds."

From inside his jacket Syzigon produced a leather pouch. He hefted it in his fist for a moment, as if he were holding something very precious, before handing it over. "Persimmon seeds," he said. "From the East. I brought them myself, all the way from a souk in Istanbul."

The gray-brown elf poured a few seeds into his hand. They were reddish brown and irregularly shaped. He smiled.

"But could we make such a seed grow in this cold and wet land?" The silvery elf frowned at Syzigon, but it was a playful sort of frown, and it hid a smile.

"A good gardener could make any seed at all grow in this wet land," Syzigon said. "And I have brought you these seeds because I know that of all gardeners, you are the greatest who ever lived."

The seeds disappeared into the gray-brown alfar's tunic.

"These seeds will be a blessing to our nursery, dwarf. Many seedlings yet unborn will bask in the rays of the sun and have cause to remember this day with joy. I am Pithsong."

"I am Tenderroot," said the silvery-skinned elf.

"I am Syzigon."

"I'm Charlie." He hadn't meant to say anything; he'd just become so entranced with the rhythms of the conversation that the words jumped out of him before he even noticed them forming. But the alfar looked at him, Charlie bowed slightly, and they smiled.

"Tell us what gift we can give you, friends Syzigon and Charlie," Tenderroot said.

"We travel to Machine-Town," Syzigon said. "Machynlleth. In the land the English call Wales, at the foot of a great mountain known as Cader Idris. It lies beyond your forests."

"It lies at the edge of our forests," Pithsong said. "We know it. The giant's seat. There was once a great kingdom there."

"A barony," said Tenderroot.

"We are pursued by enemies. They travel the roads, and we would reach Machine-Town without being seen."

"Will your enemies follow you into the woods?" Tenderroot asked.

"They may. They have followed us along the forest track. You may have seen them; they drive in a wagon of brass and steel. Their vehicle is too large for the path, and so it uproots and breaks into splinters young trees along the road's edge."

"Ah," Tenderroot and Pithsong said together.

"You would travel the Path of Root and Twig," Tenderroot

added. The way the alfar said it, Charlie could hear the capital letters in the name.

"We would," Syzigon agreed.

"We shall ask," the alfar said together.

Then they were silent, and stood still.

Charlie was astonished by the way the alfar looked and by the things they said. The conversation between them and the dwarf Syzigon seemed almost like a ritual, like a conversation that could be had a thousand times with the same words, or nearly identical words, repeated each time. He felt as if he were participating in something ancient and, if not secret, almost forgotten.

The alfar were quiet for a couple of minutes. Syzigon stood quietly too, with his hands folded, so Charlie did the same. It wasn't easy. He wanted to jump with excitement and run around the meadow.

Finally Pithsong spoke. "Your gift is great, dwarf. Your enemies are our enemies. It is no small thing that we bear other folk along the Path of Root and Twig, but we agree that we will carry your party to Machynlleth."

"Thank you," Syzigon and Charlie said together.

Tenderroot pointed at a bramble thicket at the edge of the clearing. It looked too dense to pass through, unless one had a good hacking knife or a fire to clear the way first. "The Path begins there," the elf said.

"We wish you the joy of many saplings," Syzigon said to the alfar.

"We wish you the joy of discovery and the release of homecoming at the end of your search," they said back to him.

Syzigon bowed and returned to the driver's seat of his wagon. "Climb aboard, Charlie."

Charlie did.

Then, with Tenderroot and Pithsong watching, the three dwarf wagons rolled toward the brambles at the edge of the meadow.

The alfar are said to be able to travel exceedingly quickly. It has been suggested that this perception is derived from the fact that alfar look sufficiently similar to human eyes that two alfar, hundreds of miles apart, might be mistaken for the same individual.

—Smythson, *Almanack*, "Alfar"

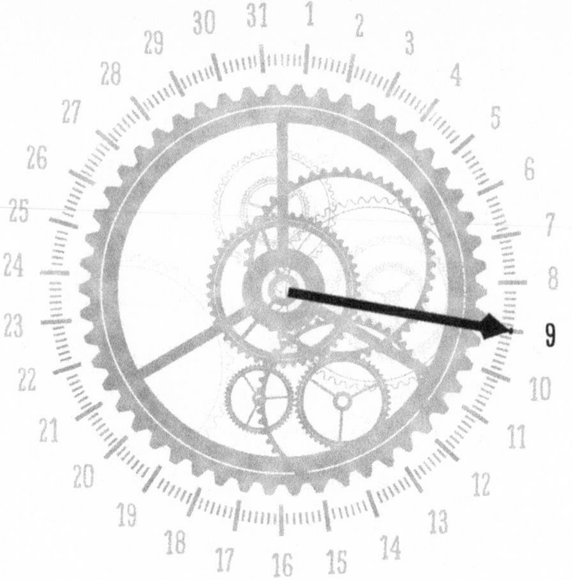

As the exhilaration of meeting his first elves began to wear off, an idea occurred to Charlie.

"Can a certain dwarf dowse for *people*?"

Syzigon kept his eyes on the brambles ahead. Atzick's donkeys were just about to enter the thicket. "Of course she can."

"Do you think she *would*?"

"For you?" Syzigon spared Charlie a quick glance. "I hope so. But you would have to ask her. I am a dwarf who can get things done, not a dwarf who tells other dwarfs what to do."

Where were Bob and Ollie and Gnat? Charlie hoped they were in a coffeehouse in Machynlleth, looking up at Cader Idris and waiting for him to arrive. Of course, if they waited there for a day or two and Charlie didn't show up, they'd begin to worry. They knew his mainspring had to be wound. Wouldn't they backtrack and try to find him in the forest?

They could be dead. The storm that had stranded Charlie alone in the forest might have crushed his friends. Could Thassia dowse for people even when they were dead?

Syzigon nudged Charlie in the ribs with his elbow. "Watch closely now."

Atzick's donkeys had pulled his wagon entirely into the brambles and stopped. Charlie watched as the brambles curled up and grew, wrapping around wheels and axles and the legs of the donkeys. Bill screamed and bucked but couldn't escape the foliage. Mary stared at her hooves.

The brambles pushed and lifted the wagon and donkeys entirely from the ground.

And then, in a flash of greenish light, Atzick, his wagon, and his donkeys were gone.

Charlie almost fell off the wagon. "Is that what's *supposed* to happen?"

"Shh."

Charlie shot a glance over his shoulder and saw that Tenderroot and Pithsong were gone. What if this was a trick? What if the alfar weren't as friendly to the dwarfs as they'd seemed?

What if they hated persimmons?

While Charlie had been looking over his shoulder, the second wagon had been whisked away, too. Now Syzigon drove his wagon into the bramble patch. Victoria took it calmly and didn't object, even when the brambles began to extend and wrap themselves around her. Bad Luck John strained and tried to run, but he was strapped to his yoke too securely to escape.

"Are you sure about this?" Charlie whispered.

"This is not my first ride on the Path," Syzigon said. "For all that Bad Luck there is complaining, it isn't his first either. Hold on."

A bar stretched across in front of the driver's seat, for holding on to, for resting one's feet on, or for wrapping the reins around. Charlie grabbed it with both hands.

Green light bathed the wagon. Charlie looked up and saw the forest canopy overhead. Wherever the light was coming from, it wasn't the sun. He looked down and saw that he had no shadow at all.

Then he looked around and had to grip the bar tight to avoid tumbling out of the wagon.

The wagon moved. Judging by the speed with which the trees rocketed past, it was moving very, very fast. Faster than Bob's flyer, faster than Isambard Kingdom Brunel's Sky Trestle in London, faster than William T. Bowen's steam-truck. Charlie couldn't tell one tree from another, the wagon was moving so fast. It shot through a tunnel of green light like a bullet down the barrel of a gun.

Below, Charlie saw brambles wrapped around the wagon wheels. Looking ahead, he saw the back of Patali and Calphor's wagon. Around its edges, blurred green motion seemed to indicate branches of the surrounding trees that reached out, grasped the wagon, and passed it on in the blink of an eye. Charlie leaned a little too far forward in his effort to see better, and a branch struck him in the chest, knocking him sideways.

He teetered and lost his grip—

and Syzigon caught him by the jacket.

"I warned you," the dwarf said. "Hold tight."

"We're going so fast," Charlie said. "Shouldn't there be wind?" Instead the air was soft and warm.

"Yes, there should," Syzigon agreed. "And yet."

Charlie watched in wonder. This would grow old, surely, but before it could, and as suddenly as the journey had begun—

it ended.

Syzigon shook his reins and clucked at Victoria and Bad Luck John, and the donkeys pulled the little wagon out of a bramble patch. Charlie looked back again just as the green light faded and was gone. Behind him he saw only forest. Yew trees, maybe—very different from the pines and oaks they'd left seconds earlier.

Ahead of them and below lay a valley. The grass was a brilliant green under a blue-gray sky, sliced into great patches by gray rock walls and dotted with white sheep. At the far end of the valley was a mountain, long and high, its lower slopes furred with forest but its upper reaches bare and rocky.

Syzigon pointed up at the gray peaks. "There's your mountain. Cader Idris."

Charlie stared. Somewhere up there was Caradog Pritchard, his bap's friend. Were there also one-eyed fish, as the medieval churchman Gerald had said? An island that sailed around its lake? Or had that all been nonsense, spouted by a madman?

Through the center of the valley below flowed a river, and on its bank stood a town. Even at a distance of a mile or more, Charlie could see that the streets crawled with horseless conveyances and that the air above the streets was thick with puffy white clouds of steam. In the center of town, at the intersection of two highways, rose a tower. Stairs climbed through the open air to connect the multiple levels, at which zeppelins and montgolfiers and other aircraft were moored.

"Machine-Town," Syzigon said. "Machynlleth."

Charlie was filled with sudden anxiety. The dwarfs were going to meet Caradog Pritchard, whom they called the Old Man. Should he travel with them and warn Pritchard? He owed that warning to his bap. If his bap had had such a warning, he might be alive today. Also, the Iron Cog had killed his father, and Charlie had a strong desire to prevent anything the Iron Cog wanted from happening—including Pritchard's death.

But what about Ollie and Bob? And Gnat? The last he'd seen the pixie, she was being blown about in a rainstorm, and the troll lawyer Grim Grumblesson had said that rain would damage her wings. Didn't he owe it to his friends to look for them? Especially since they might very well be out in the forest, looking for him?

"Do you think we got here ahead of Mr. Bowen and his steam-truck?" Charlie asked Syzigon.

The dwarf snorted. "By a day, at least. If Bowen is even coming this direction, which we don't know."

Charlie decided. "Will you excuse me, please?" he said. "I want to speak with a certain dowser."

Syzigon chuckled. "You're a dwarf born."

Charlie wasn't a dwarf and he wasn't born, either, but the

dwarf's words made him feel good anyway. He dropped to the ground. As the wagons gently lumbered down a long meadow toward a highway below, he knocked at the doors on Thassia and Atzick's wagon.

Thassia beckoned Charlie inside, where it was very cozy. Because they weren't sharing with children, Thassia and Atzick had broader hammocks, and beneath them, against the back wall, was an oblong cushion. One of the cats—one of the *sheyala,* Charlie reminded himself—lay on the cushion, licking its paws.

Thassia sat cross-legged against one wall, weaving a basket of soft wooden strips—*withies,* Charlie thought they were called. She yawned from time to time as she worked. Charlie sat cross-legged opposite her. They left the doors open, and Charlie enjoyed the sight of the forest and the hills receding behind them as they descended into the valley.

"What's the sheyala's name?" Charlie asked. It would be rude to begin a conversation by asking a favor.

"You're not here because you want to know about the sheyala," she said.

"I'm really worried about my friends."

"And you want me to dowse them for you."

"Yes. I saw you dowse the standing stones. That was amazing. And a certain dwarf told me you could use the same skill to find a person."

"A certain dwarf my sister's husband?"

Charlie thought that through. "Yes."

"You see what a good dowser I am? I dowsed your very

mind." She pulled a withy through and tightened it. "A certain dwarf is a bit nosy, but he isn't wrong."

"Would you do it for me?"

"If I can. To find a person—not just any person, mind, but a specific person—you'll need to have something of his. Something personal, something connected. It's best if you use a rod from a tree that person himself planted, but I suppose we're not that lucky."

"We're not."

The wagon bumped as it struck the highway, and then Charlie's view rotated ninety degrees. The highway was paved with huge lengths of blue slate, and behind him on the road he could see horses, steam-carriages, and other conveyances, animal as well as mechanical. A slender young woman riding on the back of a long-legged flightless bird chased a dozen white-fleeced and black-eared sheep across the highway. The shepherdess just avoided being struck by a six-wheeled cart full of coal that puffed steam out the back and had no apparent driver.

A quarter mile off the highway stood a tall wooden building. A line of men filed out of it and all the way to the road; their faces and clothing were smudged black, and they wore helmets with glowing bulbs on the front. Miners.

"An article of clothing?"

Charlie shook his head.

"A length of the person's hair? Fingernail clippings? An unwanted organ, removed and kept in a jar?"

"No. No. What?"

Thassia thought. "A longtime possession? Something really important to the person?"

Charlie considered Bob's flyer and wished he'd accidentally torn off a small piece of it when he'd fallen. "No."

Thassia sighed. "This may be difficult. I don't suppose you know a secret, something no one else knows about him?"

"Her." Ollie was careful about letting people know he was a shape-changer, but when Thassia said the word *secret,* Charlie immediately thought of Bob.

The wagon was entering town now. Charlie was surprised at how many clockwork and steam-powered devices he saw. Machynlleth, surrounded by sheep pastures and forests at the foot of a desolate mountain, looked like someone had taken Pondicherry's Clockwork Invention & Repair and stretched it out to fill an entire town. He saw foundries, piston arms, spinning wheels, people standing in oversized mechanical legs that walked them down the street, steam-spewing skeletal horselike creations pulling carts or wearing saddles, and more.

Then Charlie heard jeering. A man wearing mechanical legs picked up his pace and jogged past Thassia's wagon. Had he seen something interesting ahead?

"Her. Do you know any of her secrets?"

"Yes," Charlie said. "She has a very big secret, and I think I might be the only one who knows it."

"Easy, then," Thassia said. "We'll just need a dowsing rod. Hawthorn is best for people, and we can find hawthorn here in the valley. You'll share the secret with me; I'll use it to find your friend."

The wagon turned, and the mooring tower came into view, only a hundred feet away. It was even larger from this close distance, but Charlie didn't look at the tower or at the ships docked at it. He was too interested in what he saw at the tower's base.

"The sheyala is named Atzick, by the way."

Charlie was briefly amused that Thassia's cat shared a name with her husband. Then he focused on what he was seeing.

In front of the tower was a small square with a raised platform of slates. Around that raised platform stood a crowd of people, jeering and booing and whistling and throwing things. They threw fruit, mostly, but also dirt and stones, and Charlie saw more than one strong-stomached little boy picking up a ball of horse manure to fling.

Some of the miners were joining the crowd at the rear, jeering and cursing with harsh words.

The crowd was throwing things at three figures in the center of the platform. The three people stood, but they were bent forward at the waist because their necks and wrists had been locked into a wooden trap.

The stocks. Charlie had read about them and seen drawings, but in real life they were much more horrible.

Because, in real life, the stocks contained Heaven-Bound Bob, Ollie the snake, and the dewin Lloyd Shankin.

Once the site of Prince of Wales Owain Glyndŵr's parliament, this small market town has, due to the presence of several significant industrialists and benevolent societies, become the center of a new era of practical science and mechanical innovation in Wales. For this reason, as well as for the happy coincidence of spelling, Machynlleth has come to be called by many English speakers "Machine-Town."

—Royal Geographical Society, *Gazetteer of British Rivers, Counties, and Towns*, 1882 ed., "Machynlleth"

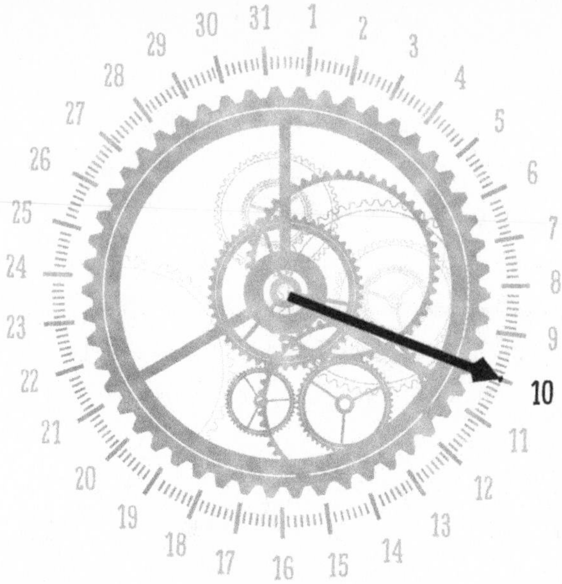

Charlie jumped from the wagon and rushed toward the stocks. He threw hard elbows to get through the crowd, and when he found himself in front of his friends, he turned around and held up his hands.

"Stop!" he cried.

For a moment, the mob froze. Then the jeering began again.

"Here now, what's this?" "You're a filthy little beggar just like them!" "Oh, look, there are *four* little turds in the gang of thieves!"

Thieves?

A long, heavy vegetable struck Charlie in the face and fell to the slates. A leek.

"Don't hurt them!" Charlie yelled.

"Hurt them? We don't want to hurt them!" A thick-bodied man with no hair and a filthy apron held six eggs clutched against his chest. "We just want to teach them what we think of thieves, boyo!"

"Oh yes, we do!" squealed the woman standing next to him. Her face was greasy; she had a matching apron and armful of eggs. "Then tomorrow we'll hurt them, but only a little bit, and only around the neck! Now get back to your mouse-eater friends!"

The aproned couple thought this was a hilarious joke. They laughed really hard for a minute, and then they pelted Charlie and his companions with all their eggs.

"Charlie?"

Charlie risked a look back and saw Bob and Ollie both craning their necks to look at him.

"You'd better run, mate!" Ollie grunted.

"I've got money!" Charlie shoved his fist into his pocket, groping for his bap's banknotes. "Are you in trouble? Is there a fine I can pay?"

"Fine? Charlie, get out of 'ere! They think you're one of us, they'll 'ang you, too."

Hang?

"What for?" he asked. A mushy ball hit Charlie in the neck, and the smell told him that he'd just been tagged with horse manure.

"Stealing my own flyer," Bob said morosely. "Ain't that just a miscarving of justice?"

"Miscarriage." A tomato struck Ollie in the head for his trouble.

Bob's bomber cap lay on the ground. Her brown hair tumbled down around her neck.

"Bob," Charlie said. "Your cap."

Ollie snickered. "Yeah, look at my mate Bob. Long hair like a girl. No wonder you never take that thing off."

Charlie stooped to pick up the cap and stopped when he saw what was inside. Folded like a little packet of papers were Gnat's wings. They were unmistakable, like the iridescent green wings of an oversized butterfly.

"Gnat?" he asked.

"She ain't dead, if that's what you're thinking," Ollie said. "Her wings got wet and they fell right off."

"An' then we lost 'er, mate," Bob added. "Or maybe she lost us. When we was arrested trying to recover my property, she got away, an' we didn't."

Stones hit Charlie, and he was glad. Stones that wouldn't hurt him might put out Ollie's eye or knock Bob unconscious. The crowd jeered louder.

"I tried to help." Lloyd Shankin stared glumly at the slates, his whole body drooping as he talked. His black coat and long face made him look like a pasty crow. "But the party trespassed against only assumed I was also a robber."

"Yeah," Bob said. " 'E wants to be a whiny dog."

"Er . . . what does that mean? What rhymes with *whiny dog*?" Charlie asked.

"It ain't a rhyme," Ollie grumbled. "It just ain't English."

"'*Gweinidog,*'" Lloyd Shankin said. "A parson, it means. I was to be a minister until recently. Until I learned I had talent as a magician."

"If you had such talent as a magician," Ollie muttered, "we'd none of us be here, would we, mate?"

Why was Ollie still here? Charlie wondered. Couldn't he just have transformed into a snake to escape?

"True. If I had a bit more talent on me, we'd have escaped. Instead I'm here with you, charged with Misdemeanor Practice of Magic Without a License from the Royal Magical Society." Lloyd Shankin sighed.

Charlie looked across the top of the crowd and saw men in long blue coats with double rows of brass buttons coming toward the stocks. Behind them, at a crossroads of two broad streets, stood a tall, narrow gallows.

He forced himself not to think of his friends hanging by the neck. "There are men coming."

Ollie looked up. "That's the gaoler and his crew," he said. "Probably come to take us back to our cell. We were only supposed to be in the stocks for an hour. This ain't the punishment; it's just advertisement for the punishment."

Bob shook her head. "Right, an' it feels like two days. Serious, mate, you better 'ightail it unless you want to spend the night with us in the rusty an' maybe get 'anged."

"The rusty?" Charlie imagined an enormous iron container with his friends inside.

"Rusty nail, gaol," Ollie said. "Ain't you learned to understand Bob yet?"

"Easy, Ollie. 'E's working on it."

"I'll be back." Charlie put Bob's cap on her head and pulled on the straps to make it tight. Then he tucked Gnat's wings into the pocket of his coat and ran. As he cut through the crowd, he took two steps out of his way to grab a ball of horse manure from a big boy's hand and smash it onto the boy's own chest.

At the back of the crowd, Charlie pushed through a curtain of miners. They resisted and swore, but they didn't stop him. Behind them, the wagons were waiting. Charlie slipped through Thassia's doors and shut them. She had lit a clutch of candles on a shelf on one wall and opened two high shuttered windows to let in light.

"You stank before," she told him. "Now you're worse."

"Thanks."

"And you see what a good dowser I am?" she continued. "You didn't even have to tell me your friend's secret."

Charlie wanted to laugh, but he couldn't. "You're such a good dowser, you're going to take me to the pixie who lost these wings in no time."

He pushed the doors open a crack and peeped out. Bob, Ollie, and the dewin were being removed from the stocks and dragged away. They were going to the gaol, Bob had said, but Thassia could help Charlie find them later, if he needed it, by virtue of Bob's secret.

"Please," he added.

"No trouble at all," Thassia said.

* * *

Before Charlie had even half explained to Syzigon what was happening, the dwarf had turned the caravan around and driven up into the hills again, searching for hawthorn. They found a clutch of the trees huddled together on the top of a crumbling stone wall between two sheep pastures.

Because Thassia insisted that the rod would only work if she made it herself, Charlie climbed the wall and then reached down and dragged her up after him. He helped her balance on top of the heap of stones as she chose a forked stick and broke it off with her hands.

Back in the wagon again, he waited while she smoothed the stick and chanted over it, rubbing Gnat's wings repeatedly down the length of the rod.

Charlie stared at the wings. Was Gnat in pain? Would the wings grow back? Was she doomed to be just an ordinary human now, but only two feet tall? Or would she grow, and become an ordinary person and full-sized? Could she accomplish three mighty feats on foot? And could she possibly be Baroness of Underthames without wings?

"Ready," Thassia said. They set out.

The sun was sinking below the horizon. Syzigon and the others stayed at the wagons, and Thassia alone came with Charlie, with the promise sworn by earth and sky that at the first sign of trouble they'd come directly back. Thassia led, swinging the rod back and forth and moving in the directions it indicated to her.

Charlie quickly learned that the rod had no interest in keeping them on a decent road. They crossed several sheep pastures and then a vegetable patch. Then they scrambled over a wall and marched across a graveyard behind a church.

It was in the graveyard that Charlie first saw the face.

"Stop," he whispered. The sun was down now.

"What is it?"

"I thought I saw someone. Over there, behind that big headstone."

"Someone you know? Or a copper?"

Charlie shook his head. "A boy's face. He was wearing a thick scarf, and a hat pulled down low."

They walked around behind the headstone Charlie was talking about. Nothing. For the second time in as many days, Charlie wished he were a tracker.

"Could have been a ghost," Thassia said.

"Do you mean a ghoul? I know about ghouls."

"I mean a ghost. The spirit of a dead person . . . you know."

"There are ghosts?"

"There are elves, and elf roads, and dwarfs, and gnomes and hulders and fairies, and machines with souls. And, as you point out, ghouls. What's so unlikely about ghosts?"

Charlie urged Thassia to walk a little faster.

On the far side of the churchyard, the buildings were taller. They were also built closer together, often sharing common walls with their neighbors. Charlie and Thassia were getting close to the center of Machine-Town, which, after all, wasn't that big.

"The rod dips, telling me we're going the right direction," Thassia said. "But it also wants to pull me upward."

"Upward?"

Thassia pointed at the rooftop of the nearest building. It was three stories tall, with a carpenter's shop on the ground floor and living rooms above that.

"Right." Charlie crouched down. "Get on my back and hold on."

With Thassia holding on to him, Charlie easily climbed up the side of the building. He went from window to window until he reached a balcony on the third floor. From there, a simple jump let him grab the edge of the rooftop and pull himself up.

"Earth and sky," Thassia said. "You're an impressive fellow."

Charlie shrugged. "I'm good at some things."

Being good at things let him help people. Lloyd Shankin had said he wanted to use his own special talents to help people. Lloyd Shankin, whom Charlie had taken for a madman, but who had tried to rescue Charlie's friends and had gotten in trouble for it.

Now all his friends needed Charlie's help.

Thassia took the hawthorn rod in both hands again and marched across the rooftops. Charlie watched her footing so that, in her concentration on the rod and its directions, she didn't accidentally drop three stories to her death down an alley.

The rod led them up and down over high-gabled rooftops. The roofs here were shingled with slate, the same blue-gray stone that paved the streets of Machine-Town. Charlie was grateful that it was dry—in the rain, the stone would be too slick to climb across.

At the peak of the last and tallest rooftop, he caught Thassia by the shoulder and pointed.

"That's the street," he said. "We've reached the end of the row. Be careful."

Thassia swung her divining tool around again several times and experienced its dip in the same place. "The rod wants us to go down a little," she said. "But not into the street, I don't think."

Charlie scanned the face of the building opposite. "That looks like an official building of some kind, doesn't it?"

Thassia nodded. "Town hall. And look!" She pointed.

Charlie saw barred windows. "The gaol. Is the rod telling us Gnat has been imprisoned with my other friends?"

"I don't know." Thassia moved the rod around again experimentally.

And then Charlie saw her.

"Stay here," he told the dowser. Carefully, keeping his center of gravity low to the rooftop, he scooted down the slate.

Just before the end of the rooftop, windows jutted out, each gabled and itself roofed with slate. There, in the angle between the rooftop and a window, lay Natalie de Minimis.

Charlie crept up to her quietly, his hands trembling. She was bedraggled and wingless, and from the way she lay, Charlie didn't know whether she was alive. He knelt over her, remembering his fairy friend as a winged terror: skewering rats with a spear, charging trolls twenty times her size, and even, on a rooftop not so different from this one, holding open Grim Grumblesson's eyelids and forcing him to jump.

Was she dead?

Then her chest moved. She was tiny, so he could barely see it, but she was breathing.

"Gnat."

She opened her eyes. "Charlie!"

She jumped onto his knee and hugged him fiercely. His hug back to her was very gentle.

"Charlie!" She waved her tricorn hat, pointing over the edge of the rooftop and across the street at the gaol. "They're going to hang the lads in the morning."

Charlie grinned. "No, they're not."

When the stars were young and hot
A certain city folk did build.
Of gold they fashioned every pot
Of wine all pools and fountains filled.

The city slumbers now in frost
Her treasures viewed by mice alone
And all upon the roads are lost
Her children nameless and unknown.

So when the stars begin to cool
And folk and stars and earth grow old
With wine again we'll fill each pool
And burnish long-forgotten gold.

—Child, *Popular Ballads*, No. 99

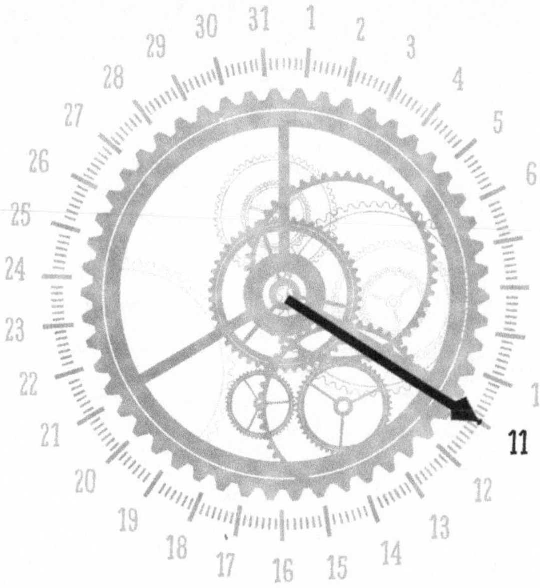

Charlie borrowed a long rope from Atzick, who offered it with a joke about taking the rope from the gallows instead. Thassia loaned Charlie a bright red cloak, with glyphs cut from gold cloth and stitched into it.

"Do you want me to actually *attract* attention?" he asked.

"The cape will make you difficult to notice. Difficult, but not impossible."

From Syzigon, Charlie borrowed tools: some fine prongs he thought might make good lockpicks, a hacksaw, and a short crowbar. He also borrowed a leather belt with multiple large pockets and loops to hang tools from.

Charlie's plan was not sophisticated. For all that it was ridiculously full of clockwork and mechanical devices, Machynlleth was a smallish town in the Welsh countryside, surrounded by sheep, forest, and mountains. Charlie was counting on the gaol being not terribly difficult to crack.

Syzigon led the caravan into town again. The dwarf wagons turned right in the center of Machynlleth and continued out the north side to a fork where the smaller, unpaved route turned and began to wind its way uphill. That way lay Cader Idris, Syzigon explained.

As Charlie walked back into town after midnight with Gnat on his shoulder, Thassia began dancing around the caravan with the Dust of Distraction in her fists.

On the way, Gnat told him what had happened since they'd parted company. It was a simple story. The storm had pulled the flyer much farther west and then wrecked it against a hillside. When Gnat and the boys had awoken to armed servants of the landowner forcing them off the hill, the flyer was gone. Suspecting that the landowner had deliberately stolen the flyer, they'd returned the next night, found the aircraft, and then been arrested. Only Gnat had managed to run away. She didn't know anything about the Welsh dewin; he must have gotten involved later.

"And the terrible thing of it is, some of these men were wearing the same pin as your Frenchman was in London. You remember? The cog-shaped pin. Do you suppose your Iron Cog could be located here?"

So Charlie recounted his adventures. As he talked, he kept turning to look at Gnat; each time, she pushed his head away, until finally he stopped.

"What's wrong, Gnat?"

"Nothing. Only don't look at me."

"Am I allowed to talk to you?"

"Aye, you are. Please finish telling me your story, only don't look at me."

Charlie sighed. "What's wrong?"

"Nothing."

"No, really. What's wrong?"

"Nothing. Only a pixie with no wings is no pixie at all. I'm nothing special; I'm just short."

Would the wings grow back? Grim had never said, and it would be rude to ask. "Well, you still frighten *me.*"

She buffeted his ear playfully, and after that she didn't object when he looked at her.

The climb up the side of the town hall only took a few minutes; the space between the main building and the tower at its corner formed a natural chimney, and Charlie just put his feet against one wall and his back against the other and pushed his way up. But it took a good long time to figure out, based on squinting past thumbs at the building across the street and counting its windows, when they were exactly over the gaol's windows, on the third floor.

Charlie tied a bowline, one of the first knots he'd learned from *Practical Sailing for Boys,* in the end of the rope. The bowline made a loop that wouldn't tighten when pulled, so it was good for lifting and lowering people; Charlie used it to let Gnat down. When she tugged on the line three times, Charlie anchored it to the battlement and shinnied down using his hands and knees.

The window to the gaol cell was barred. Inside, Charlie saw

that the simple cell had only one other exit: a single door that was a solid slab of steel. So that was how Ollie had been kept in: other than the window, there was no exit big enough even to permit the passage of a snake, and from the window it was a three-story drop. The cell also had four pallets and four wool blankets, all illuminated by a candle on a high shelf.

Gnat, Ollie, and Bob stood in the middle of the cell, locked in a whispered conversation. Lloyd Shankin leaned against the wall, whistling softly like a boy pretending he didn't want to be invited to dance.

"Pssst!" Charlie called.

Bob bounded to the window. "Charlie, mate!" she whispered. Ollie crowded in behind her. "What's the plan?"

Charlie tied another bowline around his waist. "Plan A," he said. "Lockpicks." He produced the prongs and passed them to Bob.

Bob passed them right back. "No good. The door's solid an' I can't reach the lock."

"Plan B." Charlie handed Bob the saw. "You start working on the bars from that side."

"What will you do?"

Charlie produced the crowbar. "I'll work on them from out here."

Lloyd Shankin cleared his throat softly. "I'm sorry I don't know any songs about escaping from prison."

Bob didn't spare him a glance. "As am I. An' I'm also sorry you don't know any songs about calming down angry judges or about recovering a stolen flyer."

"Yes, well, in hindsight the absence of a good prison-escape song seems a glaring omission." One of Lloyd's eyes looked at Charlie and the other looked at the door, but the dewin's split gaze no longer seemed ominous to Charlie. It was almost charming.

Charlie turned to Ollie. "Why didn't you just, you know, sneak away?" He didn't specifically ask why Ollie hadn't turned into a snake, because he didn't know how much Lloyd Shankin knew. Ollie was sensitive.

"I ain't leaving my mate Bob, am I?"

The street below Charlie was lit by gas flames within tall iron poles. Those flames cast light upward, but only dimly, and Charlie found himself working within the long black shadow of a gargoyle beneath him. Perfect.

Bob filed and Charlie banged at the mortar around the tops and bottoms of the iron bars. Ollie sat on his pallet and pretended to snooze, and Gnat listened at the door. Bob and Lloyd were the ones they had to get through the window, of course. Gnat could already squeeze between the bars, and in a heartbeat Ollie could be a slender snake.

"You're quite a brave boy, Charlie," the dewin said.

"That's Charlie." Ollie beamed.

"How did you come to be with Bob and Ollie, Mr. Shankin?" Charlie asked.

"After meeting you, I looked for your friends." Lloyd Shankin folded his hands behind his back and thrust his chest forward as if he were reciting. "Your words . . . touched me."

Charlie paused. "What words?"

"I said I was the guardian at the gate, boyo, welcoming you to the fairy world on your adventure."

"I remember. I thought maybe you were mad."

"Ah, well, you weren't the first one. I meant nothing by it; I was just being clever. But you said that *you* might be *my* guardian at the gate, and that got me thinking. I *was* on an adventure, so what kind of adventure did I want to have?"

"He decided he wanted to help us," Ollie added. "Lucky us."

"You got to Machine-Town ahead of me," Charlie said. "I thought I took a fast road."

Lloyd clapped his hands. "One of the love songs I know has this line about wearing a hat and going on a journey. I found I could make my step very light with it. So I did. And I ran."

"You were looking for my friends."

Lloyd nodded. "And when I got to town, there was a trial being held out on the square. I recognized Bob and Ollie from your description, so I tried to speak up for them."

"Speaking up wasn't the problem," Ollie said. "The problem was you trying to cast a spell."

"Yes. Well, I did sing a short englyn to try to grant me a silver tongue. Charisma. To be more persuasive."

"What's an englyn?" Charlie asked.

"'Tis a song-spell," Gnat said. Charlie looked at her over Bob's shoulder, and she shrugged. "Welsh and Pixie are related languages."

"Are they?" Lloyd Shankin asked. "How interesting. Well, I'm afraid the judges heard my englyn and, ah, were not amused. They took me for a conspirator and threw me into the stocks with the lads."

Charlie managed to work one bar out of its setting. He passed it through to Bob, who slid it under her pallet. Then he joined Bob in working on the second bar. Bob had cut most of the way through it at its lower end, and Charlie wedged the crowbar behind it.

"Let me try to lever this one," he suggested.

Bob stood back.

Charlie braced himself with one hand on the remaining solid bar and pushed.

The bar budged, snapping through where Bob had sawed it, but only an inch, and then the crowbar slipped, jumped from Charlie's grasp, and fell to the street below.

Clang!

Charlie looked down and couldn't see the crowbar. At least it hadn't hit anybody. On impulse he looked up.

A face looked over the edge of the roof and down at him. A boy's face, with a thick scarf and a hat pulled low.

A ghost's face?

"Voices!" Gnat called. "And footsteps, coming this way!"

"The 'eck," Bob muttered.

Charlie looked at the window. There wasn't enough room for Bob and Lloyd to get out yet, but there would be if he finished removing the second bar.

He made a decision. "Stay back."

Bracing himself with the last bar, he grabbed the one that was partially out and yanked.

He felt energy burn within his chest, arms, and legs. He grunted. His grip threatened to slip, so he tightened his fist, pulled harder . . . and the bar bent up and out of the way.

Lloyd Shankin's eyes grew very large.

"Ollie!" Bob threw herself out the window headfirst. Charlie barely had time to get out of her way, and then she was anxiously scrambling up the rope.

Gnat followed. She didn't have wings, but she bounded from the floor right up to the window and tumbled out, and then she was up the side of the building after Bob. Lloyd Shankin took his coat off and hung it over his shoulder; without it, he turned out to be quite thin, and he slipped through the bars easily.

Ollie stood, hesitated, and snuffed out the candle with his fingers. With the cell plunged into blackness, Charlie heard muttering and a soft, familiar *bamf!* He smelled rotten eggs, and then a yellow snake slithered out of the window and up his arm and settled around his neck.

As fast as he could go, Charlie raced up the wall. He pulled himself arm over arm, and his feet scaled the slate almost at a run. If he'd had fingers of flesh and blood, the skin would be ripped from them by the pace he kept.

Bob made it over the lip of the roof, with Gnat and Lloyd Shankin right on her heels, and Charlie immediately behind the dewin. As he tumbled onto the roof and Ollie slithered away, Charlie hauled the rope up after him.

Would the cloak of not-being-noticed hide the rope hanging over the edge of the building if anyone looked? He doubted it.

Loud whistles from below confirmed his doubts.

"Come on." He stood.

And there, on the gable of the roof thirty feet away, stood the boy in the scarf.

Charlie looked at him. Something was wrong with the boy. He was unnaturally still, like an acrobat or a statue.

There was something naggingly familiar about him, too.

The boy turned and disappeared down the far side of the roof.

"Come on." Charlie ran for the tower at the corner of the building, dragging the rope behind him. His friends followed.

A parapet ran around the outside of the tower and, at its nearest, came within twenty feet of the town's big airship mooring tower. That was too far for any of his friends to jump, but it wasn't too far for Charlie. With one end of the rope still tied around his waist, he tied the other to the railing of the parapet.

Then he jumped.

He rolled to a stop on a landing twenty steps below one of the mooring platforms. After picking himself up, he retied his end of the rope to the staircase's iron railing.

The rest was easy.

Bob crossed the rope upside down, holding on with her hands and knees. When she hit the ground, a yellow snake dropped from her pocket, and Ollie rolled away from her in a cloud of smoke.

By then, Gnat had joined them.

Lloyd Shankin came last. He crawled slowly but resolutely. Charlie thought he saw the dewin's lips moving as he dragged himself along, and he wondered if the Welshman was singing a spell to help himself. An englyn.

After pulling the dewin over the railing by his shoulders, Charlie jumped back across the gap to the town hall. Below, in the yellow gaslights, he could see searchers running through the street. Having untied the rope from the parapet, he hopped across again to join his friends and pulled in the rope.

But his friends had disappeared.

"Psst!" he heard from above. Gnat's tiny face peeped from the door of a zeppelin's gondola, and Charlie climbed the stairs and entered the airship.

Inside, his friends were slapping each other on the back so much it made the zeppelin rock. This time Lloyd stood with the others, giving and accepting slaps with an uncertain smile on his face. He looked like the least mad person in the world, no matter what his eyes were doing.

Charlie's hands trembled.

"Bob," he said. "Could you wind my mainspring a little?"

As Bob wound Charlie, Ollie turned to the dewin. "So you was saying how you only recently learned to do magic."

"Yes!" The Welshman was staring at Bob's work on Charlie's back, but he tore his gaze away. "I had had terrible dreams on that Saturday night, you see, and the next morning I was in chapel and we were singing. 'Bread of Heaven,' you know."

Charlie shook his head. The chimney sweeps looked at each other and shrugged.

"We don't know, mate," Ollie said.

"Right." The dewin cleared his throat. "'Bread of he-eaven,

bread of he-eaven,'" he sang. "And what do you think happened?"

"Somebody gave you bread," Ollie guessed.

Lloyd laughed. "There was already bread there, on the table, and when I sang, it rose up off the board and floated."

"You've got my intention now," Bob said.

"Attention." Ollie nudged his friend with an elbow. "And then?"

"Well, that was it," Lloyd Shankin said. "Reverend Jones was inclined to see the event as annoying rather than miraculous, and I was out of the chapel."

"'Ard luck, my china," Bob said. "An' so now you've come 'ome to lick your wounds?"

"No." The dewin's voice became quiet. "I came here to help you, as I said. And also to spend a night on the Cader."

"Shh," Charlie said. "Do you hear something?"

They waited two hours, until the east was beginning to grow light. Then they crept down the mooring tower to the ground. Bob wore Thassia's cloak, with Ollie in snake form in her pocket and half the cloak draped over Lloyd Shankin. Charlie walked behind them, his hands in his pockets and with his eyes on the ground, with Gnat by his side.

They passed the gallows, and Charlie looked away.

They came to a line of miners, trooping along the highway in the direction of the mine. Charlie and his friends stood aside and let them by. Charlie caught a few curious stares, but none of the miners looked in the chimney sweeps' direction; Thassia's cloak was working.

No one gave any of them a second glance as they walked right down the main street past the town hall and then all the way to the dwarfs' wagons. Even though he knew where they were, Charlie walked by the wagons three times before he could see them under Thassia's warding.

Once inside the wagons, Bob, Ollie, and Gnat promptly fell asleep. Charlie sat outside with his back against a wagon wheel and the sheyala Atzick on his lap, rubbing the big cat behind the ears and enjoying the morning sunshine with Lloyd Shankin.

"You're a very special boy, Charlie Pondicherry," the dewin mumbled as he dozed off.

The persistent notion that dwarfs eat mice is to be explained by the constant presence of their sheyala cats, coupled with an old folktale. As related by a dwarf informer to Blenkinsopp (1832), that tale tells of a famine in the dwarfs' legendary homeland. After the failure of the city's water sources in the face of a three-year drought, the dwarf race was on the brink of extinction. The dwarfs' sacrifices to their ancient gods were answered by the sudden appearance of a pride of the sheyala, each animal bearing a mouthful of live mice.

Clarence's suggestion (1810) that the eating of mice is a ritual act of unknown significance performed at unknown times and places by adult dwarfs is to be dismissed out of hand.

—Smythson, *Almanack*, "Dwarf"

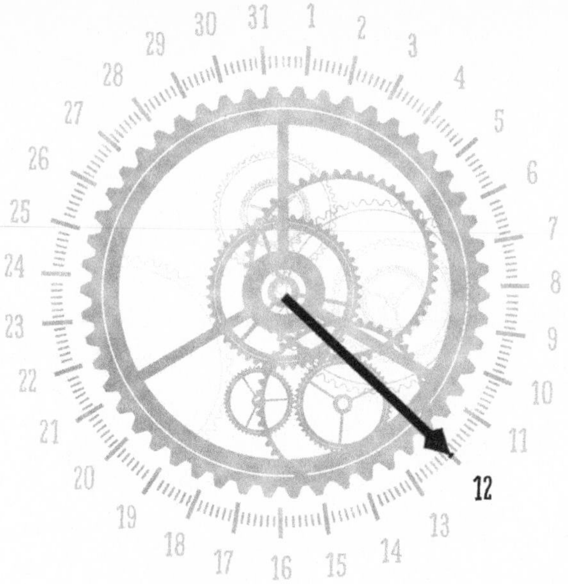

"We have to take the long way," Syzigon explained. "This highway winds all around Cader Idris into the valleys between Idris and Snowdon—that's the mountain to the north of it—and there's our gate."

"Is that the front door?" Charlie asked.

"The Old Man has no front door, not as you're thinking of it. All his doors are hidden. That's the door our wagons can reach, because the roads run to it. But that's a lot of traveling on the highway for you, and the shorter road runs up the mountain."

"Besides which, we're wanted criminals and should stay off the main roads." Lloyd Shankin looked up at the rocky ridges. "Charlie, before you leave this place, you must get a look at the sea."

It seemed like a random comment. "The sea? Are you thinking of sailing away?"

"Thinking of buried houses." Lloyd nodded toward the west. "They say that the waters out just beyond the shore here cover the Drowned Hundred. A hundred is a place, something like a county. There's an old story, and songs, you know, about a flood that destroyed the entire hundred. I've heard that fishermen sometimes look down from their boats and see the houses."

The three of them sat on stones beside the wagons in the morning sun. Syzigon peeled an orange, and Charlie accepted a pip. He slowly sucked at it, just to be able to share in the meal with Syzigon. Lloyd Shankin had his own orange and had nearly finished it.

"So I'll take my friends up the straighter road?" Charlie asked.

Syzigon laughed. "It's not straight by any means; it's just short. And it's steep, so you'd better watch your ankles. But it's the most direct road. I've been watching, and no one's gone up this morning."

"So no police," Lloyd said.

"Thank you," Charlie said.

"Just shepherds and madmen." Lloyd Shankin grinned, his eyes wandering apart. "Like your Caradog Pritchard."

Charlie nodded.

"What's more," Syzigon continued, "we'll stay here as long as we can, and misdirect any searchers who come looking for you."

"How do I find the Old Man's . . . door?"

"If you've never been through it, I will tell you right now, you don't find it. No, what will happen is this: The Old Man will send someone to look at you. If you pass his tests, if you seem right, the Old Man's servants will bring you to him."

That sounded fine to Charlie. He would tell the Old Man's servants about his father, Rajesh Pondicherry, who had once been known as Dr. Singh and who'd been a friend of the Old Man. Caradog Pritchard. Even if they wouldn't let him in, he could at least pass on the warning that the Iron Cog was coming.

Not just coming, if Gnat's eyes were to be trusted—and her eyes were very, very sharp. The Iron Cog was already in Machine-Town, and more of its minions were on the way.

Once he passed on his warning, though, Charlie had no idea what he'd do. Sitting with Syzigon and eating an orange, he considered joining the dwarf caravan. He could travel and collect things.

Have a folk.

"Thank you for everything," Charlie said to Syzigon. He and Lloyd each shook the dwarf's hand.

"This isn't good-bye," the dwarf said. "I'll see you in a couple of days."

Before Charlie and the dwarfs parted company, Thassia gave him a compass. It was lodged in a battered brass case so thoroughly worn that the degree numbers around the outside had mostly been rubbed off.

"The needle looks strange," Charlie said. "Is it a splinter of wood?"

"This will always lead you to a certain dwarf's wagon," Thassia told him. She pointed at Syzigon and Yellario's wagon when she said it. "Though it won't tell you how far, or what obstacles might lie in the way."

"And why does it point at that wagon in particular?" he asked.

She looked surprised. "And here I thought you were beginning to understand us. It's because a certain dwarf is a dwarf who can get things done. And it's because that splinter of wood came from his wagon."

Charlie led his friends up the Cader Idris road, which very quickly became a footpath. Charlie's last glimpse of the dwarf wagons—Thassia had dropped the Wards of Distraction, and the carts were eye-catching with their red and gold paint—was from a track scant inches wide. As the wagons disappeared, so did Machynlleth, leaving Charlie with a view of more distant forests and pastures.

The valley was forested. It was damp with the waters of a rivulet that bounced and rolled down from the mountain, leaving splashes of bright green moss on a broad channel of stones and filling the valley with gnarled but cheerful little trees.

"Doesn't this feel like a pixie place?" he asked.

Gnat stopped her march and looked around. She huffed and puffed from the hike, which Charlie wasn't used to. Usually, the pixie flew, and her flight seemed effortless. "In fact," she said, "we've passed markings. Doors. But they're old and faint. Pixies lived here once, but 'twas a long time ago."

Charlie looked at Gnat, standing on the trail. "How long, do you think?"

Gnat shrugged. "I've no way to know, short of asking."

Lloyd Shankin stopped the bouncy tune he'd been muttering under his breath. "Hundreds of years, I think. Before I was born. Before my great-grandfather was born."

"Oh, I see. . . ." Charlie looked at his feet. It wasn't what he'd meant, but now he was too embarrassed and afraid to say what was really on his mind.

"You mean how long until my wings grow back, don't you?"

Charlie couldn't meet Gnat's gaze. Staring at his shoes, he nodded.

Gnat sighed. "If I could perch in a proper fairy nest and molt, not long. A day. Two at most."

"Molt?" Charlie knew what molting was. It was when an animal's skin all came off and there was a new and slightly different animal underneath. He had a hard time imagining Gnat molting.

Or perching.

"Aye," she said. "If I'd a nest and a bit of quiet in which to spin a proper cocoon, my wings would return in no time at all."

"I wish the gaoler hadn't taken away my book and pen," Lloyd said.

"You spin cocoons?" Ollie sat down on a cushion of moss and stared.

"And otherwise?" Charlie asked.

The set of Gnat's mouth was flat, and her eyes were fixed

on a distant patch of forest. "And otherwise, I don't know whether they shall."

Ollie squinted at Gnat. "Do you lay eggs?"

Bob swatted Ollie on the top of his head. "That's personal, mate."

"I don't mean *her,*" Ollie objected. "I mean, you know, fairies."

"That's it—this conversation 'as become entirely too analogical." Bob spun on her heels and started hiking up the mountain again.

"Do you mean anatomical?" Charlie followed Bob up the track.

"That's what I said!" Bob yelled over her shoulder.

Then she stopped. Stared at the path in front of her.

"The 'eck."

"What is it?" Charlie picked up his pace to catch up, but Bob didn't answer. When Charlie reached her, he looked with her at the damp earth.

There was a paw print. Just a single one, in a soft patch of dirt surrounded by stone.

"Dog?" Charlie asked.

Bob knelt on the stone and spread her hand as wide as she could. The span of her hand from the tip of her thumb to the end of her pinky was not as broad as the paw print.

"If that's a dog, Charlie, then it's the size of an 'orse."

"Maybe it ain't a dog, then," Ollie said as he stepped up. "Maybe it's a wolf."

"Cŵn Annwn," Lloyd Shankin said. It sounded like *coon-*

ANN-noon. "The Hounds of the Lord of the Dead." He stood tall, looked about, and inhaled as if he were trying to suck the entire mountain into his body. "This is fantastic."

"It ain't fantastic if it eats us, mate," Ollie said.

"Maybe it's a . . ." Charlie tried to think of some harmless creature, but the size of the print boggled him. "Maybe, whatever it is, it left this spoor on its way off Cader Idris forever." He liked the word *spoor.* Using it made him feel like Allan Quatermain.

Gnat stood beside the paw print and shrugged. "This animal went *up* the mountain." Then she continued on the trail. "Wild animals mostly leave folk alone."

Bob followed. "'Oo says as it's wild?"

Ollie trailed after his friend. "Giant Welsh attack dogs. I never should have left London."

They approached the timberline, the line of altitude on the mountain where the trees stopped growing and the mountain became bare grass and rock. High up on the rock, there were still patches of unmelted snow.

Movement off to the side, in a thicket of trees and tall brush, caught Charlie's eye.

He froze.

Could it be a giant dog?

He was unarmed. They were all unarmed, except for Gnat.

If only Lloyd Shankin knew a good song about lightning bolts.

Charlie was a stone's throw behind the others. It was possible he hadn't been spotted.

Slowly, he sank to a crouch. Easing to one side, he pressed himself into a patch of tall grass and watched the thicket.

There it was again, a flash of movement and, clearly framed in a dappled patch of sunshine, black-and-white fur.

Charlie wished he could whistle, like Syzigon. On the other hand, a whistle that alerted his friends might also alert the lurking creature.

Charlie scrabbled about in the grass until he found a pebble. Rising as little as he could off the ground, he bent back his arm and let fly with the rock.

He nailed Ollie, right between the shoulder blades.

Ollie turned around, saw Charlie, and frowned.

Charlie pressed a finger to his lips. He pointed at the thicket. He pantomimed a four-legged beast.

Ollie's eyes grew wide. He nodded, then turned, took a couple of quick steps to catch up to the others, and said something Charlie couldn't hear. They kept walking.

Moving on all fours like an animal, Charlie crept sideways. He kept his friends in sight; their path rose above the thicket on an eyebrow of earth and turned past it. Charlie scrambled across splotchy grass and behind a long finger of stone, and then he saw the fur again.

Just a patch, black and white.

The creature was lurking in the thicket. It was watching them.

Charlie picked up the biggest stick he could find. He slipped through a stand of trees and snuck toward the thicket. He could see a cave opening, low and partially covered by bushes.

The creature watched his friends. Charlie saw upright ears, the back of a round head.

He noticed, too, that Bob had picked up a large rock in the turn of the path. And Gnat wasn't leaning on her spear like a walking stick now, but held it ready to stab.

His friends passed right above the creature.

The creature moved, and Charlie charged.

"Pondicherry's!" he yelled, and crashed into the thicket with his stick raised high. Bob and Gnat jumped into the thicket from above while Lloyd Shankin raced around to the side of it, all three of them screaming bloody murder, and Charlie suddenly smelled rotten eggs.

The creature whirled to face Charlie.

It was a rabbit.

It was as tall as he was.

And it was wearing a red-checked dress and a kitchen apron.

And spectacles.

Foretelling the future is an uncertain art. The possibility that a magician could know events to come raises such complex philosophical challenges that the Royal Magical Society's official position is that accurate prophecy does not exist. Persons interested in knowing what will happen tomorrow are best advised simply to wait to find out.

—Smythson, *Almanack*, "Scrying"

13

Charlie and his friends stopped. Charlie had his stick raised over his head, but the sight of the big rabbit wearing little round lenses made him feel ridiculous.

Also, the rabbit struck him as familiar.

He dropped the stick.

Bob followed his lead, tossing her rock into the bushes.

Bamf! Ollie rose from the thickets in his boy shape. He stepped toward the rabbit but then stepped back again, uncertain, his hands dangling at his side.

“The Hound isn’t abroad yet,” the rabbit said. “But you can’t stay out here much longer. Night is falling.”

The rabbit’s voice sounded like a cheerful old lady’s. English, though not a London accent. And there was a twangy, slightly metallic element in her speech.

Gnat looked at Charlie and arched her eyebrows.

Lloyd Shankin's eyes quivered with delight, at slightly different speeds.

"Listen to your auntie, now." The rabbit reached forward and laid a paw on Charlie's wrist. The paw wasn't exactly like a rabbit's paw should be. The digits were longer than he would have imagined, and almost like fingers. "With night comes the Hound. Do you wish to die, boy?"

"No," Charlie said. "But who are you?"

"And how do we know we can trust you?" Ollie added.

Charlie thought about Syzigon's instructions. The dwarf had said that Charlie and his friends would meet one of Caradog Pritchard's agents and be tested. Only if they passed the test would they be allowed into his realm. Could this rabbit possibly be in the service of the Old Man?

Could it be a shape-changer, in fact, who could also assume the form of a giant hound?

And then he remembered: in his dream, the only dream he had ever had, hadn't his bap been wearing *exactly this dress and apron*?

The rabbit gasped and clapped her hands to her apron. "Betsy's sake, children! Don't you have the sense to know a friend from an enemy? I'm your old auntie, Aunt Big Money. I've been watching you come up through my woods and I see you need taking care of, so here I am. Come on in the house and get some shepherd's pie."

"We don't need taking care of." Ollie thrust out his chin and planted balled fists on his hips.

"I dunno." Bob slipped a finger under her bomber to

scratch her scalp. "I reckon I might 'ave a use for a wedge of shepherd's pie."

"Your house is still on the Cader, is it?" Lloyd asked.

She nodded.

Charlie saw the others looking to him for a decision. If they had to, he supposed, they could defend themselves from Aunt Big Money. From a hound that left the tracks they'd seen lower down the mountain, though, he wasn't so sure. Even if the hound didn't belong to the Lord of the Dead.

"I would love some shepherd's pie," he said. "And I never turn down an offer of help."

Aunt Big Money patted Charlie on the cheek. "You learn this much good sense at your age, I shudder to think what a font of wisdom you'll be at mine."

Aunt Big Money whirled abruptly and ducked into the hole at the back of the thicket.

Charlie hesitated. Ollie pointed at the hole and grinned, a treacly sweet exaggeration of a smile. "Go on, then, mate. Follow your old auntie."

Charlie stooped and stepped into the hole.

Steps led down. They were made of flat slates, very smooth, and they were well swept. The walls were of hard-packed white chalk. Charlie hadn't seen chalk since he'd come out of the Path of Root and Twig; where had Aunt Big Money gotten hers? A kerosene lantern hung above the steps, casting a greasy yellow light upon Charlie's descent. Bent over as he was, Charlie had to press himself against the wall to avoid bumping his head on the lantern.

At their bottom, the steps opened into a long, narrow room.

The ceiling rose several feet, so Charlie straightened up. Against one wall was a broad stone hearth, with a fire burning on a thick pile of embers and multiple pots hanging from iron hooks. A teakettle sat at the edge of the fire, gently piping steam.

A long table of thick, scarred planks filled the room. It was laden with bits of string, tall stacks of books, scraps of note-filled paper, sealed packets, jars containing withered roots, eyeballs in liquid, small animal skulls, and stranger things. At the end of the table stood a rocking chair beside a pair of knitting needles and a basket of yarn in many colors.

The wall opposite the hearth was covered from floor to ceiling by a cabinet with a thousand tiny drawers. Each drawer was carefully labeled with a bit of paper pasted to the front of it, the neat letters on the paper identifying the contents of the drawer. Charlie leaned in to read some of the slips of paper: COMFREY, ST. JOHN THE CONQUEROR, PLANTAIN, ALOE, MANDRAKE.

Charlie heard his friends' footsteps on the stairs behind him.

"Books," Lloyd Shankin said reverently.

"It's like a library, innit?" Bob said, pointing at the drawers.

"What do you know for libraries, mate?" Ollie's voice was sour. "You ain't never been in a library."

"Yes, I 'ave," Bob said. "Many times. 'Ow do you think I researched the design of my flyer? An' libraries 'ave card caterpillars." She gestured at the wall of tiny drawers again. "Like this."

"Catalogs." Charlie had read about libraries.

Ollie frowned. "Where was I, then? I would have helped

you, if I'd known you wanted to go to a library and read its card catalog."

Bob shrugged. "I did some of my research before I knew you, Ollie. An' some of it was while you was busy doing other things."

"Well, ain't you the mysterious one?"

Bob grinned at her friend. "I 'ave depths about me, Ollie, I 'ave."

Aunt Big Money shuffled into sight from around the bend of the room. She carried a tray bearing empty teacups and saucers, along with a loaf of crusty bread and a tall brick of butter.

"You've a lovely home," Gnat said to the rabbit.

"Thank you," she answered. "Now sit down and eat."

She brushed aside clutter on the table to make space for her guests, then produced plates and silverware from a cabinet in the corner. Gnat pointed out (she was short enough that she could see this) that there were stools beneath the table. Charlie, the dewin, and the chimney sweeps pulled stools out and sat, and then the rabbit brought out a round iron pot full of crispy golden mashed potatoes.

"I'd murder for that shepherd's pie right now," Bob said cheerfully, "but I'm right glad I don't 'ave to."

Beneath the mashed potatoes lurked layers of peas, carrots, leeks, tomatoes, and minced lamb. Lamb had been one of Bap's favorites. Charlie put his hand in his peacoat pocket and fingered his bap's broken pipe stem, then accepted only a small portion of shepherd's pie and a cup of tea.

"Do you have any music books?" Lloyd Shankin leaned

conspiratorially toward Aunt Big Money as he asked. "Or poetry?"

The rabbit shrugged. "I have what I have; you can look and see for yourself. Up on this mountain, most of the poetry doesn't come out of a book, if you know what I mean."

The dewin stared at her with quivering eyes and slowly nodded.

"This is a comfortable home for such a wild place." What Charlie wanted to ask was *Who are you really and what are you doing living up here on this mountain?* but that would have been rude.

Aunt Big Money also had only a small portion of food in front of her. "They say a person who spends a night alone on Cader Idris comes down mad, or a poet." She smiled. "Of course, that isn't true. I can't rhyme to save my life."

Ollie poked his fork into his shepherd's pie as if he suddenly wondered what was in it.

"I'm glad I'm not alone," Charlie said. "How about the Old Man, then? Caradog Pritchard? Is he mad, or a poet?"

"He might be both." The rabbit cocked her head to one side and then the other. "Betsy's sake, he's at least *mad.* He'd have to be, to make a poor little creature like me."

Make?

Before he could say what was on his mind, Aunt Big Money continued. "You know, they also say the Cŵn Annwn hunt this mountain, and that if the Hounds catch you, they take you to Annwn's realm and you can never leave."

"You see?" Lloyd murmured.

"And that's true, is it?" Gnat knelt on her stool to be able to reach her plate, and it took her both hands to productively use her fork.

Aunt Big Money shook her head. "There's only the one Hound, and he's a recent arrival. Of course, if he catches you, he'll kill you, and as far as I know, you don't come back from that."

Lloyd Shankin looked disappointed; Ollie snickered.

"When you say Mr. Pritchard *made* you," Charlie said slowly, "do you mean . . . does someone have to come wind you up, from time to time?"

"I have friends in Mountain House," the rabbit said. "But you didn't come here to talk about boring little details like that, did you?"

"No?" Charlie didn't think the details were either little or boring.

"You came here for a scrying."

Charlie nodded, wondering what that could mean. It sounded like magic, but magic was something that folk did, and each folk, or each nation of humans, had its own magic. Turkish dervishes, Dutch ichthyomancers, troll blood witches. Welsh dewins.

Hadn't Aunt Big Money told him that she was a clockwork creature, just like him? That someone from Mountain House came here and kept her wound?

Could a clockwork device perform magic?

He caught Ollie's eye and saw by his wrinkled brow that the chimney sweep was also baffled.

"Listen to your auntie, now," the rabbit said. Then she got to work.

She grabbed a bowl of brown eggs and moved it to a spot on the table nearer the fire. Then she folded her apron several times over to make a thick protection for both hands. Bending down, she grabbed something in the fireplace, something that had been lying buried under glowing coals. She heaved it out and laid it on the floor beside Charlie.

Charlie again remembered his dream. In his dream, his bap had pointed at the embers of a fireplace just like this one and said he had something to show Charlie.

And hadn't Bap also had a lady's voice, with a metallic edge to it? Had Charlie really been dreaming of Aunt Big Money? And how was that possible, before he had met her?

But Charlie couldn't really ask any of this, let alone the biggest question: How could Charlie dream at all?

Charlie forced himself to pay attention to what was happening in front of him.

The object Aunt Big Money had dragged from the fireplace was a flat, circular stone with carvings on it.

Charlie examined the stone. The images were of figures, folk and animal, as well as signs Charlie couldn't identify. They formed a spiral that ran continuously from the outside edge of the stone into the center. At the same time, certain images in the spiral, by the way they faced, seemed to divide the stone into four quarters. The positioning of other images created tiers; Charlie counted seven—three with figures facing the top of the stone (from his point of view) and four with figures facing the bottom.

It was so beautiful he reached a finger out to touch it—

"Stop!" Aunt Big Money hissed. She had an egg in one hand, and she waved Charlie back. "You'll only burn yourself, and you'll wreck the scrying to boot."

Charlie sat back.

The rabbit held the egg up to her mouth and whispered to it. "Mammy Bammy, song and sooth, about this boy tell me the truth."

"That's a rhyme," Ollie muttered.

"It's a song," Lloyd added.

Aunt Big Money spun her arm in a single vertical circle and slammed the egg down on the stone. Yolk and white splattered in all directions, sizzling as the egg cooked on the hot stone, and she stooped to look at it closely. Then she stood and looked Charlie in the eye. "You are a wanderer," she told him. "Your path will take you far from home, but if you are true to it, it will always bring you back again."

Charlie had nothing to say, but the rabbit didn't seem to expect anything. She was already grabbing a second egg and whispering to it. "Mammy Bammy, first and last, tell me about this child's past."

Again she slammed the egg onto the hot stone and stooped to read it.

"Good thing I already ate." Ollie elbowed Bob in the ribs. "Or my mouth would be watering." Bob ignored him and focused on the rabbit.

Aunt Big Money addressed Charlie again. "You have a deeper past than you know. You must understand that every person has a spark of heaven in him, and right next to that spark of heaven and tied up with it is a terrible, terrible knot of hell. You are no different."

Charlie expected another wisecrack from Ollie but heard nothing. He looked at the chimney sweep and was surprised to see a tear glistening on each cheek.

Aunt Big Money grabbed a third egg. "Mammy Bammy, stitch and suture, has this boy a golden future?"

She slapped the third egg onto her scrying stone, then grabbed Charlie by the back of his neck and dragged him forward, forcing his face toward the hot stone and the cooking trails of egg.

"Your turn," she barked. "Look!"

Megalohomo gigas (common name: giant)—The natural philosopher William Blake demonstrated (1804) what folktale had long claimed: that the aboriginal inhabitants of this island included not only pixies but also giants.

—Smythson, *Almanack*, "Giant"

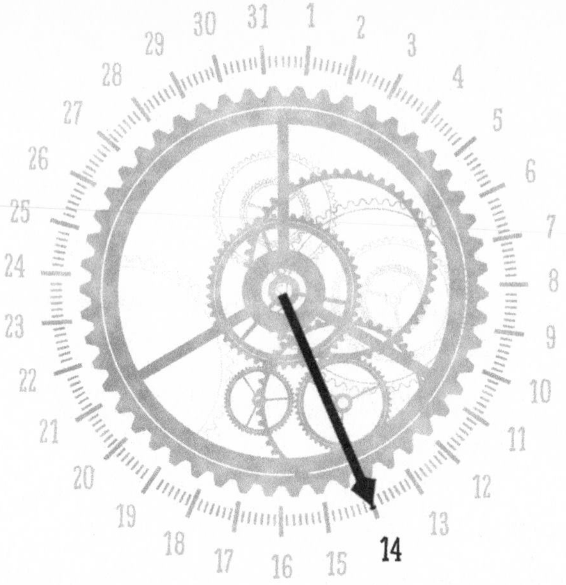

14

Charlie sank into the stone.

He felt the spirals rise more than he saw them. The scratches in the stone received the meat of the cracked eggs and swelled, gaining dimension and substance and spinning around him in a cyclone.

He cried out wordlessly.

Then he felt a soft, slightly furry hand on the back of his neck.

"There is no vision without danger, boy. Look while you can. Look and live!"

Charlie looked. He saw a pit, with great ribs of stone arcing up to a pinprick of light far over his head. He saw the mound of a grave, marked by a white stone with no words on it. A boy stood beside the tomb with his head down and his hands folded, as if he were weeping.

Then the boy looked up, and Charlie knew the boy was keeping a secret.

"That's me," Charlie said.

"No vision is so simple!" the rabbit barked. "Look!"

A city burned. The great river winding through the city's heart smoked and bubbled, and the reek of charred flesh filled Charlie's nostrils. Folk with strange masks that made their faces look like those of birds ran back and forth in the flames.

People ran from the bird faces, but the bird-faced folk carried weapons. Charlie didn't recognize the weapons; they looked like simple tubes, but when the bird folk pointed them, fire spouted from the tips.

"Know death!" the rabbit whispered in Charlie's ear. He could no longer feel her hand or see her. "Death waits for everyone! Know death and fear it not!"

The sky tilted. Stars sank on the wrong horizon, and strange stars rose. Charlie stood on a high place, on the peak of a great rounded rock. Before him raged a giant. Roaring and grabbing with enormous hands, the giant charged at Charlie. Charlie ducked under the first attack and dodged the second.

On his third lunge, the giant wrapped his arms around Charlie, and they both fell from the stone. Charlie wailed as he plummeted through the air.

"I don't want to! I don't want to!" he howled in his vision.

"Don't want to *hurt him*!" Charlie cried, and the orange glow of embers told him the vision had ended. He crashed to the ground.

"Done!" Aunt Big Money shouted.

Charlie opened his eyes, feeling suddenly cold. The pit, the fire, the dome-shaped rock were all gone. He lay on the packed-earth floor of Aunt Big Money's burrow, staring at the ceiling.

Bob knelt by Charlie's right side, and Ollie by his left. "Charlie," Bob said, shaking Charlie's hand. "Are you all right, mate?"

Charlie shook. His head was full of fire, and darkness, and his own death.

"I'm fine," he lied.

Aunt Big Money bent down, scooped up her scrying stone with both hands wrapped in her apron, and slid it back into the embers. Lloyd Shankin leaned back on a stool and stared.

"Well, I ain't doing *that* for love or money," Ollie said.

"No," Aunt Big Money agreed. "You're going to bed."

Charlie looked at the stairs. The light was out, and it was dark outside. He didn't want to stay, but he was afraid that if he left, the Hound would find him on the mountain and tear him to pieces.

"She's right, Ollie," he said. "Get some sleep."

Aunt Big Money lent them each a blanket. No one said much while they sat sipping hot tea, and then the rabbit showed them to a room with beds of soft moss to lie on and piles of dry leaves to heap over their blankets.

"What about the Hound?" Gnat asked.

"The Hound will not get into this burrow," Aunt Big Money assured her. "Not tonight."

Gnat and the sweeps tunneled into the leaves to rest. Lloyd

did the same, but he took three books with him from Aunt Big Money's stacks.

"I'm not a sleeper," Charlie said.

"Neither am I," Aunt Big Money said.

Charlie and Aunt Big Money sat at her table. She refreshed a pot of black tea, then a pot of red tea. He sipped and read and stared into the fire, shuddering at the occasional sound of a beast howling.

In the middle of the night, when his friends' breathing was regular and the embers had burned low, Charlie spoke. "This is not the first vision you've sent me."

Aunt Big Money smiled. "Clever boy."

"Who are you?"

"I'm your auntie," she said.

"Isn't that just your name? Aren't you just *called* Aunt?"

"In your case, Charlie, there's more literal truth to it. You'll understand that soon enough. And you're asking good questions, because I've shown you troubling things, and you want them explained."

"Of course I do."

Aunt Big Money nodded. "But understand this: just because I have the power to show you a vision doesn't mean I can see the vision myself, much less *explain* the vision to you. Call me a witch, call me a seer, but my power is to give vision to others. Most of all to you, Charlie."

"I didn't come here looking for visions."

"No?" The rabbit smiled. "Well, then I'm glad I was here to point you in the right direction."

Aunt Big Money closed her eyes as if in sleep. Since that seemed to end the conversation, Charlie returned to his book.

* * *

While it was still dark, Lloyd Shankin crawled out of the leaf pile, replaced the books he'd borrowed, and put on his hat.

"Where are you going?" Charlie asked the dewin, but he knew the answer.

"I never did spend the night on the Cader, boyo." Lloyd smiled. "And now that I *have* done it, I've not done it alone."

"Be careful," Charlie said.

Lloyd patted the chalk wall thoughtfully. "Yes," he agreed. "Most of the time. But I don't think you get to be a dewin, a real dewin, by always playing it safe."

He doffed his hat, and Aunt Big Money rocked once in her chair in salute, and then the Welshman disappeared up the stairs and was gone.

* * *

Aunt Big Money woke Charlie's friends at first light by cooking thick strips of bacon on a flat black griddle on the coals. Charlie, having watched the meat sizzle and grow crisp only inches from the spiral-engraved slate in which he had seen dark portents of his own future, waved away the offer of food and had a last cup of honeyed red tea instead.

"And the whiny dog?" Ollie asked around a mouthful of bacon.

"He's taken his own road," Charlie said.

"I 'ope 'e finds the poetry 'e's after, an' not the madness," Bob said.

Then Aunt Big Money led them out of her warren by a different tunnel. They emerged next to a small pasture containing half a dozen very large goats.

"You won't want to walk." From a deep pocket in her apron the rabbit produced leather bridles. "These goats are surefooted. They won't complain. And they know the way."

"You want me to ride a goat." Ollie stared at the animals. They were shaggy and white and the size of ponies. Their horns were bigger than their heads and curled back from their foreheads in brownish-gray spirals. They munched mouthfuls of grass and stared back at him.

"Your choice," the rabbit said. "Everything in this life, in the end, comes down to your choice." She looked Ollie in the eye, and her face grew stern. Not unkind, but very sober. "Even when facts and events are beyond your control, you always have the choice of how to react to them."

Ollie backed away from Aunt Big Money, looking at his feet. But when she held out the bridles again, he was the first to take one.

"No saddles?" Bob asked. "No stand-ups?"

"Stirrups," Charlie said.

"You won't need them. These goats are used to bearing riders."

Charlie looked to Ollie, expecting to hear a harrumph of some sort. Ollie was still inspecting his own shoes.

Charlie almost fell over the goat and off the other side trying to mount, but Aunt Big Money showed him how to sit, and what to do with his knees, and how to not let the goat have too much slack in its bridle so it wouldn't run away with him. When he finally got confident that he could ride the animal, he found that the others were ready, too.

Gnat led out. The goat seemed quite large under her; she had to scoot forward and sit with her legs around its neck, more like a mahout astride an elephant than an equestrian atop a horse.

Charlie leaned over to whisper to Ollie.

"Are you all right?" he asked the shape-changer. "You seem a little . . . not-Ollie."

Ollie snorted. "Can't a man think a little without everybody wanting to launder his socks?"

It wasn't a simple yes, but even though Charlie guessed *something* about Aunt Big Money or her den was bothering his friend, Charlie decided to leave him alone. Ollie had shared secrets before; he would talk when he was ready.

Charlie followed Gnat, and the sweeps came after.

At the next crest above the forest, just before losing sight of the rabbit and her remaining goats, Charlie stopped his goat to wave at her. She waved back and then disappeared down her burrow.

Was she the emissary from the Old Man who was supposed to test him? He was troubled by the visions he'd seen in the grooves and egg patterns of her hot scrying stone. He was more troubled by the fact that days earlier she had sent him a vision from hundreds of miles away and wouldn't—or maybe couldn't—explain it herself. But she had gone out of her way to help Charlie, and that was a lot.

The goats climbed with little guidance. They were calm, leaping from rock to rock with casual grace, and the party wound its way up a wide valley past empty sheep pastures and past the foot of high cliffs. Along the way, Charlie shared a few things he'd learned in his travels and in his reading the night before.

"*Cader* means 'chair' in Welsh," he told his friends. "So Cader Idris is the seat of Idris, and Idris was a giant in ancient days."

He explained this as they were coming up into the highest valley of the mountain. It was horseshoe-shaped and ringed on three sides by high gray cliffs, so it did look something like a seat. In the middle of the valley floor lay two lakes. Small islands dotted both lakes; Charlie squinted, but none of the islands were moving.

"A backside to fill that chair would be very large indeed," Ollie said. Charlie was glad his friend's sense of humor was coming back. "A giant with a bottom that size could destroy St. Paul's just by sitting on it."

"Or the 'Ouses of Parliament," Bob agreed. "An' Westminster Abbey at the same time."

"Or all of Machine-Town," Gnat said.

"His rival was another giant in the same neighborhood. One day they fought, and Idris killed the other giant."

"Most likely with his enormous rump," Ollie suggested.

"The place where Idris buried the other giant is called Yr Wyddfa." Charlie was pretty sure he was pronouncing the Welsh name wrong, but he tried: *uhr WITH-vuh.* "In Welsh, that means 'the burial mound.' It's another mountain, north of here. If we get to the top of Cader Idris, I guess we'll see it. They're the two biggest mountains in Wales."

Charlie's goat turned at the edge of the lake and headed for a narrow slit of rock that climbed steeply up the cliffs. The crack was choked with boulders and didn't look passable, but the goat took the passage without slowing down. It scrambled to the top of the first boulder, then jumped to the second, then bypassed the third entirely by springing up sideways onto a tiny shelf. The ledge was so small that Charlie could barely see it, but his goat wedged its feet into the gap and balanced there.

Charlie just held tight and let the goat have its way.

Looking down, he saw his friends doing the same.

Charlie gripped the reins and let his goat continue.

Halfway up the crevasse, a particularly massive piece of fallen rock jammed the canyon, creating a space large enough for ten or twelve people to stand on. Or even pitch a few tents.

This was no dead end—Charlie saw how he could clamber on all fours and get farther up the chasm—but the goat just stopped. And waited.

Charlie climbed off.

The view from this height was spectacular. He saw the horseshoe-shaped valley below with its two lakes, and the trails he and his friends had followed to get there. He saw the patches of snow at eye level now, and realized that they weren't so small after all. He saw black birds perched in the rocks along with gray-and-white gulls. How far were they from the sea?

He saw the upper reaches of the wood farther down the slope. He couldn't see Machine-Town, but he saw the rising plumes of smoke and steam that told him where it was. He saw miles and miles of forest and pasture stretching off into indistinctness in the south.

One by one, his friends reached the top and stepped down from their goats. There was no grass to eat, but the goats were content to stand.

Ollie arrived last. "Dead end?"

A voice came from behind Charlie. "What do you want?"

Charlie turned.

Standing with them on the shelf was the boy with the thick scarf and the low-pulled hat.

This pixie colony once existed in the mountains of north Wales. The baronesses of Giantseat were vassals of the princes of Powys, and it is generally believed that the barony was destroyed in the revolt of Owain Glyndŵr, the last native Prince of Wales.

—Royal Geographical Society, *Gazetteer,* "Barony of Giantseat"

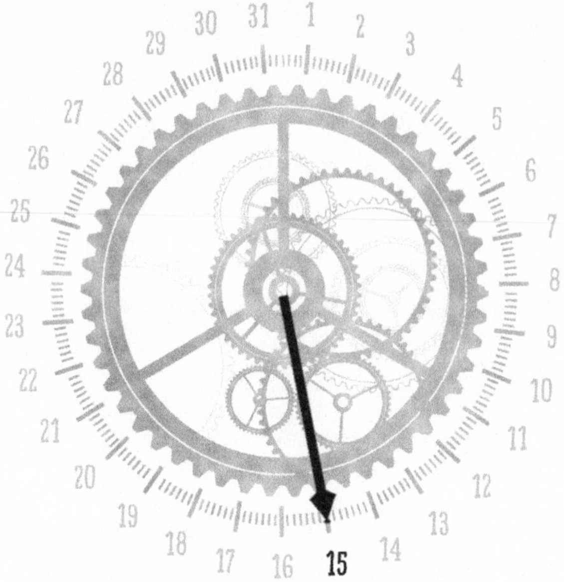

Charlie froze.

The boy was pale. Wisps of dark hair poked from under his hat, and a black coat covered his entire body.

"We want to speak with Caradog Pritchard. The Old Man."

"Caradog is a crazy old fellow who used to herd sheep on this mountain. The Old Man is just a legend. I can't help you with either one."

"Who are you, then?" Ollie demanded.

"What do you mean, following us?" Bob added.

"Maybe you'd better go back down the mountain." The boy stared at them. His eyes were a very pale blue.

Charlie knew.

"The Old Man is your father," he said to the boy.

"Why do you say that?" the boy asked.

"I don't know whether you have a mother," Charlie said, "but the rabbit seer Big Money is your auntie, isn't she?" So what had she meant when she hinted she was Charlie's auntie, too?

"You're guessing."

Charlie was hesitant about his final guess, though. If he was wrong, he'd drive the boy away.

"Were you there when your father made her? Or was it the other way around? Did she care for you? Like a nurse? Like a . . . nanny?"

As Charlie asked each question, the boy fidgeted more. By the end of the questions, he was grinding his heels into the stone of the shelf and shaking his head.

"Charlie," Ollie muttered, "what are you getting at?"

"You don't know anything," the boy said.

Charlie took a step forward, and the boy stepped back.

Charlie stopped. "I'm Charlie. I'm like you."

Ollie and Gnat stared. Bob nodded, as if she'd known all along.

"Nobody's like me." The boy stepped back again.

"You could tell me your name," Charlie suggested. "That wouldn't hurt, would it? And maybe after we talked, you would decide we could go meet your father. Together."

The boy cocked his head to one side. "Did Aunt Big Money show you this road?"

Charlie nodded. "She gave us the goats, and the goats brought us here."

"You should go now. Aunt Big Money was wrong. This is not my father's house; it's just a place where I come to see the view. The goats know the way here because they're my beasts. But I've been watching you, and I don't think you're friends."

"We're friends."

"You're criminals. Thieves and gaol-breakers."

Charlie frowned. He jabbed his finger at the boy. "Look, we've come a long way to bring your father a message. I want to see him now!"

The boy looked down. "He's not here."

Charlie stamped his foot. "Where is he?"

The pale boy pointed his finger past Charlie, into the horseshoe-shaped valley. Charlie turned around to look.

The boy pushed Charlie.

Charlie fell. It wasn't a single straight drop, which might have left him shattered, but a series of short falls. Charlie bounced from one boulder to the next, rattling and tumbling one direction and then the other until he came to a rest on a patch of earth and grass on the valley floor.

He hurt.

He had landed on his back, so he could see what was happening above him. The pale boy must have done something to the goats, because they came bounding down the crack, scattering in different directions as they went. Ollie and Bob stood on the shelf shouting at the pale boy, who leaped from crack to crack as nimbly as his goats, charging up the crevasse.

Charlie hurt, but he wasn't angry.

He understood the pale boy. The boy knew he was a

clockwork person and he was sensitive about it. Maybe it was a secret, or maybe it was a source of embarrassment or fear. Charlie had pushed him too far, and the boy had done what was necessary to escape.

The boy knew Charlie was clockwork, so his push probably hadn't been intended to kill. That realization didn't make Charlie hurt any less, but it helped him not be angry with the boy.

Frustrated, yes. But not angry.

He wished he knew the boy's name.

Charlie rolled to his feet as one of the goats approached him. Raising his hand, he waved gently and made soft, comforting noises. The goat slowed. Charlie ripped up a handful of grass and held it out to the animal. When it came to him for a bite, he gently took the bridle and mounted the creature.

He needed to help his friends.

Charlie failed to collect the other goats because they charged away when he approached. One goat turned out to be enough. Bob rode it down from the mountain, Ollie let himself down in the form of a yellowish snake, and Gnat agreed to ride on Charlie's back as he climbed down himself.

By the time they reached the shore of the lake, the sun had dropped beneath the cliffs to the west. Ollie came out of his snake form shivering, and all Charlie's friends looked to him.

"It isn't long until sunset," Charlie said. "Let's go as fast as possible, without anybody falling and getting hurt. I think we can get down off the mountain, or at least to Aunt Big Money's burrow, before dark."

Bob led the way on the single goat and set the pace. Ollie

rode with Bob, curled in thin yellow snake form around the mountain goat's enormous horns. The goat didn't seem to mind. Charlie ran behind, with Gnat on his shoulders.

"Just don't stab me with your spear," he told her.

Charlie stopped to take one last look up at the cliff face. No sign of the nameless pale boy, or of his recluse father.

He sighed.

Then he turned and ran.

As Charlie followed Bob's goat in a long leap down from a hump of stone, he heard the Hound howl. It was a throaty sound, full of hunger and despair. He couldn't tell what direction it came from.

"HRAAAAAAOOOOOOOOOOOOOOO!"

"That sounds like no dog I've ever heard," Gnat said, right in Charlie's ear. She rode him standing up, with her left hand gripping his hair and her spear in her right.

"For one thing, it's much too loud," Charlie said.

"Aye. And also, it has in it a touch of something else. The hateful wail of a lost soul, I think."

That thought didn't comfort Charlie. He jogged forward a little faster. Catching up to and running side by side with Bob, he struggled to keep his balance on loose stone and grass as the shadow in the valley deepened. "What do you think, Bob?"

"We ain't making it to the bottom of this 'ere valley, mate!" Bob shouted. She held the goat's reins in one fist and kept her other hand on Ollie, holding him steady as the goat shook and bounced. "We ain't even making it to the rabbit 'ole."

Ollie hissed.

"Ollie 'ere thinks 'e's gonna bite the 'Ound an' Bob's your uncle."

"And if the Hound bites him instead?" Gnat asked. "Remember the size of that paw print."

Charlie shuddered. "Either way, I'd rather not have to find out."

"HRAAAAAAOOOOOOOOOOOOOOO!"

The howl this time came from directly behind Charlie, and it was much closer. He looked over his shoulder as he ran, slowing so as not to stumble.

A star or two began to twinkle in the deep indigo of the sky. The Hound was a shadow in Charlie's sight, a darker blackness in the shade that now swamped the valley from cliff to cliff.

The Hound's head and neck rose silhouetted against the stars. The beast's head was enormous. It might have been Charlie's imagination, but he thought he saw, low beneath the Hound's forehead, a dull red glow where its eyes should be.

Charlie wondered for a moment where Lloyd Shankin was, but he couldn't spare the dewin much thought.

"Faster, Bob!" Charlie spun his own face about and pushed his legs.

"Tell it to the goat!" Bob yelled. "I'm already going as fast as I know 'ow!"

"Veer right!" Gnat shouted.

She pointed with her spear. Charlie saw a cliff face, ghost white in the moonlight, with a boulder leaning against it.

He turned toward it anyway. Instead of running downhill, they were now running perpendicular to the slope, toward the wall of the valley.

“What do you see?” he yelled.

“ ’Tis a big-folk gate!”

Charlie knew what that meant: an entrance into a pixie realm that was big enough for humans to fit through. Though the one big-folk gate he had seen, in London, had also been big enough to accommodate a hulder.

“And the Hound? Will it fit?”

“I’ve no idea!” Gnat shouted. “All I can do is read the signs!”

Charlie looked back over his shoulder and saw the Hound, closer than ever.

They weren’t going to make it.

He reached back and plucked Gnat from his shoulders with both hands.

“What are you doing?” she yelped.

He didn’t answer, just placed her on Bob’s back. She grabbed Bob’s chin straps like reins and glared at Charlie.

“Charlie Pondicherry, don’t be doing anything stupid now.”

“Right.” Charlie wished he had a weapon. “You don’t either. Get inside that gate and stay down until morning.”

He stopped. There were rocks at his feet, so he picked one up in each hand and turned to face the Hound.

It was enormous, and it bore down on him with the speed of a train. Charlie threw the first rock.

The Hound was so big it wasn’t possible for Charlie to have missed, but if he’d hit it, the Hound didn’t show any sign. It rushed onward.

He could hear its heavy breath.

“Clock off!”

Charlie crouched and threw the second rock. This time he

was sure he hit the Hound, and squarely in the middle of its big head. But the monster just shrugged and shook itself, the way Bap would have done when he was bitten by a fly.

From a rocky outcropping, the Hound leaped into the air, straight at Charlie.

"HRAAAAAAAOOOOOOOOOOOOOOOO!"

Charlie sprang forward from his crouch, right at the Hound.

They collided in midair, claws raking Charlie's chest, and crashed together to the stony ground.

Riddle me, riddle me, one, two, three
What sleeps in a nest, but not in a tree?
Darker than dark, still it can see
Riddle me, one, two, three

Riddle me, riddle me, four, five, six
A home built of stone, a bed of sticks
Ten thousand candles, without wicks
Riddle me, four, five, six

Riddle me, riddle me, seven, eight, nine
Perched on your nests, all in a line
It's time for sleeping, children mine
Riddle me, seven, eight, nine

—Child, *Popular Ballads,* No. 121

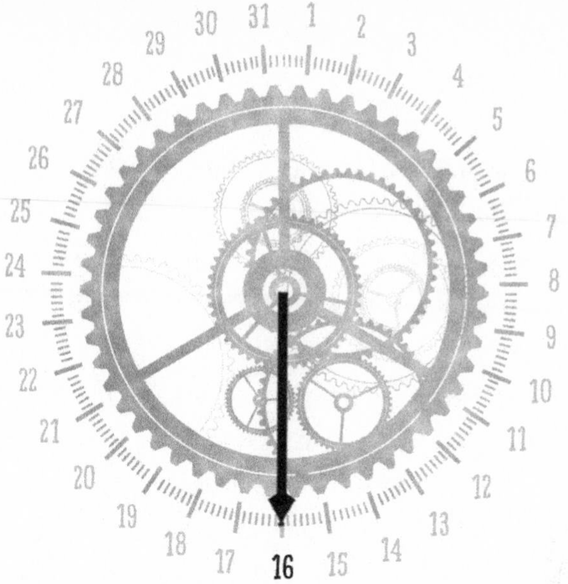

Charlie and the Hound rolled.

The Hound stretched its powerful jaws wide and strained to close its mouth on Charlie's head.

Charlie was tough, but he wouldn't survive having his head bitten off.

He punched his fist into the Hound's nose.

The inside of the nose was warm and wet. Charlie didn't think about what he was touching. As he and the Hound rolled again, and rocks pummeled Charlie's back and neck, he just shoved his fist in deeper.

The Hound yelped.

Its yelp was not as terrifying as its roar.

Charlie pushed his arm in as deep as he could go.

Then he scratched.

Charlie dug his fingers into the walls of the Hound's nasal passages and scraped.

"SKYEEEEEEAAA!"

The Hound squealed. It was a high-pitched sound that still managed to have in it a rumbling bass note of menace. The Hound lurched sideways onto its shoulders, stopped their collective roll, and kicked Charlie in the chest with both its hind legs.

When the legs hit Charlie, three things happened. First, he noticed something that surprised him. The Hound's face was flesh, bone, and blood. The inside of its nose was the inside of a flesh-and-blood nose. Its teeth were the bone teeth of an immense animal that wanted to feed on flesh.

But its hind legs were metal. They were covered in fur, and beneath that fur springs and steel.

Second, Charlie was thrown from the Hound and through the air. The stars spun over his head and in front of his eyes and then reached down to punch him to the ground like a thousand tiny, glittering fists. He rolled again, this time alone, and bounced up the low incline of a small rock ridge.

Third, Charlie hurt.

"Ow . . ."

Charlie staggered to his feet, shaking his right arm to try to fling off the sticky fluids that had come out of the Hound's nose. He wished he had his friend Grim Grumblesson's Eldjotun, the immense hand-cannon that could, the salesman had assured Grim, put down any beast in Britain.

But he didn't. He had nothing but himself, and he was facing a ferocious dog the size of a horse, with metal body parts.

What hope did Charlie have?

The Hound rose again. Its squealing stopped and it looked straight at Charlie. Its teeth were enormous in the moonlight, and its eyes burned a low red color.

The Hound was not natural. It was a creature of sorcery or machinery or both.

Who could have made it?

That was a question for another time. Charlie braced himself. The Hound jumped forward again—

Charlie dropped flat on his back.

He watched the Hound pass, snarling, over him, a shadow blocking out the stars and stinking of flesh and oil. Then he rolled to his feet and jumped after the Hound.

He didn't have to win this fight. If he could keep the Hound occupied long enough, Charlie's friends could get through the big-folk gate and into the pixie habitat under Cader Idris and be safe.

Probably.

Charlie grabbed the Hound's tail, as near its base as he could, and held on.

The Hound felt him. It whipped around and tried to pounce on him, but as the front half of the Hound moved, the hindquarters followed, and the Hound's own motion yanked Charlie out of reach of the Hound's teeth—barely.

The Hound's tail was also not flesh and blood. It was wrapped in fur, but as the tail whipped side to side, Charlie felt ball bearings within the tail roll back and forth against each other.

The Hound snapped at Charlie again and missed. The

stink of its breath made Charlie tremble, but he felt elated. The Hound had missed! Had Charlie found the one place in the world safe from the monster—attached to its own body?

Wham!

Charlie slammed into a boulder. He let go of the Hound's tail and bounced in the grass. In an instant, a paw the size of Charlie's head was upon him, pressing down into his chest and squeezing him.

The Hound didn't need to bite Charlie's head off. It could shatter him with its weight alone.

"HRAAAAAAOOOOOOOOOOOOOOO!"

The Hound roared into his face, hot and wet. Charlie was trapped.

"De Minimis and Underthames!"

The last thing Charlie expected, staring gigantic canine death in the face, was the arrival of a billy goat. But just as the Hound opened its jaws, a goat hurtled in and butted the Hound in the temple with both horns.

The Hound shook off the blow, turned to roar at the goat, and saw the goat's tiny rider, Natalie de Minimis—

who shoved her spear into the Hound's eye.

The yelp of pain that rang from the Hound as the pixie's spear punctured its eyeball nearly deafened Charlie. The Hound reared back, and the spear went with it, flinging both Gnat and the goat into the darkness. The Hound batted at its face, roaring and shrieking.

Charlie ran.

"Gnat!" he shouted.

The pixie popped up in the tall grass, and as Charlie passed, he scooped her up in both arms.

"Please tell me the big-folk gate is this direction!" he shouted. With Gnat in his arms and no need to slow his pace for Bob, Charlie unleashed the full power of his legs. He still had his small limp, but he flew over the grass and stone.

"Over there!" Gnat pointed, and Charlie adjusted his course slightly.

As he approached the cliff and its boulder, he saw Bob and Ollie. They stood on the top of the boulder—no, that wasn't quite right: they stood in a seam of the cliff face just above the boulder. That must be where the gate was. The boulder made a sort of staircase that led up to it.

Ollie and Bob cheered.

"Faster, Charlie!" Ollie yelled.

Behind him, Charlie heard the heavy footfalls and the breathing of the Hound. Mixed in with those sounds now was a terrible, bloodcurdling whimper, punctuated every few moments by a dark *"Yap!"*

"Look over my shoulder," Charlie said to Gnat. "Tell me exactly when the Hound pounces."

She looked. "Not yet."

Charlie sprinted.

The cliff came closer. The chimney sweeps crouched down and backed into the seam. Charlie could see the big-folk gate now. There was no way the Hound could fit through.

But could Charlie make it in time?

"Not yet."

The cliff drew closer. Still Ollie and Bob disappeared into the seam.

Charlie was almost there. He saw the pits and striations in the boulder he would need to run up.

"Now!"

Charlie slid to the ground.

He protected Gnat with his body, fearing that the Hound might land on them and tear them both to shreds. But again the Hound passed over him, yowling its bafflement.

As the Hound passed Charlie, Charlie rolled back up to his feet—

jumped, still holding Gnat—

passed over the head of the Hound—

which snapped at him and missed.

Charlie turned sideways just in time to dive into the seam of the rock, a split second before the Hound crashed against the opening, roaring and pounding at the stone.

Gnat wiggled in his arms, and Charlie let her go. They crawled into the darkness, anxious to get out of reach of any stray paw the Hound might venture into the cave. When he'd gone as far as he dared, crawling totally blind, Charlie collapsed.

For a few seconds, he lay in silence.

Then he heard a throat being cleared.

"Well, I 'ope the goat made it."

As is fitting for a charismatic, heroic Bronze Age culture, pixies are renowned for the taking of trophies.

—Smythson, *Almanack*, "Pixie"

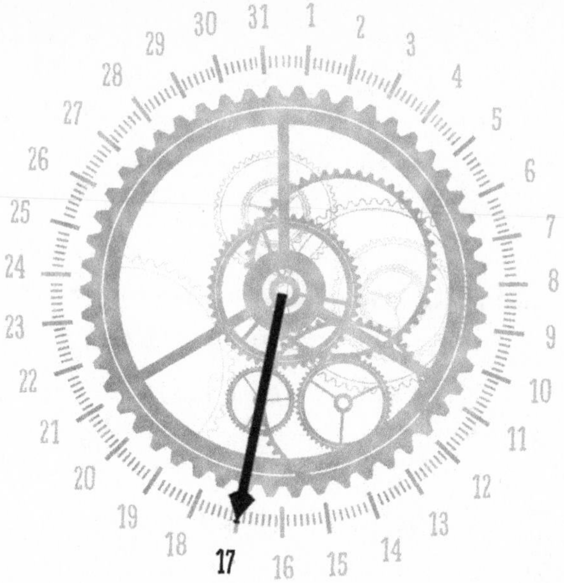

"Gnat," Ollie said. They still sat in total darkness. "Ain't you got to defeat three big beasts to be able to go home?"

"That's right!" Bob's voice was enthusiastic. "I 'ad forgotten. Two more beasts to go!"

"Defeat," Gnat said. "Not *escape.* And they don't need to be beasts. But aye, I must perform three mighty deeds."

" 'Ow will your folk know you've done it?" Bob asked.

"Yeah," Ollie chimed in. "How will they know you ain't just pretending?"

There was a moment's silence before Gnat spoke. "They'll know."

No one had anything to add to that.

"Well, I might as well be in a pig's intestine, for 'ow much I can see."

"Ain't this a fairy kingdom?" Ollie added. "Where's the, what do you call it, the glow-weed?"

"Gloom-moss. Aye, there was gloom-moss here, once. The stubs of it still cling to the walls. But 'tis shriveled up and dead many a year now."

"What else do you see?" Charlie had forgotten that Gnat's vision worked in complete darkness.

"This barony was called Giantseat." Gnat's voice was sad. "I can read its welcome signs. It ended in fire."

Charlie shuddered.

"That's cheerful," Ollie said.

" 'Ow about a way out? If we 'eld 'ands, an' watched our 'eads, could you find us another road out?"

"Or we could lie right here," Ollie suggested, "take a nice little nap, and just walk outside the way we came in once the sun's up and the Hound goes away."

"Aye, if we knew for sure the Hound would go away with the sun, which we do not."

"The rabbit said the Hound came with nightfall," Ollie reminded them.

"First of all, just because the 'Ound comes with nightfall don't mean the 'Ound leaves with sunrise. Maybe the 'Ound comes with nightfall an' it don't leave until it eats you. An' second, Ollie, you're putting an awful lot of weight on the words of a rabbit."

"She seemed trustworthy."

"She might be the most trustworthy witch rabbit as ever lived, mate. It just ain't like you to do the trusting."

"She's interesting. She's a witch, and I don't think she's a liar. . . ." Ollie's voice trailed off.

"I trust her, too," Charlie said.

Another silence.

Something Aldrix had said to him was ringing softly in the back of Charlie's mind, and he had to share it. "The Old Man lives in a maze."

" 'Ow's that, mate?"

"Al—one of the dwarfs, the young boy, said the Old Man lived in a maze. I was imagining that it was some kind of building. You know, a maze on the top of Cader Idris."

"There ain't a maze on the top of Cader Idris," Ollie pointed out.

"Right." Charlie let it sink in.

"You're saying it might be in Giantseat that he lives," Gnat said. "In the old barony."

"Maybe. Or maybe Giantseat, I don't know, connects to the place where he lives. Think about the boy we saw up on the mountain."

"I'm thinking about him," Ollie agreed. "I'm thinking about me giving him a black eye for throwing you over that cliff."

"Where did he come from?" Charlie asked. "He was awfully high on the mountain to be rambling. He lives up here, somewhere, but the only buildings I've seen are the crumbly old shepherds' shelters made of stone. And what was it Aunt Big Money called it?"

"Mountain 'Ouse. I 'ear what you're saying, Charlie. Them

piles of rocks the shepherds sleep in to keep out of the rain just ain't grand enough to quantify as Mountain 'Ouse."

"Qualify, Bob."

"That's what I said. An 'ouse with a name ought to 'ave, I dunno, *servants.*"

Bob was right. Syzigon had even said the Old Man had servants. Charlie thought a little more. "So we haven't seen the whole mountain. For all we know, just at the top of that little canyon there's a big mansion, and that's Mountain House, and it's big enough for my friend to call it a maze."

"Or perhaps 'tis Mountain House we're standing in. Aye, I'll lead you."

"Right," Bob said. "Deeper in it is. Only remember, Gnat, you ain't the tallest of us, an' now you're on foot. I'll keep an 'and out in front of my 'ead just in case, but don't go dragging us into knee-'igh tunnels. Not without warning."

"I'll go second," Charlie said. "It won't matter if I bump my head."

"It'll matter," Ollie said. "Only you're tougher than Bob."

" 'E's tougher than you, too, china."

"Yeah. But I won't be bumping my head on anything. I'll be hugging the ground and following you by smell."

"By smell?" Charlie asked.

Ollie muttered. *Bamf!* Rotten eggs.

Of course. "Right, then. Let's join hands and get going."

They linked hands and Gnat led them.

Both Charlie's hands were full, so he banged his head once or twice, but the pace was slow, and the bumps didn't hurt much. Gnat was very good about leading him over smooth footing.

They walked a long time in the dark. Charlie smelled water and heard it dripping. He heard scurrying noises in the corners of the cave.

"Tell me that ain't motleys," Bob said, using her rhyming-slang word for ghouls.

"Nay, 'tis nothing so dangerous. All manner of things live in caves, most of them sightless, colorless, and harmless."

"I reckon we all know this is the moment when Ollie would crack a joke about pixies," Bob said. "In 'is honor, let us imagine what 'e might 'ave said if 'e wasn't a snake at this moment."

" 'And not just the ones in tricorn hats,' " Charlie suggested. He tried his best to say it in an Ollie voice, but it wasn't quite right.

" 'I don't know about 'armless,' " Bob tried. " 'I know from experiment they've got gaols.' "

"Experience, Bob."

" 'Ush. I'm being *Ollie* now."

" 'If they're so sightless,' " Gnat said in a pretty good Ollie imitation, " 'who's leading this caravan?' "

Ollie hissed.

Then there was light. Green and blue, ahead.

Gnat picked up the pace. Charlie staggered, trying to keep up as he dodged stalactites and stalagmites. When he could see well enough, he dropped Gnat's and Bob's hands and broke into a run.

The light came from a hole in the floor. Charlie lowered

himself to all fours, just ahead of Gnat, and looked down through the gap, which opened into the ceiling of another large cave.

The cavern below reminded him of Underthames. It was large, and gems sparkled on all the walls and in the ceiling. Nests lay scattered about the chamber, and on the far side stood structures Charlie couldn't quite make out.

A stream ran down the middle of the chamber. On the near side of it, the nests were burned completely, or scattered. But on the far side of the water, they were intact.

"The 'eck," Bob said over her shoulder.

Gnat said nothing. In the light shining from Giantseat's crystals, Charlie saw tears on her face. Ollie coiled up beside Charlie's hand and lowered his serpentine head into the opening, tongue flickering in and out.

Charlie decided to climb down. He rotated, still on hands and knees. In the shadows, he scrabbled about until he found a raised ridge, a seam in the floor he could grab with his fingers. Then he backed his legs and body over the lip of the hole until he was dangling.

"There would have been a ladder once," Gnat said. "I suppose it burned up in the same fire that wrecked everything else."

"Careful, Charlie," Bob said.

He let himself go.

He bent his knees on impact and he rolled down a short slope. Then he stood, swept some of the dirt off his coat with his hands, and hiked up the slope to stand under the hole in the ceiling.

"Who's next?" he called.

Bob promptly jumped down the hole. Charlie caught her in his arms, bowing slightly from the weight, and set her down.

"Thanks, mate."

Then Ollie dropped down, still in the form of a snake, and finally Gnat. Charlie caught them both. Immediately upon touching the ground, Gnat marched briskly off toward the unburned part of the chamber.

"Let's find your Caradog Pritchard," she said.

Ollie took his boy shape again, and Charlie and the sweeps followed the pixie.

On the other side of the stream, Charlie expected the cavern to be *less* desolate. Instead, it was *more.* It felt *haunted.* As they walked past nest after nest, Charlie hoped a tricorn hat would peep out, or a piping, silvery voice would shout a greeting, or pixies in arms and armor would emerge to shout a challenge.

None of that happened.

They crossed a path, a road that led among the nests, and Gnat turned to follow it.

"These nests," Bob said as they marched. "If we was to wait—say, camp 'ere a day or two—you could put up your cocoon in one of these an' molder an' get your wings back, right?"

"Molt," Charlie said.

"That's what I said, molt."

"I could." Gnat didn't slow down.

"An' why don't we do that, then? You go all butterfly on us while we enjoy this light show, maybe eat a few sightless,

’armless things. I could stand to catch up on my sleep, even after last night.”

“Aye. And when we’ve warned Caradog Pritchard, I might come back here and, as you say, go all butterfly.”

“Right.” Bob pulled her bomber down tighter on her head. “Mission first.”

On a rise surrounded by empty nests stood a paved floor and a ring of carved stone columns. The structure reminded Charlie of a similar pavement and ring he’d seen in Underthames, Gnat’s home.

Gnat stood silently looking at it. Was she thinking of her barony?

Or of her cousin Seamus, who’d said she was his own true heart, but who was betrothed to her ruthless cousin Elisabel, the Baroness of Underthames?

Either way, Charlie didn’t interrupt her.

When her thoughts were finished, Gnat led them farther along the path and deeper into the chamber. Down the far side of the rise and around the corner, the cavern ended abruptly. Not in a natural stone ending, but in a solid steel wall.

Set in the center was a door-sized rectangle, also made of steel. It had no visible knob, latch, or keyhole.

“Well,” Ollie said. “I reckon we found Mountain House.”

Though Scotland Yard continue to ask the public to come forward with any information regarding an organization called the Anti-Human League, some of London's elder folk think the investigation has taken a wrong turn. "I cannot say it any more simply," said Mr. Grim Grumblesson, a lawspeaker who practices in Whitechapel. "There is no such thing as the Anti-Human League. If there were, I'd have heard of it. Now I stand ready, as I'm sure all folk stand ready, to assist the government in its investigation. Only let's not chase shadows, shall we?"

— "Explosions Investigated," *Daily Telegraph*, 26 June 1887

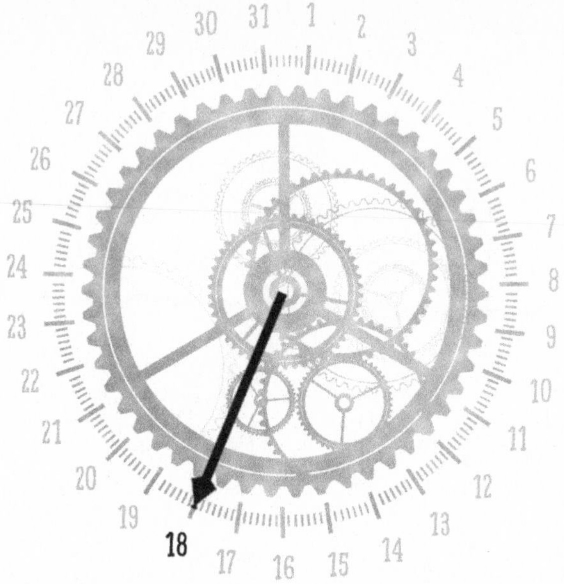

Ollie knocked on the door.

When there was no answer, Charlie joined him. He banged as hard as he could. He even kicked to try to make the loudest noise possible, and it was very loud indeed.

Boom! Boom! Boom!

Nobody answered.

Bob, meanwhile, had become interested in the edge of the steel sheet, where it joined the natural stone wall of the cavern.

"What do you see, Bob?" Charlie asked. "A way in? Is there a crack?"

"Not a way in," she said. "Not unless you're a lot stronger than I think you are. I reckon even a crew of 'ulders with crowbars would find themselves stuck if they was trying to peel back this sheet by strength of 'and."

"What is it, then?" Charlie banged several more times on the door.

"Look at these bolts 'ere." A thick band of steel skirted the wall, folded in an L shape that allowed bolts to be sunk into the steel wall and also into the stone. The aeronaut pointed at the large-headed bolts themselves.

Charlie looked. The bolt heads were six-sided. Within each bolt head, there was a hexagonal depression.

He shrugged. "They're bolts, Bob. I'm not sure what you're seeing."

"I ain't sure what I'm seeing either." Bob's eyes narrowed thoughtfully. "I need to think on it a little more."

BONG!

A ringing noise filled the cavern, so loud it hurt. Charlie covered his ears and turned around.

Ollie had a rock the size of his head, clutched in both hands. He raised it overhead, stepped back, and charged the steel door again.

BONG!

And again.

BONG!

Huffing and sweating, Ollie threw the rock aside. "If that don't get us a little attention, nothing will."

Charlie and the sweeps waited, and still no one came.

Charlie only realized Gnat had left them when she reappeared, a disappointed look on her face. "Giantseat has other passages and chambers," she reported. "Every passage leading in this direction ends in a sheet of steel."

"Well, the mountain didn't grow this wall." Ollie kicked it with his boot to show which wall he meant. "The pixies didn't build it. It wasn't the Hound. I guess that leaves your man Caradog Pritchard. He's an inventor like your dad, yeah, Charlie? An engineer? So I reckon this is Mountain House, all right."

"Caradog Pritchard." Bob scratched under her bomber. "An engineer."

" 'Tis no use, lads." Gnat surveyed the steel wall and sighed. "If they haven't heard us by now, they won't. And if they haven't opened to us by now, I don't expect they'll do that, either."

Ollie yawned. "Then I've got a plan to propose. Are you going to get all shirty with me if I flop down in a pixie bed to sleep for a few hours?"

Gnat shook her head. "I'm pleased my folk can offer you this much hospitality. We can catch a few hours' rest and leave in the morning. More likely than not, the Hound will have disappeared by dawn."

"Agreed." Ollie was already crawling into the nearest nest. "And then I've got a question to ask Aunt Big Money. It's nice in here, by the way. A bit dusty."

"What question?" Charlie asked.

But Ollie was already snoring.

Bob started climbing in after him.

Gnat looked at Charlie. "What's next?"

"I know there's another way into Mountain House. It's the way the dwarfs took, on the north side of the mountain. So we can hike over the ridge and drop down that side, try to find the door."

"Something's not right."

Charlie looked around at the empty Giantseat. "You mean this?"

Gnat shook her head. "Nay, the destruction and abandonment of Giantseat happened ages ago. I mean that the dwarf told you someone would let us in if we climbed the valley. And that didn't happen. Was the dwarf lying? Was he confused? Has something changed recently?"

Charlie nodded slowly.

"I'm only saying, we need to be careful."

"I'll think about it. You get some sleep." Charlie patted the nest from which Ollie's and Bob's snores could now both be heard. "Are you sure you don't want to . . . spin a cocoon?"

"I could do it," Gnat said. "I can feel the power in these old nests, still." She pointed at the gemstones on the ceiling, but she didn't say anything about what might connect the stones, the lights, the nests, and her ability to spin a cocoon. "But it would take too long."

"Maybe you could spin a cocoon around the lads." Charlie grinned. "Grow them each a nice pair of wings."

Gnat laughed. "Bob might like that. I'd be interested to see what became of Ollie the next time he changed shape."

Charlie imagined Ollie as a yellow snake with iridescent green butterfly wings, and he laughed pretty hard, too.

The two of them climbed into a second nest, because the sweeps entirely filled the nest they'd chosen. Gnat crept near the edge of the nest and curled forward into a ball, resting on her forearms and knees.

Charlie realized he'd never seen Gnat sleep. She must not require sleep very often; on the first night of their journey from London, she'd stayed awake and spent her time scouting. He looked at Gnat and imagined how she would look with her wings still on. The wings would be upright, which made sense because it would protect them from being bruised or broken, but it would also be beautiful. Gnat in her sleep would look sort of like a magical butterfly-flower.

"You're amazing," he said. "I don't know if you know that."

"No, Charlie." Gnat yawned, raising her head from her forearms for a moment. "You're the amazing one. I'm just a pixie."

And then she fell asleep.

Charlie stretched himself the length of the nest. Although from the outside it looked like it was made of sticks, the inside was lined with softer things: feathers, strips of cloth, dried grass, moss, fur, even old pixie wings, which were slightly fuzzy to the touch.

Charlie anchored himself firmly with his toes in the bottom of the nest and found that he could just reach the nest's edge. There he folded his forearms and settled his chin onto them. He wasn't curled into a ball, but with his head on his arms, he felt as if he were Charlie de Minimis, pixie adventurer, come to rest in his hereditary family home of Giantseat.

He gazed around at the nests, the light, the stone ruins.

In the ruins, he saw a flash of movement.

It was tiny. He'd only seen it for a second.

But it wasn't a colorless cave-dwelling thing. Charlie was sure he'd seen a person in a black coat. A person he'd seen before.

He considered his options. He could call out, but he thought the pale boy would disappear. He could try to avoid alarming the boy by approaching him openly and alone. But the last time he'd done that, the boy had thrown him down a cliff.

Charlie decided to sneak.

Keeping a careful eye on the stone ruins, Charlie slipped over the back of the nest. Crouching in its shadow, he felt around on the ground and gathered up three pebbles.

It would help that the light in the cavern was irregular and of many colors.

Charlie needed to distract the boy so he could move closer. He sighted carefully, aiming at the stream running down the middle of the chamber, and threw.

Plunk!

As the stone hit, Charlie was already on the move. He carefully watched the pillars on the small rise, he moved in a low crouch, and he cut right, heading toward the ruins at an angle. His chosen route was not the most direct, but it would keep him generally out of sight.

No sign of the pale boy.

Charlie hunkered down again behind a nest.

His view of the pillars on the knoll was from a different angle now, but he still didn't see the pale boy. He aimed at the stream again, but this time at a spot a little farther away from the hill and to the left.

His aim was slightly off. He heard the rattle of the pebble striking stone and bouncing and then the plunk of it falling into water.

He was rewarded with a view of the boy. The mysterious boy of the mountains and rooftops who had been following Charlie for several days stood with his back to Charlie now, peering in the direction from which the noise had come.

Charlie tiptoed forward, eyes on the boy, careful not to risk detection by attempting too big a gain. Eight quick steps forward cut the distance between the two of them in half, and then Charlie ducked behind a nest.

His mind was full of questions for the pale boy: Where is your father? What is his connection with dwarfs? Why won't you let us see him? What's the Hound, who made it, and what is it doing?

And also: What was it like, learning you were not made of flesh and blood? Does your father love you? Do you wish you were his natural son?

Do you feel lonely?

With his third and final pebble, Charlie aimed to his right. He chose a nest this time, because it would be an easy target to hit, and also because a noise in a stream might, after all, be a fish.

He dropped the pebble right into its center with a soft rustle.

Then he sprinted, quick and silent as he could manage, into the middle of the pillars.

But the boy was gone.

Charlie looked around, baffled. He saw no sign the boy had ever been there.

"Come back!" he called softly, not wanting to wake his friends. "I just want to talk to you!"

Nothing.

"Won't you tell me your name?" Charlie pleaded.

Silence.

And then, a few paces from him, Charlie saw a flash of bright color at the edge of the stream. Not a gemstone, but cloth. He walked to the stream and picked up what turned out to be a pair of striped trousers.

"Like a dwarf's," he said out loud. The trousers were striped white and purple, they were wet from the stream, and they looked new.

Charlie looked around again. He saw no sign of the pale boy and no sign of any dwarfs, so he turned back and rejoined his sleeping friends to wait out the night.

Draco draco (common names: dragon, wyrm)—Dragons were once considerably more common in these islands than they are today. In our time, dragons are only to be seen in Britain as trained beasts of war in military regiments, or wild (and to be avoided) north of the Grampians.

—Smythson, *Almanack*, "Dragon"

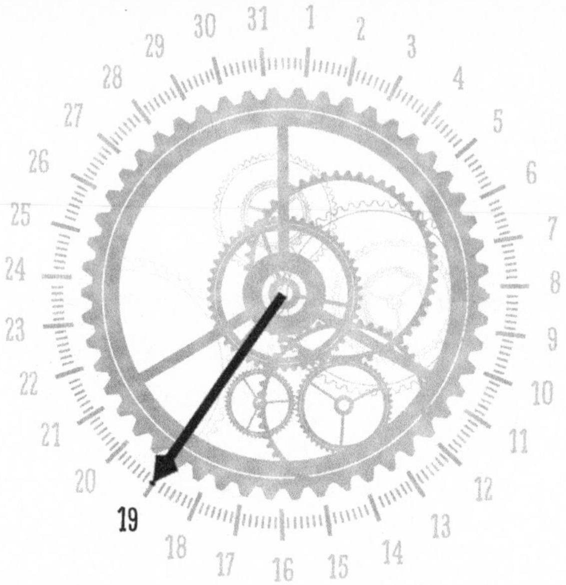

After his friends woke up, they went back to the big-folk gate. They traveled a slightly different road this time, Gnat scouting the path. After a few minutes, the gloom-moss again disappeared and they walked in darkness.

Ollie went out the gate first, in snake form. When he came back, he reported that there was no sign of the Hound.

This turned out to be not quite true. When Charlie dropped from the rock seam to the valley floor, he saw multiple enormous paw prints and great scuff marks where the Hound and his battle with it had left very big, very definite signs.

But the Hound itself was gone.

In the sunlight, Charlie showed his friends Thassia's compass. He felt silly using dwarf terms to explain it, but the words seemed appropriate. "The compass points to the wagon of a certain dwarf."

"Which one?" Ollie asked.

"A certain dwarf who is my friend. Who can get things done."

Bob scratched her scalp under the bomber. "If 'e can get things done, can 'e get us into Mountain 'Ouse?"

Charlie shrugged. "I hope he can. He's the one who sent us up the mountain in the first place, but I think he knows another way in."

"Well, then 'e sounds like the right dwarf for us."

Ollie crowded close to Charlie to look at the compass. "Which way's it point now, mate?"

Charlie looked. The compass pointed them north and east, up over a ridge that was steep, but not a sheer cliff. "Over the mountain."

Ollie appeared disappointed. "What if we was to drop in and say hello to Aunt Big Money first? Thank her for the goats."

"We'd better do that later," Charlie said. "Once we get into Mountain House, I think we'll be able to talk to her all we like."

"Maybe she can get us into Mountain House."

"She tried, mate, remember? Those were 'er goats we rode up the 'ill, an' they took us right to that bloke on the mountaintop. If the rabbit could get us in to see the Old Man, I reckon it would 'ave already 'appened."

Ollie looked down at his feet, but he nodded. "Right, then. Let's go climb over this mountain."

They climbed. Charlie had to slow his pace to match his friends'. Gnat was tireless, but once their path began to lead them up the slope on the other side of the valley, the chimney sweeps panted and gasped for breath.

At a rest stop near the top of the ridge, Bob swept the breadth of their panoramic view with her arm. Below lay the valley, and below that the forest, and the trail leading down to the dark woods and bright pastures around Cader Idris. Off to the right, billows of steam suggested where Machynlleth was, and beyond it Charlie could see the dark blue arm of the sea.

"All that, mate?" Bob said. "You can't see that in London."

Ollie didn't even look. "You mean you don't *have* to see it in London. Instead you can see theaters, and buses, and coaches, and costermongers, and cobblestones, and gaslight, and everything else that makes up civilization."

"But this is England. You love England, don't you? You've been a queen-an'-country lad since I met you."

"I love England, all right," Ollie agreed. "But this is *Wales.* And even if it *were* England . . . it ain't London. You and I have talked philosophy before, Bob. Everything outside London is rubbish."

The hike over the mountain took the better part of the day. As they crossed near a particularly craggy peak, Gnat drew Charlie's attention to a ring of boulders. The rocks were the size of hansom cabs, and they stood shoulder to shoulder in a perfect ring.

"Standing stones," Charlie said. "Ancient crossroads."

"Oh, aye?"

Charlie nodded. "A good place to contact any elder folk who may be living on this mountain, but I don't think Caradog Pritchard is one of the elder folk."

Gnat laughed. "Charlie, you know many things. Sometimes you know less than you think."

"What is it, then?"

"Go on, take a look."

Charlie climbed onto Bob's shoulders; from there he dragged himself to the top of the nearest stone. Then he lay on his belly, extended a hand down, and pulled her up to join him.

Ollie flopped into the grass and stared at the sky.

The space enclosed by the ring was full of ashes and cinders. It was depressed in the center, but not in a perfect bowl shape—the depression was oblong and winding.

"What is it?" Charlie called to Gnat. "Old volcano?"

The pixie laughed again. "Dragon's nest."

"The 'eck!" Bob jumped down as if the stone she was standing on had burst into flame. Charlie looked a little longer.

"No eggs," he reported.

"Aye, and no dragon, either. Or we'd have seen it long since."

"Could this be what happened to the pixies of Giantseat? Did they fight a war against dragons?"

"You don't really fight wars against dragons," Gnat said. "You can leave them alone. You can hunt them down. Or you can run screaming in fear with your hair on fire. But to answer your true question, aye, perhaps. Perhaps the folk of the barony tangled with a clutch of dragons and got the worse end of it. Or perhaps not. One way or the other, this mountain has history."

"And mysteries," said Ollie.

"An' secrets," added Bob. " 'Op on down now, Charlie. It'd be a real shame if some dragon took this very moment to decide 'e wanted to reoccupy this very comfortable-looking old nest."

Charlie jumped down.

"Dragons." Ollie snorted. "Something else you don't have to worry about in London, mate."

The descent down the far side of the mountain was much faster than the climb up. Charlie found his biggest challenge was keeping his footing. The compass occasionally led them to cliff tops or tangles of fallen trees, but nothing so big they couldn't get around it with a few minutes' extra work.

To their north, ahead of them as they dropped into the valley on the other side of Cader Idris, stood more mountains. They were mantled in dark green by thick forest and had shoulders of gray slate, but the peak looming above them was white with snow, though it was the end of June.

Snowdon. Yr Wyddfa. The burial mound.

Finally the road came into view. As they descended through dark-leafed deciduous forest, Charlie scanned the track, hoping he'd see red-and-gold wagons, but he didn't. Of course, maybe they were under some enchantment of Thassia's, and he was just failing to notice them. Or maybe, since the needle pointed straight, the wagons were *beyond* the road. Maybe they were on another road, past this one and over the next hill. The compass didn't tell Charlie anything about *how far away* Syzigon's wagon was.

But Charlie still felt a little nervous.

" 'Ere now, what's that?"

Charlie snapped out of his thoughts. To his left, from the west, a vehicle approached. For a moment, Charlie expected to see Syzigon's red wagons, or maybe the wagons of a different dwarf family.

Instead he saw William T. Bowen's steam-truck.

He dropped behind a fallen log and his friends dropped with him. They were high enough on the hill that he didn't think anyone would spot them, but he didn't want to take any chances.

He himself could see Bowen quite clearly. The incorporator who had kidnapped the boy dwarf Aldrix stood at the wheel of his steam-truck and beamed at the road as his giant India rubber tyres pounded over its slates. That sight alone would have made Charlie uncomfortable, but there was more.

The deck of the steam-truck was packed with men.

They weren't in any sort of uniform, but they were big men, and armed; Charlie saw rifles and pistols and scatterguns. Most of them also had knives hanging from their belts, and a few had actual swords.

"Beautiful," Bob whispered.

Charlie stared at his friend.

"I mean the machine," the aeronaut protested. "Not the babblings on back."

Charlie looked to Ollie to explain.

"Babbling brook, crook," he said.

"Where do you think they're bound?" Gnat asked.

"I'm more worried about where they're coming *from*," Charlie said.

He watched the steam-truck rattle along the highway, concerned that the rough men standing on its deck would jump off and come looking for him and his friends. But the steam-truck didn't slow down, and when it had gone, Charlie glanced down at his compass.

"I think we're close," he said.

He was *afraid* they were close. What if Syzigon had encountered William T. Bowen again, and this time it had gone worse for the dwarfs?

They descended the rest of the hill and crossed into the center of the road without seeing any sign of the wagons.

"Keep your eyes open," Charlie said. "Remember, dwarf wagons can be very difficult to spot."

They crossed the road through a stand of pines. Beyond that, they descended another slope and crossed a brook . . . and Charlie accidentally kicked a pile of red wood.

Ollie cursed. "Where did that come from?"

They stood in a small meadow Charlie hadn't noticed. A wagon rested across a pair of fallen logs at the edge of the meadow. It had no wheels. And in the center of the meadow, at Charlie's feet, was a pile of red-and-gold-painted wood. Charlie saw spokes and shingles in it and knew immediately that the wood was the remains of one or more of the dwarf wagons.

He caught a sob of shock before it could escape his chest.

"Syzigon? Thassia? Yellario?" He wasn't really sure he should use their names so conspicuously, but he was terrified.

"My friend!" Syzigon stepped from behind a screen of thin young pines. His face was streaked with smoke and sweat, his jerkin was torn, and the braids of his beard were thrown back over his shoulders. In his hand he held a hammer, and behind him came the other dwarfs and Lloyd Shankin. "You've come back to us in our hour of need."

Dwarfs are a practical folk who value accomplishment. This is evident in their constant boasting about the leaders of their caravans that they are dwarfs who can get things done.

—Smythson, *Almanack*, "Dwarf"

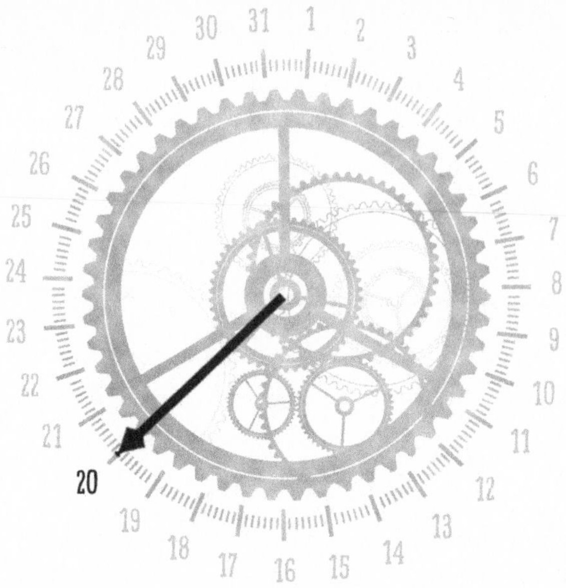

"It seems I am to find myself perpetually in your debt."

Syzigon sawed lengths off a board Yellario had cut and planed.

Under Bob's direction, Ollie, Gnat, and Lloyd Shankin had put the wheels back on the least damaged wagon and had nearly finished assembling the second vehicle. Because all three wagons had suffered serious damage—scorched and shattered boards, snapped yoke poles—the third was taking longer to repair. Charlie, Yellario, and Atzick worked on this one under Syzigon's leadership. They picked suitable trees, felled them, cut and shaped the trunks into boards, and then painted them.

The dwarf elders played with their grandchildren and watched five of the donkeys. The three sheyala stalked Bad

Luck John through the woods; he had kicked his hobble in two and pulled up his picket, but the tassel-eared cats kept him from getting very far.

"We're just helping," Charlie said. "Except for Bob, we're not particularly good help."

"That yoke pole was a tree you uprooted with your bare hands." Syzigon pointed at the pole in question. "And the dewin has a song that blends a seam in wood down to nothing."

"He does?" Charlie changed the subject and lowered his voice. "What happened?"

"The Old Man's gate is blocked. Guarded by his enemies. They fired on us and chased us away. A certain dwarf was able to hide us, but not before they wrecked our wagons. Praise earth and sky, none of us were hurt."

"Just a little scorched." Charlie watched Lloyd Shankin sing as he held a board in place for Ollie to drive nails into it. The dewin had a hole the size of a large ham burned through his coat.

"Just a little." Syzigon gestured at the Welshman. "A certain singer showed up as we were running and tried to help."

"*Did* he help?" Blending a seam in wood sounded useful, but Charlie had a hard time imagining Lloyd summoning lightning or doing anything else that might be helpful in a fight.

Syzigon shrugged. "He tried."

"Well, our shortcut didn't turn out much better." Charlie looked into the stand of pine trees where Patali and Aldrix were counting a tree's branches and guessing how tall it was.

In the early-evening shade, Thassia stooped over the boards already painted red and added gold characters onto all sides, chanting with each stroke of her fine brush and sprinkling Dust from a pouch onto each character as she completed it.

Syzigon grunted. “You survived, though.”

“We all did. Will the Old Man escape?” Charlie asked.

“The Old Man is cunning,” Syzigon said. “And he’s armed. He knows these enemies well.”

“I still don’t know them.” Charlie frowned. “What do they want? Why do they do the things they do?”

“They kidnapped your father,” Syzigon reminded him. “And they killed him. Does it matter exactly why they did it?”

Charlie wasn’t sure. He changed the subject. “Will you tell me what you do for the Old Man?”

“We’re finders.” Syzigon shrugged. “When we bring the Old Man the items he asked us for on our previous visit, he gives us a new list.”

“What sorts of things does he ask for?”

“Our wagons are small. We bring him spices, seeds, oils. Also unusual feathers and other rare animal parts. Precious metals. Gems. Very small, specific machine parts. And before you ask, I don’t know what he does with any of it.”

“There must be other dwarfs who help him,” Charlie said, guessing from Syzigon’s own words. “And some of them have bigger wagons.”

“The Old Man has a foundry. I’ve known dwarfs who bring him ore, or large tooled items—pipe, tubing, cogs, and so on. None of them wear our colors.”

What was going on inside the mountain?

Syzigon cleared his throat. "You are welcome to come with us. We'll be going east in the morning. We don't have room for your friends, but we can share some food with them and help them find their path. And you are welcome with us for as far as the road goes."

"You won't deliver what you were bringing?"

Syzigon opened his hands helplessly. "I don't see how we can."

Charlie rocked back on his heels. The man his father had called Caradog Pritchard was surrounded by his enemies, and they were openly firing weapons. Whatever Charlie's warning might have been worth a few days earlier, now it was surely worth nothing.

Was his journey over?

* * *

Later, Charlie found himself alone for a minute with Lloyd Shankin. "How did you get back to the dwarfs?" he asked.

Lloyd smiled. "I sang my way here."

"And . . . you spent the night on the mountain? How was that?"

Lloyd's smile only got wider, and his eyes twinkled like the stars over Cader Idris.

* * *

Over plates of stew and thick black coffee, Charlie and his friends talked. They spoke openly with the adult dwarfs, Aldrix and Yezi having already gone to bed in the first of the repaired wagons, bundled in leather and silk.

"We ain't finished yet," Bob said. "That man needs 'elp."

"When did we become the Help Everybody Association?" Ollie objected. "There's widows and orphans and prisoners all over this world, and here you go wanting to help some random chap on a hillside."

"Helping people is a good thing." Lloyd Shankin pointed at Charlie with a spoon. "Isn't it, Charlie?"

Bob crossed her arms. " 'E ain't random. 'E's Charlie's dad's friend, for starters."

"I feel the same way," Charlie said. "It *is* good to help people when you can, and this is not a random old man. Also, the Iron Cog killed my bap. Anything I can do to stop them, I want to do it."

"Charlie's my mate," Ollie said. "I owe him. But this ain't a lark like going down old Pondicherry's chimney, Bob. This is dangerous."

"We've done dangerous before, Ollie, you know we 'ave. An' this Old Man, I think 'e's someone special."

"Is he as special to you as Aunt Big Money is to me?" Ollie's face was red. "Because I really wanted to talk to her again, and *that* wasn't going to be dangerous at all, and instead we climbed over the mountain and here we are, talking about risking our lives for some mad hermit."

" 'E ain't a mad 'ermit," Bob said. " 'E's important."

"Caradog Pritchard! Important?" Ollie snorted. "I'd never heard of him until I met Charlie."

“ ’E ain’t using ’is real name.” Bob looked solemn. “That’s because everybody thinks ’e’s dead.”

Ollie stopped his rant. “You say he ain’t using his real name, and you obviously think you know what his real name is. You’d better tell us.”

“It was the ’ex bolts, see?” Bob looked to Charlie.

Charlie shook his head. He had no idea what Bob was talking about.

“Those bolts in the steel wall in Giantseat. I got to thinking I’d seen bolts like ’em before. You know, an ’ead with six sides, an’ inside the ’ead an infestation with six sides again.”

Charlie considered that one for a moment. “Indentation?”

“You’ve got it. I ’ad to think about it a bit, an’ then it came to me. The Sky Trestle.”

That was the train that ran over rooftops and viaducts in London. “I remember the Sky Trestle,” Charlie said.

“The Sky Trestle ’as such bolts. An’ the reason it ’as them is the bolts were invented by the man who built the Sky Trestle. ’E used them on all ’is big projects, an’ as far as I know, nobody else ever did.”

Charlie gasped. “Isambard Kingdom Brunel?” The dwarfs recoiled in shock. “He’s dead! He died almost thirty years ago! Are you saying Isambard—”

“Enough!” Syzigon snapped.

“Excuse me.” Charlie slowed down. “And you think this person . . . you think he’s alive.”

“That’s the Old Man,” Bob said. “An’ . . . you know. Who I said. An’ Caradog Pritchard. All one fellow.”

“That’s mad,” Ollie said.

"Is it?" Bob stood up, the straps of her bomber bouncing around as she spoke. "Think about it. Brunel dies, what, about thirty years ago. Only 'e doesn't die. 'E gets kidnapped by the Iron Cog an' 'e 'as to work for 'em. Or maybe 'e doesn't realize as they're evil at first, an' 'e's in 'iding because it's sensitive work. Like for the queen. Later 'e changes 'is mind an' runs away from 'em, with 'is friend Mr. Pondicherry, and like Mr. Pondicherry, 'e stays in 'iding because now the Iron Cog wants 'im dead. The timing is right."

"Yeah, but . . . *Isambard Kingdom Brunel*?" Ollie kept his voice down almost to a whisper, but the dwarfs still frowned. "He's one of the greatest engineers who ever lived, isn't he? The man's famous. He's on monuments. His face is all over Waterloo Station. He's the Duke of Wellington of machine-makers."

Bob flapped her arms. "That's the most perfect thing! 'Oo did you think we was going to find when we got up that mountain an' knocked on the door? Punch an' Judy? Spring-'Eeled Jack? The Prince of Wales? No, it was going to be an engineer an' an inventor, it always was. An' it 'ad to be a really good one, someone as good as Raj Pondicherry, someone 'oo could build *amazing* things."

"Like the Articulated Gyroscopes." Ollie's face was thoughtful.

"Like *Charlie*!" Bob pointed.

Just like me, Charlie thought, remembering his attempts to corner the pale boy in Giantseat the night before. The possibility that Caradog Pritchard, his father's old partner and fellow refugee, might be Isambard Kingdom Brunel made Charlie intensely proud. Why couldn't his bap's face be in murals in Waterloo Station, too? He put his hand in his pocket and took out the stem of his father's pipe.

Ollie stood up slowly. He faced Bob as if to speak but stopped, looking at Charlie's hands. "Mate . . . is that yours?"

Charlie shook his head then nodded. "It was my bap's. It's broken, and I lost the other half."

Ollie frowned and plunged his hand into his own jacket pocket. "Did the other half look like this?" In his palm he held the missing cherry-colored bowl of Bap's pipe, with the gold panthers painted on it in a ring.

"Thank you." Charlie's voice trembled slightly.

"You're my mate." Ollie smiled. "I found it in my pocket while we was in gaol."

Somehow, in the storm that had wrecked the flyer, Ollie had ended up with the other half of Bap's pipe. Charlie took the bowl and pressed it against the end of the stem—only the tiniest crack showed that the pipe wasn't actually whole. "We rescue the Old Man."

"I see it." Ollie nodded. "We'll go rescue the man, if we can. I only have one request."

Bob's grin nearly touched both her ears. "Name it."

"I want to talk to the rabbit. I'll help you save the Old Man, and you help me see Aunt Big Money again."

"Of course, mate," Bob agreed. "Can you tell me why?"

Ollie blushed and looked at his feet. "I . . . I've got a question for her. It's kind of personal."

Bob nodded. They both spit in their palms and shook.

“I think the two goals are ’ighly contemptible.”

“Compatible, Bob.” Lloyd Shankin saluted the aeronaut with a spoon to the brim of his hat and one eye drifting left.

Charlie turned to look at Gnat, who had sat through the entire conversation without speaking. “What do you think?”

“My mother’s throne, three great deeds, and Charlie Pondicherry.” Gnat smiled gently. “I’m with you, Charlie.”

“All right, all right,” Ollie said. “But all-for-one-and-one-for-all ain’t a plan. What are we actually going to *do*?”

“I’d ’ave thought that was obvious,” Bob said. “We ’ave to steal back the flyer.”

* * *

Nearly twenty-four hours later, Charlie lay on his belly on a mound of dirt beneath a tree. The tree was one in a grove of chestnuts within the park attached to the largest house in Machynlleth.

The largest house by far.

Machine-Town Palace, Syzigon had called it as he drove his wagon through the night to get them here. Lloyd had said the Welsh name for it was Plas Machynlleth, which sounded pretty similar. The palace stood on the edge of town, and its wrought-iron gates bore the gigantic initials *WTB*.

Climbing up onto Ollie’s shoulders and peeking through parted ivy into a carriage-house window, Bob had reported seeing the steam-truck.

William T. Bowen. The man who had kidnapped Aldrix,

who drove the enormous steam-truck, who wore a pin that marked him as a creature of the Iron Cog. This was his house, and he had the flyer.

"Really," Charlie said to his friends, who lay in the dirt beside him, "I'm not sure how this could be worse."

"We need the flyer," Bob said. " 'Ow else can we reconvene the mountain?"

"Reconnoiter," Ollie said. "He's right, Charlie. It'd take us much too long to tramp about the slopes of that hill to look for more secret entrances and gates or to find your boy with the pushy hands. Plus, if we're in the air, we ain't getting bit by gigantic black dogs."

"Don't be so sure the Cŵn Annwn can't fly." Lloyd Shankin's voice sounded nervous, but that might just have been because lying on his stomach pushed all his breath out of his lungs. "The old stories are full of surprising detail about Death's Hounds."

"That monster on the mountain isn't one of the Cŵn Annwn," Charlie said. "It's a machine. At least in part."

Syzigon had driven down long and winding lanes to bring Charlie and his friends to the far edge of the park from the house. The park was bigger than the town, and included meadows, small artificial hills, and groves of well-ordered trees. There was also a perfectly circular lake, a stone's throw from the palace itself, with a statue in the center of an angel holding an astrolabe and a gearwheel. Lights glowed beneath the surface of the lake.

Thassia had insisted on coming with them. She lay with

them in the dirt now, chanting and turning from side to side, dowsing with a forked hawthorn rod. Charlie thought she was using her magic to keep a watch for enemies.

The palace was three stories tall and had a parapet around the edges of its peaked roof. The two upper stories rose only over the central portion of the house, like a tower. The ground floor spread more widely—Charlie counted ten large windows on the back side of the first story alone, all of them floor-to-ceiling big, with triangular lintels over the tops that looked Greek or Roman.

Around the front side of the building, carriages—some horsed, but most of them powered by steam—had been unloading visitors for an hour. The windows were full of light now, and getting lighter by contrast as the sun set. Through the windows, Charlie saw servants bringing in food for guests in black evening wear. The guests sat around an immense dining room table, and on a stand in the middle of that table sat a gleaming, unusual centerpiece—

Bob's flyer.

Si hei lwli, 'machgen i
Mae'r llong yn hwylio i ffwrdd
Si hei lwli, 'machgen i
Mae'r capten ar y bwrdd
Distaw, distaw, af drwy'r drws
Cysga, cysga, 'machgen clws
Si hei lwli, 'machgen i
Nes cawn ni eto gwrdd

(Si hei lwli, my child
The ship is sailing away
Si hei lwli, my child
The captain is on deck
Quietly, quietly, I'll go through the door
Sleep, sleep, my beautiful child
Si hei lwli, my child
Until we meet again)

—"Si Hei Lwli," traditional Welsh lullaby

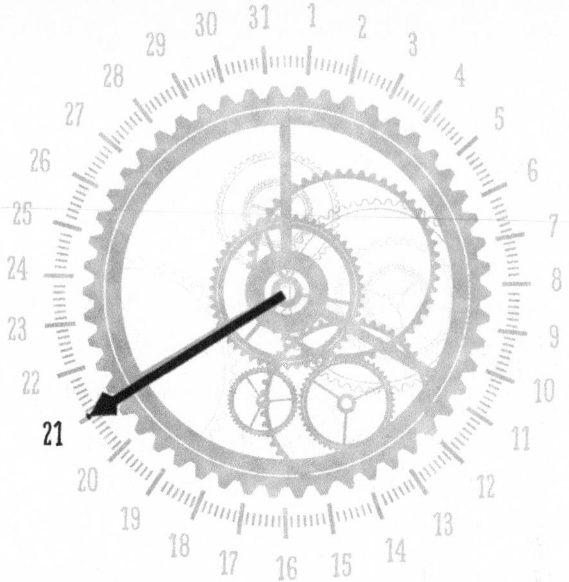

"Right." Bob's voice was gloomy. "We'd better go 'ave a closer look, at least."

"Wait." Thassia took the Dust of Distraction from inside her leather jerkin and held it ready in her hand, right next to her dowsing rod. "Now you can go."

Bob sprang to her feet and walked briskly across the grass, almost too fast for Ollie to keep pace. Lloyd Shankin followed with Thassia; he hunched low so she could share her cape with him.

Charlie brought up the rear with Gnat. He looked left and right but saw no guards, and then he was pressing himself up against the wall outside the dining room with his friends.

"Look at that." Lloyd Shankin pointed to the house's main gate, at the end of the drive. "Isn't that sad?"

"I'm sad the gate is shut," Ollie said. "We might need to run out that way."

"What's sad about it?" Charlie didn't know what Lloyd was trying to point out.

"The initials shaped into the iron, you see. You'll remember what they said on the outside?"

"WTB," Charlie said.

Lloyd nodded. "Look."

Charlie looked and read. "*GTB.* The letters on the outside and the letters on the inside are different. I don't understand."

Lloyd Shankin frowned. "The man's name is *Gwilym* Bowen, and he remembers it. That's a Welsh name. But he tells the outside world his name is *William;* that's the English version. Sad."

"He's given up his folk," Charlie said. "That's what you're saying."

"For wealth." Lloyd sighed.

"'E's not the one you should be feeling sad for at this moment." Bob put a finger over her lips. "Now 'ush."

They listened.

". . . for that report, Brother Daniels. It's gratifying to see that the society continues to take in more funds in dues, fees, royalties, and business profits than it spends in expenses. That bodes well for the continued success of our mission. I'm sure you'll all join me in thanking Brother Daniels for the fine work he continues to do in his position as lodge comptroller."

Charlie didn't know the voice. There was a round of applause for Brother Daniels, punctuated with cries of "Hear, hear!"

"They don't sound like an evil organization," Ollie whispered. "They sound like a gardening club."

"Please join me also in welcoming our host, Brother William T. Bowen, who will report on the status of Project Icarus." Applause.

"Gentlemen, welcome." Charlie recognized Bowen's voice. He listened to what the incorporator and kidnapper said, but at the same time he examined the building and the grounds for anything that might suggest a useful plan.

"I appreciate your coming here on short notice. As you all know, we have been aware for some time that one of our traitors was operating somewhere in the region of northern Wales. It has been my special portfolio to find Mr. Brunel and return him to the society, living or dead."

Bob stiffened.

"I say," muttered a trembling voice. "It mustn't *always* be *dead*."

"You will say you prefer *living*, no doubt." Bowen's voice assumed a placating tone. "And of course I do as well. But remember this, Brother Preece: we are building a new world here. One day, when Europe—no, when the *world*—lives in a state of leisure, peace, and universal good health, served and protected by machines and guided by the Iron Cog, we will look back at those who have died along the way with gratitude. The men we must kill today we will tomorrow see as heroes to the cause, as necessary sacrifices. And though some of us here, perhaps many of us, regard Brunel as a friend . . . well, the only true sacrifice is to surrender something—or some*one*—we hold dear. Is it not so?"

Brother Preece said nothing. Was he nodding silently?

Bowen cleared his throat. "We have long known that our *friend* Brunel uses certain families of dwarfs as his carriers and go-betweens. Surveillance of those families has been difficult, given the peculiarities of dealing with *semihomo barbatus,* but we have made excellent progress in identifying the families in question, infiltrating or turning them, and recruiting others."

Applause.

"Bob, can you drive a steam-carriage?" Charlie asked.

"If it's a mechanical device"—Bob jerked a thumb at her chest—"count me in."

A plan was beginning to form in Charlie's head.

Bowen wasn't finished. "But I must give credit to our colleagues pursuing the other turncoat. After years of searching, and months of careful arrangements, they were able to find the traitor Dr. Joban Singh."

Charlie shot his hand into his coat pocket and clutched Bap's pipe fragments.

"Dr. Singh could not be persuaded to rejoin us, but the operatives of Project Icarus eliminated him."

The biggest round of applause yet.

"We knew him as a friend. We recognized him as a threat. We should also remember Singh as a fallen hero. A moment of silence, please."

The applause stopped abruptly and silence followed. Charlie gritted his teeth and struggled not to yell. He felt friends grab both his shoulders and squeeze.

"Sadly, you will have heard of the failure of Project Galatea.

The queen sleeping in Buckingham Palace tonight is not the queen we would have wished. However, out of the failure of Galatea, and the success of Icarus in London, we have received important information. Here to recount their success are Brothers Heinrich Zahnkrieger and Gaston St. Jacques."

Heinrich Zahnkrieger!

Charlie risked leaning out from the wall a bit so he could look in the window. Sitting around the table were men in black evening wear. One of them, sitting just twenty feet from Charlie, was the kobold Heinrich Zahnkrieger. Charlie had known Zahnkrieger all his life as his father's partner, Henry Clockswain, only to find out too late that the kobold was an enemy and a traitor, and part of the conspiracy that had killed his bap.

"This flyer," the kobold began, standing on his chair as he spoke so he was tall enough to be seen, "is captured enemy property. The scoundrels flying this device thwarted our attempt to . . . to improve Queen Victoria's political and social views. Their vehicle here reminds us both of our defeat and of the swift vengeance we mete out to those who stand in our way."

Charlie wanted to rush in and grab the little kobold by the throat. Instead he explained his plan to his friends. Bob and Gnat jogged away to do their part, though not before Bob shot longing looks over her shoulder at the flyer.

Thassia chanted, sprinkling Dust about Charlie in large quantities.

"I'll leave, too; there are too many of us for that flyer."

Lloyd Shankin turned to go, then hesitated. "But I think I have a song that may be useful here."

"'Bread of Heaven'?" Ollie suggested. "Fly us all right out of here, wouldn't it?"

Lloyd smiled and then sang a single verse in Welsh. The tune had the slow rise and fall of a lullaby, and the words several times included a phrase that sounded like *see hey loolie.* "That will help."

Thassia finished as the kobold was wrapping up. "And so we telegraphed to Brother Bowen that our turncoat was likely living in the vicinity of the mountain Cader Idris, and calling himself Caradog Pritchard."

Telegraphed!

Before Charlie had left London, the information that Caradog Pritchard was Isambard Kingdom Brunel, the great inventor and builder and refugee from the Iron Cog, had reached the Cog's men in Wales. Charlie's mission had been a failure before it had even begun.

"At which point," Bowen resumed, "we laid siege to the mountain, including by releasing Brother St. Jacques's Hound."

"Don't think of it as *my* Hound." Charlie recognized the voice; the speaker was the Frenchman he thought of as the Sinister Man. Charlie peeked, and he saw the man sitting a few seats down from Heinrich Zahnkrieger. "Think of it as *our* Hound."

"And your—that is, *our*—other agent?" Bowen asked. He had a note of impatience in his voice. "The rakshasa?"

"Being procured." Gaston St. Jacques smiled blandly. "A

shaitan is not an easy creature to find in the best of cases, due to its nature. A shaitan who will work with us is still more of a challenge."

"But surely," Bowen said, "you are the man for the job. Should the siege persist, and should the rakshasa's services be necessary."

St. Jacques's smile didn't falter. "Surely."

"You ready, mate?" Charlie asked Ollie.

The sweep nodded.

Charlie shook Thassia's hand. "Thank you."

She winked, pulling her rune-stitched cape over her head and throwing its edge over Lloyd Shankin. Before they had taken three steps, Charlie had lost sight of them.

Charlie and Ollie crept to opposite ends of the dining hall. Ollie bent to pick up a rock, and they looked at each other.

Charlie held up fingers and counted down. Three . . . two . . . one.

Ollie smashed the window nearest him with the rock.

Diners jumped up from the table.

Except that some didn't. Some fell forward onto the table, snoring.

Ollie reached in to grab the handle and open the door. As he stepped inside, Charlie jumped through the window nearest him.

The diners who were alert turned to look at Charlie, but they had a hard time focusing on him. Especially when Ollie started his act.

Ollie clapped his hands. "Gentlemen! Your attention!"

Most of the men looked his way, though a few persisted in trying to stare at Charlie. Two more collapsed into sleep, one on a convenient sofa and the other on the floor.

Ollie muttered something. *Bamf!* He became a yellow cobra.

Shouting began. "Loup-garou!" "What is this?" "Bowen!" "St. Jacques!"

Bamf! Ollie was himself again.

Charlie was too far away to smell the stink of rotten eggs, but some of the diners held their noses.

"Gentlemen!" Ollie clapped his hands and began to dance a little jig. It wasn't a very good jig, but it didn't have to be. It just had to attract attention.

William T. Bowen, who wore a top hat and a ribbon on his chest in addition to his bottle-green coat and tails, lurched toward Ollie—*bamf!*—just as Ollie turned back into a snake.

Charlie jumped onto the table, kicking dishes aside, and noticed that Gaston St. Jacques was drawing a pistol from his jacket.

Charlie sprinted down the table. Wineglasses and china shattered as he crushed them underfoot, and when he reached the flyer, shining and polished and perfect-looking, with the Articulated Gyroscopes buckled into their correct position, he grabbed it.

The diners who weren't already asleep or standing pulled back, yelling, but very few of them looked directly at Charlie. Dwarfish magic, Charlie thought cheerfully.

One of the few who did, though, was Gaston St. Jacques.

Something about Charlie caught his attention, and he turned to look at the last second—

just as Charlie kicked him in the face.

St. Jacques went down without firing a shot.

Heinrich Zahnkrieger stood up, his hands on the table in front of him.

Charlie happily jumped. He landed with both feet together, stomping as hard as he could on the kobold's fingers.

Zahnkrieger fainted.

Somewhere behind him, Charlie heard shots.

He reached the end of the table and jumped to the floor. At the same moment, Ollie hurtled toward him—*bamf!*—and in midair became a snake.

Charlie grabbed his friend with one hand and kept running, right out the window, with the flyer on his shoulders.

Ollie slithered up Charlie's arm and settled around his neck.

Behind him, Charlie heard more shooting. He turned and raced toward the circular drive.

He'd told Bob to get any steam-carriage she could and be ready. As Charlie looked now at the line of carriages, he didn't see the aeronaut. Just black-suited drivers stumbling back in surprise as he charged through their ranks.

Crash!

The huge sound of splintering wood and shattering metal caught Charlie by surprise, but the instant he heard it, he knew where it had come from: the carriage house.

That was farther than he'd intended.

He ran faster.

For a moment, he thought his own speed would be enough and the flyer would pick him up and carry him away. But it didn't, and as he reached the carriage house, he saw the vehicle of Bob's choice and the back of her bomber cap as she worked the steering wheel, grinding a tight turn.

Bob had stolen William T. Bowen's steam-truck.

Charlie grabbed the ladder on the back of the steam-truck with one hand and gripped the flyer tightly with the other. A few seconds of climbing and he collapsed, with Bob's flyer, onto the deck of the steam-truck.

Ollie slithered away and took his human form again, and Gnat emerged from the wheelhouse, laughing. The three of them looked back to see a swarm of lights around the steam-carriages and a cavalcade of horses rushing past the parked vehicles, their riders brandishing long guns.

"Bob!" Charlie called. "Go faster!"

Britain glories in its participation in all the great international fraternal organizations, including the Knights Templar, the Freemasons, the Rosicrucians, and the Benevolent Society of Mechanicks, Engineers, and Friends of Industry.

—Smythson, *Almanack*, "Fraternal Societies"

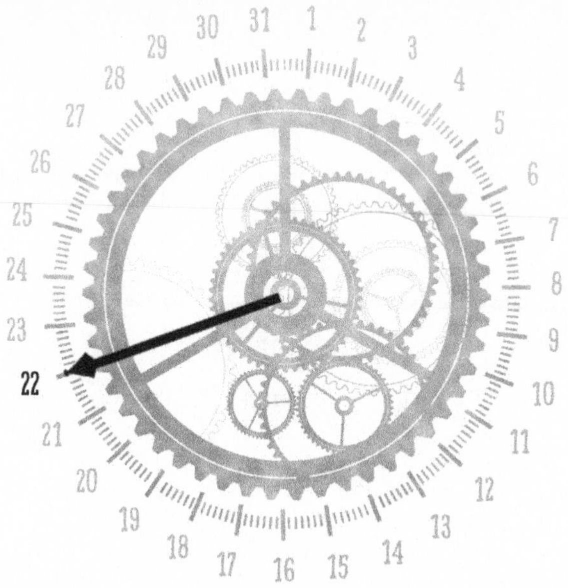

Crash!

The stolen steam-truck knocked open the iron gate at the end of the drive without slowing down.

Bob raced at breakneck speed along the narrow lane leading to the highway. The branches of the trees overhanging the lane had been trimmed to form a tunnel, big enough for the steam-truck to pass through without hitting anything.

Bang! Bang!

The horsemen were gaining on Charlie. They were a rough-looking lot, dressed in dirty clothing that didn't match, and they were shooting. Fortunately for Charlie, it was hard to aim while galloping.

Still, Charlie ducked low to the steam-truck's deck. He

kept one hand on the flyer and wrapped the fingers of the other through the grate of the deck. "Ollie!" he shouted. "Is there anything useful belowdecks?"

Ollie obligingly slipped below. Gnat followed.

The junction with the highway approached. To the right stood a row of gray stone buildings: a bakery, a butcher's shop, and a bookstore. To the left was an open pasture.

Charlie's plan was to turn right. He'd told Bob that. Right led back to Cader Idris, and higher cliffs.

Bob turned left.

She swerved without warning before reaching the highway. The steam-truck took the low stone wall surrounding the pasture at an angle, bouncing high into the air.

With one hand tethering him to the deck and the other holding the flyer, Charlie was floating for a moment—

and then crashing back down to earth.

Sheep scattered in all directions. Charlie half expected to see flattened white puddles of fluff behind the truck, but either Bob tried to avoid hitting the sheep or they were quick enough to get out of the way.

Some of the horsemen stopped, surprised by the sudden turn. Others galloped ahead to the junction. A few jumped their horses over the wall and came after the steam-truck directly.

One fell asleep and tumbled forward off his horse over the remains of the wall. Lloyd Shankin's lullaby, Charlie thought.

"Bob!" Charlie shouted. "I said *right*!"

Bob looked over her shoulder to shout back. "If we was to

go right, mate, I'd 'ave to slow down. 'Ow d'you feel about playing 'ost to a party of those 'orse-riding gents?" She turned back to the wheel.

Charlie looked back at the men chasing them. Rattling down the lane behind the horsemen, steam-carriages were now catching up. These had men with guns standing at the rear and leaning out the windows; the carriages were a much more stable platform for shooting than the back of a horse.

Bob shattered a wooden gate at the far end of the pasture and turned left again. On the highway the steam-truck began to really pick up speed.

The first horseman pulled up to the back of the steam-truck. He grinned at Charlie, flashing broken yellow teeth surrounded by an unshaved, scarred face, and then he disappeared from Charlie's view as he jumped on the ladder.

The horse immediately slowed down and turned off the path. Charlie braced himself. He couldn't let go of the flyer, and he was afraid to let go of the deck. He prepared to kick.

The man's head appeared at the top of the ladder, and then his shoulders, and finally he pulled himself up onto the deck. He climbed to one knee, drawing a pistol from his belt—

and a chair hit him in the face.

Charlie saw a split-second look of astonishment before the attacker fell backward off the truck.

Ollie emerged from the hatch. He had another chair, which he pushed against the back of the wheelhouse, and two shovels.

"Good idea," Charlie said, "but I don't have free hands."

Gnat popped up from belowdecks. She had a short length of rope and a knife. "But a moment, Charlie, and I'll have you free to fight." She quickly knotted the flyer's main harness to the deck with her rope.

Charlie scrambled to grab one of the shovels from Ollie just as a second attacker jumped onto the steam-truck. He grabbed the lattice of the deck with both hands and started pulling himself up.

Charlie and Ollie simultaneously cracked their shovels down on the man's hands. He groaned, and Ollie pushed him away with a shovel like a bargeman pushing away a bit of floating refuse.

The flyer rose into the air fast as any kite. With a loud pop, it hit the end of its tether and the rope went taut.

"We're going to need a cliff or something!" Charlie called to Bob.

"We're going to 'ave one! Smell that?"

Charlie sniffed. "Salt?"

"That's the sea, mate. Likely a cliff there, an' if not, we're going fast enough to launch without one, I reckon. Breeze at our backs ain't idealistic, but I expect we'll fly."

"Ideal. It isn't ideal."

"You've got it."

"Let me do the flying," Charlie said. "I'm stronger."

Bob nodded.

Had he hurt her feelings? Charlie didn't have time to worry about it now. The houses had given way to forest and pasture. The horses had fallen behind. The steam-carriages were gaining, and the first was nearly upon them.

The steam-carriage's driver hunched low over his gears on the high coachman's seat. Behind him, a fat man on the right squinted at Charlie along a rifle, and a tall man on the left brought a scattergun up to his shoulder.

"Get down!" Charlie yelled to his friends.

He grabbed the second chair and threw it at the windscreen.

Crash!

Shattered glass jumped; the chair hit the driver in the chest.

Boom! Bang!

Both men's firearms went off, but thanks to the steam-carriage's sudden swerve left, they missed. The carriage disappeared into a tangled green thicket.

More carriages were coming, and Ollie had disappeared.

"Any sign of a good place to launch?" Charlie called to Bob.

Bob pointed.

Ahead of them and to the right lay the sea. Under the surprisingly strong light of the stars, it was a dark blue, empty plain. Between the highway and the water stretched a short, rocky slope and a strip of white sand.

But where Bob pointed, the rocky slope rose to a black cliff.

"Go!" Charlie patted Bob on the shoulder and turned to face his attackers.

Objects began erupting from the hatch. Mattresses. A bucket. A whole shelfload of books, one at a time. Ollie and Gnat were heaving up everything they could get their hands on.

When a broken toilet bowl came up the hatch, Charlie almost laughed. "That's enough!"

He started with the books. He wanted to read their spines, then open and leaf through them. Depending on the book, he might glance at the last page first, or the introduction, if it wasn't too stuffy. Then he'd lie on his stomach under the gaslight and enjoy each volume for hours.

Instead he forced himself not to even look at the titles. He grabbed the first book and threw it.

Under an onslaught of hurled literature, the next steam-carriage pulled back. From fifty feet away, the men leaning out the vehicle's windows took careful aim.

Bang! Crash!

The first shot knocked out windows in the wheelhouse. Ollie and Gnat fell to the deck and shoved objects off the back of the steam-truck as fast as they could.

Fortunately, Charlie had a good throwing arm, and the driver of the steam-carriage had underestimated his strength. Charlie picked a heavy book this time, and he couldn't help noticing that it was a copy of *Mrs. Beeton.* Compact, but solid.

He took aim, threw, and hit one of the shooters squarely in the face. The man dropped his gun, waved his arms wildly, and fell right out the window. Carriages behind him swerved left and right to avoid hitting the fallen man.

Charlie picked up the shovel. He gripped it like a javelin, bullets whizzing past him. Starting with his back against the wheelhouse, he took three short steps and hurled the garden tool.

The shovel sailed through the air, spiraling slightly, until it struck the first steam-carriage right in the thicket of gears and guiding levers at the driver's feet. The driver braked and another vehicle struck him from the rear.

The others passed the wreck and accelerated.

The steam-truck lurched right, and immediately the ride was much bumpier. Charlie looked forward and saw that Bob was now driving across a field. Ahead, the cliff drew near.

"Now!" he shouted to all his friends.

Quickly he stepped into the flyer's harness and strapped himself in. Ollie shoved the toilet off the back of the deck to trip up the pursuers, and then—*bamf!*—he was a yellow garter snake, sliding up Charlie's leg and into his peacoat.

Bob jammed a stick into the spoked wheel to hold it steady and then scrambled to join Charlie. She laughed as she buckled herself into the front position of the flyer. "I ain't used to being the pretty lady."

Inside Charlie's sleeve, Ollie hissed.

Gnat gripped Charlie by the calf. "I'll just have to hold on," she said. In her right hand she still had the little knife, and she laid it against the length of rope that anchored Charlie and the flyer to the steam-truck. "Tell me when!"

Charlie nodded. He crouched, bracing himself to jump at the right moment. The water of the bay swung in and out of view. Behind him, he heard gunshots, and with a high-pitched whine, bullets ricocheted off the truck very close to him.

With a final big bump, he felt the front of the steam-truck tip downward and begin to fall.

"Now!" he shouted to Gnat.

Charlie was watching the bay as its entire surface suddenly

spread out before him, but he felt the tension of the rope dissipate and the flyer's sudden strong desire to rise.

"Run!" he yelled to Bob.

They took two steps forward—

they jumped onto the wheelhouse as it tilted down and away from them—

and they sprang up into open space.

Charlie flapped the flyer's wings as hard as he could.

Changing temperatures also cause the so-called "sea breeze," which blows toward the sea by night and toward land by day.

—Royal Geographical Society, *Gazetteer,* "Prevailing Winds"

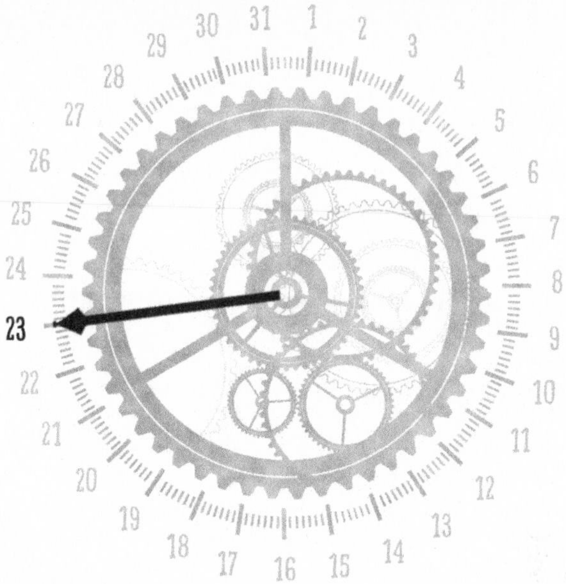

Charlie flew.

Up and away from the men shooting at him, with a stiff breeze at his back coming off the mountains. As he wheeled right, out of range of his attackers and back toward land, the breeze pushed under the wings of the flyer and raised him.

Charlie looked at the water below for evidence of Lloyd Shankin's Drowned Hundred, but didn't see any houses beneath the waves. The starlight on the water turned the entire sea a sparkling, opaque silver.

"You're a natural, Charlie!" Bob called over her shoulder.

"Your flyer is beautiful!" he yelled back.

"We 'ave your bap to thank for that!"

As the nose of the flyer lifted and turned toward land, Charlie saw the full expanse of the night sky. There was no moon, and it was dark enough that all the stars were visible. He nearly dropped the handles in astonishment. It reminded him of the gemstones in the walls of the pixie barony.

"The sky!" he gasped. "I've never seen anything like that!"

"Well, you wouldn't, mate," Bob shouted over the breeze. "Not living inside a shop as you did. Even out of doors, London's got too much fog and too many lights to see the night sky properly."

Ollie the snake hissed.

"That's Ollie reminding us 'e likes London!" Bob laughed. "We know, my china! We know!"

Charlie flew over a small village at the mouth of the river, just a handful of yellow lights in the darkness. Ahead he saw the many glaring lights of Machine-Town. A string of lights dotted the highway from Machynlleth to the sea. How many men did the Iron Cog have, anyway?

And what was all that talk about building a new world and about his bap being a sacrifice? And who was Gaston St. Jacques, that the Hound belonged to him and that he had some kind of contact with shaitans? Charlie knew very little about shaitans, except that they were dangerous.

Veering left, Charlie was immediately over the lower flanks of Cader Idris. He aimed for the summit. He was going to find the pale boy.

As Machine-Town disappeared over the shoulder of the mountain, Charlie felt he was rising to enter a field of pure light. Angels, he thought. This must be what it would be like to rise to meet them.

"Charlie," Bob called. "It occurs to me I ought to 'ave asked you a question."

"What is it?"

"When was the last time your mainspring was wound up?"

Charlie thought about it. "Last night."

"An' you been jumping an' running a bit, 'aven't you?"

Charlie saw her point. "I'll fly lower."

He was careful not to fly *too* low. A glint of red that might have been merely a stray reflection, or a trick of the light, reminded him that the Hound stalked this mountain at night. The Iron Cog's creation had nearly killed Charlie the last time they'd met, and he couldn't count on being lucky enough to find a big-folk gate a second time.

He headed for Aunt Big Money's burrow. The witch rabbit might know where to find the pale boy. Also, Ollie would be pleased to see her again, though Charlie wasn't quite sure why.

At least he knew why the pale boy was afraid of him now. His home had been surrounded and his father attacked. Charlie would explain that he was not an agent of the Iron Cog. Not a *creature* of the Iron Cog, he corrected himself, since the pale boy had to realize that Charlie was a device like him.

Charlie brought the flyer down at the top of the forest, just above Aunt Big Money's cave. Ollie instantly assumed his boy form.

"Thanks, Charlie!" His face wore an enormous grin Charlie was more accustomed to seeing on Bob's face. Ollie immediately jogged down the hill toward the burrow.

Charlie shrugged out of his harness. "Let's stay in pairs. Can you two watch the flyer?"

Without waiting for a response, he trotted after Ollie.

At the top of the mound of earth covering the burrow, he stopped. Ollie stood below him, looking at the warren entrance. His mouth was flattened into a thin line.

"Ollie?"

The chimney sweep didn't answer.

Charlie dropped down and landed next to Ollie, and he realized Ollie was in shock.

Aunt Big Money's burrow had been destroyed. The neatly packed chalk of the walls was shredded and the slates of the staircase ripped out. Charlie could see the marks of the work, and they weren't the tracks of shovel and mattock—they were enormous paw-shaped gouges.

The Hound had opened the entrance to Aunt Big Money's burrow. The hallway looked like a raw wound.

Ollie stepped forward.

"Stop!" Charlie said. "The Hound may be down there."

Ollie kept walking.

"Ollie . . ."

"I have to see it for myself," Ollie said. He eased his feet into the destroyed passage, spread his legs for balance, and then slid down into Aunt Big Money's warren.

Charlie shook his head, but he followed.

Aunt Big Money's main chamber was shattered. The fireplace was cold. The hundreds of drawers of herbs and other simples were ripped out and smashed. The great table that had once presided over the center of the room was split in two.

And lying on the floor, between the two halves of the table, was the witch rabbit.

She was mangled. One arm was missing entirely, and her torso had been ripped open. The sight of gears and pistons spilling out of her split chest struck horribly close to Charlie's heart. He imagined himself lying there in her place.

Ollie sniffed.

Charlie put a hand on his shoulder. "I'm sorry, mate."

"Maybe she's not dead. Maybe Brunel can put those gears back where they belong. Maybe Bob . . ." Ollie looked to Charlie.

Charlie wished he had answers. He shrugged.

Ollie abruptly sobbed. "Don't you see? She gave me hope."

"Hope of what?" Charlie remembered the visions the witch rabbit had shown him, of a pit with a tomb at its depth, a fire along a boiling river, and a giant who wished to kill him. None of those images gave Charlie anything resembling hope.

Before Ollie could answer, Charlie heard a growl at the top of the entry passage.

He was unarmed. Charlie grabbed one of the table's thick legs with both hands and yanked as hard as he could. The leg came away in his hands with a loud *CRACK!* Charlie stepped to the bottom of the passage, club raised over his head.

At the top of the passage crouched the Hound. It growled and sniffed, thrusting its face into the opening. Its one eye gleamed red; the flesh around the other eye was swollen over it.

Charlie considered his options. Ollie could probably escape on his own, as a snake. But Bob and Gnat didn't have that luxury. The slope of the mountain here wasn't steep enough for Bob to launch the flyer.

If Bob and Gnat weren't already dead.

The Hound threw back its head and *ROARED!*

Charlie charged.

It was a desperate act. The smarter move would have been to back deeper into the burrow, look for a smaller exit through which the Hound couldn't follow, or a tight space in which the Hound's size would be a disadvantage.

But that would have left the Hound free to attack his friends.

Charlie took the passage in a single leap and caught the Hound by surprise. Even as his feet touched down on the ground, Charlie swung his table-leg club at the Hound's muzzle.

The Hound ducked, and the club hit it in the shoulder—

CRACK!

And snapped in two.

With a lunge and a shake of its head, the Hound battered Charlie, hurling him through the air. Charlie slammed into the hillside and dropped to the ground behind a patch of briars.

He climbed to his feet just in time to see the Hound tossing a large yellow constrictor from its mouth.

"Ollie!" Charlie stood. "Bob! Get out of here!"

Before he could charge again, the Hound saw him and *ROARED!* It lunged forward—

Charlie dodged to the side—

and the Hound fell over, whimpering.

Charlie hit the ground at the same moment, puzzled. But through the briars he saw Gnat, nearly underneath the giant Hound. She held her knife in one hand and a large splinter of wood in the other.

There was blood on the splinter and blood on one of the Hound's paws.

Gnat dived forward, driving the splinter deep into the flesh under an uninjured paw.

The Hound shrieked, then lunged forward, snapping its jaws at Gnat. Gnat leaped straight into the air, and the huge yellow teeth snapped shut on empty space.

She jumped with such grace and energy, she looked as if she were flying.

Gnat rolled in midair at the top of her leap, and she came down on the back of the Hound's neck.

Charlie climbed to his feet and struggled forward through the briars.

Gnat planted her knife in the Hound's good eye.

With a *ROOOOOOOAR!* that echoed off the cliffs like thunder, the Hound rolled over and threw Gnat off. It gnashed at her again and again, but it was blind now. Charlie stopped his charge, afraid he'd be crushed by the huge animal in its thrashing.

Gnat didn't step back.

She grabbed another splintered piece of Charlie's club. She ducked one bite attempt, and then a second, and then, as the jaws snapped at her a third time, she dropped to one knee and planted the splinter like a spear.

The Hound bit over the splinter with all its weight, driving the sharp wood deep into its own brain.

It fell, shaking as it died.

Charlie staggered forward. There was blood everywhere, and he didn't know whose it was. "Ollie?" he called. "Bob? Gnat?"

"Yeah," Ollie groaned. He crawled out of a thicket of bushes, clutching his leg.

"'Ere, Charlie." Bob slid down the bank from above. She hobbled and held one arm gingerly, but her eyes glittered.

No answer from Gnat.

Charlie grabbed the Hound by its shoulders and pushed with all his strength. He felt his inner mechanisms strain to deliver more power, and with a grunt he shoved the Hound aside.

Gnat lay on the ground, covered in blood. In one hand she had her knife and in the other a long, sharp tooth, which she must have pulled from the Hound's mouth.

She opened her eyes, looked up at Charlie, and held up the tooth.

"That's one great deed." She grinned.

Charlie wanted to laugh, but he suddenly realized they were not alone. On the other side of the Hound's body stood the pale boy. He looked at Aunt Big Money's ruined burrow with sad eyes, and then at the Hound.

"She was my friend," the boy said.

"She was mine, too," Charlie answered.

"My name is Thomas."

There once was a young man who loved a maid, but when he asked her to marry him, she said she could never marry a man who had no name.

"I don't understand," he said. "My name is Hans."

"That's no name for a married man," she told him. "Go and find a real name."

So the young man journeyed far and wide, looking for a real name. He translated his name into many languages. He attended university courses. He sat in a cathedral and had many learned discussions, and then he came home, with the intention of proposing to his sweetheart again.

The night before he arrived again in his village, he was sleeping under a tree in the forest when he heard a yowling. When he investigated, he discovered that a large, somewhat strange-looking cat had been caught in a badger trap and could not get out.

"Hold on a moment," Hans said, "and I will free you."

"I will give you nothing for it," the animal said. "I am a cat, and I owe you nothing."

Hans freed the cat anyway, and before it left, it turned and looked at him. "My name is Merry Merry Topkins," it said. "Now you and I are kin and kind."

—Jacob and Wilhelm Grimm, *Children's and Household Tales*, "Merry Merry Topkins"

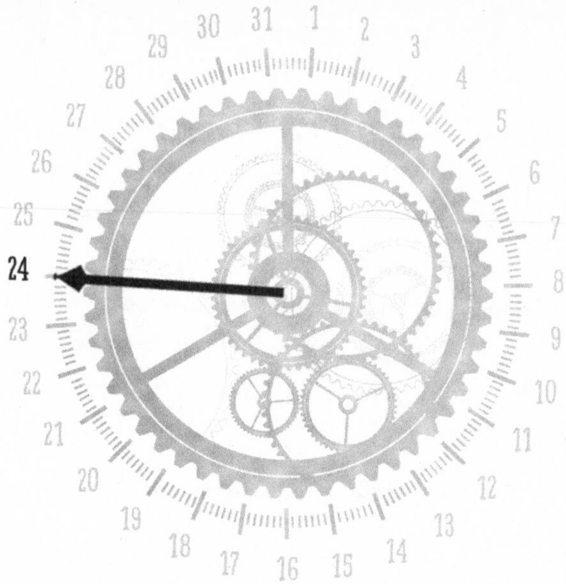

"If you're lying to me, I'll take terrible revenge."

Charlie and his friends stood again high in the crevasse, having reached the spot in Bob's flyer. The night was chilly, but the only one who seemed to suffer was Ollie. He had a bandage around his torn leg, and he wore Thomas's scarf around his neck.

Charlie had an idea what *terrible revenge* might be. He'd read *The Count of Monte Cristo,* and besides, he had his own desire to exact terrible revenge on the people who'd killed his bap. Stomping Heinrich Zahnkrieger's fingers and kicking Gaston St. Jacques in the face didn't begin to cover it.

He nodded his acceptance. "We're not with the Iron Cog. My bap—that's my father—and your father worked together.

My bap made me the same way your father made you, and he sent me to warn your father."

That almost makes us brothers was the thing he didn't add.

Could he and Thomas together be a folk? Not by the dewin Lloyd Shankin's definition, since they didn't share stories. Or did they? Did they share a story that went back to the stories of their fathers? A story that included, in different ways, the witch rabbit Aunt Big Money?

And what was it the rabbit had said to him? *You have a deeper past than you know.*

"I 'ave to say," Bob added, "I am a great entomologist of your father's work."

"Enthusiast, Bob," Charlie said.

"That's right."

Thomas reached into a crack in the rock, and the rock wall that had been a featureless slab of flat stone revealed a door that swung inward.

Beyond were stairs leading down. Gas sconces in the walls provided light. Thomas gestured and Charlie led the way. The cold breeze on the back of Charlie's neck stopped when Thomas shut the door.

Other halls crossed their path, and at each turn Thomas pointed the way. Charlie couldn't be sure, but he thought they traversed identical hallways more than once. Was Thomas leading them in circles?

They were walking through a maze.

Ollie leaned on Bob for support, and Gnat walked at Charlie's side. She carried the little knife she had taken from William T. Bowen's steam-truck—the knife she had used to slay the giant half-flesh, half-machine Hound—tucked in her belt. The Hound's tooth hung on a thong tied around her neck. She walked with her head held high, and Charlie didn't think she could look any better, however glorious a pair of wings she might have on her back.

Charlie saw dwarfs in the complex as they passed through, but he didn't recognize them, and none were dressed in the red and gold colors of Charlie's dwarf family. He saw devices, too, things that moved about on wheels or springs or stalking legs. But nothing that resembled Thomas and him.

"Here it is."

Thomas pushed forward and joined Charlie at the front. They stood at a door that looked like many others they had passed. Thomas opened it without knocking.

The man behind the door was definitely Isambard Kingdom Brunel.

"The 'eck."

Charlie recognized the man from his daguerreotype in the *Almanack,* from the Sky Trestle tokens, from the murals in Waterloo Station, and from pictures he'd seen of the great inventor in newspaper accounts of how his impressive engineering feats, such as the Sky Trestle, the Great Western Railway, and the Gibraltar Mooring Tower, were faring, years after their builder's death.

Only he wasn't dead.

He stood in front of Charlie, large as life, with bushy white side-whiskers and the stub of a cigar between his teeth. He was significantly older than he'd been in any of the images Charlie knew, but his back was straight and his grin was fierce.

When he saw Charlie, he removed the cigar and pointed at him with it.

"By Jove," he said. "You must be Joban's boy."

Charlie had only heard the name Joban for the first time earlier that evening, but the Iron Cog's men had called his father Dr. Singh when they'd captured him, and again at Waterloo Station. Joban Singh must have been his father's name before he fled the Cog and changed it to Rajesh Pondicherry.

"My father named me Charlie. Charlie Pondicherry."

"You're perfect." Brunel didn't take his eyes off Charlie, though Bob was beginning to fidget. "You're a work of art, Charlie, do you know that? Your father always had a flair for the stylish."

"I'm a boy," Charlie said.

"Of course you are." Brunel nodded. "And have you met *my* boy, Thomas?" He grabbed Thomas by his shoulders and drew him closer.

"Thomas is a boy . . . like me." Charlie wanted to say so much more. This man was taller than his bap, and older, and had a fair English complexion, but standing in his presence and talking about being a boy made Charlie feel as if he were talking with his bap. "He brought us here."

Brunel clapped his hands. "So we all understand each other. Excellent! Now tell me, what else have you learned?"

"Papa." Thomas's voice had a plaintive note in it. "They killed Auntie."

Isambard Kingdom Brunel looked at Charlie and his friends, puzzled.

"Not us, sir." Bob's voice shook. "We're the greatest admirers of your work."

"Ah, no. You mean the Iron Cog." Brunel pulled at his hair with both hands. "Bowen and his snotty, pretentious middlemen, who think they own the world because they buy and sell commodities and get to meet the queen once in their lives. The meddling little conspirators who think they have the power and the right to fix everything. The Iron Cog killed poor Big Money."

"The Iron Cog killed my father, too."

Brunel looked at both boys with a furrowed brow.

Thomas nodded. "It was the Hound."

"My bap was killed in London. By a Frenchman named Gaston St. Jacques."

"St. Jacques?" Brunel's eyebrows jumped to the top of his forehead. "The rogue!"

Charlie remembered seeing his bap dead, a tiny dot from a great height. He didn't mean to, but he made a single sound, like a sob. He realized Thomas had made a similar noise.

"Here, now." Brunel dropped to his knees and opened his arms. The boy stepped into his father's embrace, and Brunel wrapped one arm around him. "She was a good auntie. She served her purpose well."

"She took care of me," Thomas murmured.

There were tears in Brunel's eyes. "She did more than that, son. She was your prototype. Big Money showed us we could do it!"

"You mean build . . . make a person?" Charlie asked.

Brunel laughed, a gut-deep sound that was full of sorrow. "Yes, among other things!"

"She gave me visions," Charlie said. "She made me dream dreams and see things."

"Did she?" Brunel looked surprised. He still had one free arm, and he beckoned Charlie forward. Charlie stepped into the embrace of Isambard Kingdom Brunel and restrained more sobs. Brunel was warm and smelled of tobacco, and he held Charlie's head tight against his shoulder. "Joban was a good man. The best."

Goodbye, Bap, Charlie thought.

"She did more than that." Ollie was suddenly lively, though still leaning on Bob. "She was a witch."

"Yes, she was." Brunel released both boys from his hug and stood. "Well, that was half the point, wasn't it? We needed to see if we could build a magician, as well as a creature with free will."

Build a magician? Prototype? But what did that mean about Thomas? Was he some kind of wizard?

And what did it mean about Charlie?

"You're a magician yourself, Mr. Brunel." Bob grinned a wider grin than Charlie had ever seen on her face.

Brunel laughed. "The lads of the Cog think so, too. You might think *they're* the greatest admirers of my work, the way they keep trying to get their hands on it."

"What do they want?" Charlie asked. "What's the new world they talk about building?"

"Hmm, they want power, I think. You'll learn, Charlie, that when people in this world organize themselves to achieve an objective, most of the time the objectives are depressingly the same. Power, money, pleasure, and pride. There are exceptions, and they are as noble as they are few. For every hospital, there are a thousand professional associations."

"So why do you say it's *power* they want?" Bob asked. She stood on her tiptoes and grinned from ear to ear.

"Hmm? Simple. Because they already have the other three. Because the reason Joban and I fled their company was that we learned they were planning to use our . . . *creations* to impersonate monarchs and prime ministers, and other influential people. The new world? In the end, however they dress it up as a paradise of no work and no pain, I think it's only a world in which the Cog rules. Because I know many of them personally, and they are a pack of power-hungry, ankle-stinging scorpions. Mind you, by some accounts, that makes them extremely ordinary people."

"Too right," Ollie muttered. He kicked his toe at the floor.

Brunel noticed Ollie's injury. He produced a chair from behind him and pushed it toward the wounded sweep. "Forgive me my denseness, young man. Have a seat."

Bob dropped Ollie into the chair, and Charlie finally took a moment to look at the room. There was a central table, surrounded by chairs and covered with schematic drawings. Speaking tubes and periscopes jutted from a panel running around all four walls at waist height. Overhead, the ceiling was glass, and through it Charlie could see a few bright stars twinkling, even with the light filling the room from gas sconces in the walls.

"Is this a control room?" he asked.

"Good intuition," Brunel said. "Are you a mechanick, or has your father got a room like this?"

Charlie shook his head. "My father's workshop was much smaller than yours."

"I'm a mechanick." Bob's grin seemed wider than her head. "An' an aeronaut."

Brunel patted her on the shoulder and she beamed. "Very good," he said. "I hope you take good care of Charlie."

"I do my level best. It'll be easier, as we've got 'is spare bits back now."

Brunel gestured at the panels. "The viewers let me see tactically sensitive places around the mountain. Entrances, key air vents, the water supply, and so on. When I built this refuge, I hoped I'd never need the viewers. I'm certainly glad I have them now."

"Did you know you were building so close to the Cog's people?" Charlie asked.

"Bowen and his Machine-Town lot? Ha!" Brunel's laughter shook his entire chest. "Of course I did; I had been one of them and I knew just where they were having their little monthly meetings! I built here to keep an eye on them, and I had dwarfs and other friends bring me what I needed."

"Until they found out you were here. And they released the Hound on your mountain." Charlie's shoulders slumped. "That's my fault."

"Nonsense! It was bound to happen sooner or later." Brunel rapped his knuckles on the nearest viewer. "And I had plenty of time to get prepared."

"An' the speaking tubes." Bob pointed. "They let you give instructions."

Brunel nodded. "Mostly to automata. Servants who are powered by springs and cogs. I have very few servants of flesh and blood."

"I've seen some dwarfs," Charlie said.

"They're not servants. They're business partners! I hire a few dwarf families to find certain things for me."

"Like certain dwarfs I know whose colors are crimson and gold."

Brunel arched an eyebrow at Charlie. "Hmm. Someone here has spent time among the cat friends."

"I don't talk to the dwarfs much," Thomas said. "They make me nervous." He crept around and stood behind his father.

"Thomas is shy, you see," Brunel said to Charlie. "It keeps him from approaching people who might be dangerous."

Charlie thought back to one of his last conversations with his bap. "I'm disobedient," he said. "A little. It keeps me from *cooperating* too much with people who might be dangerous."

Brunel clapped his hands again. "Oh, well done, Joban!"

"So what are you doing?" Charlie asked. "What are the dwarfs collecting for you?"

"Well, right now, I'm mostly preparing to flee. Today, in fact, as the Cog has found me and I'm under assault. Since you're here, I expect you should plan to come with me, so I'll show you my airship shortly."

"What about all this stuff?" Bob gestured with both hands,

as if trying to encompass the entire mountain in her arms. "You just plan to leave it, do you?"

"Why not?" Brunel shrugged. "It's toys, all of it. I don't need it, and it won't help the Cog any. The things I need for my . . . *plans* are in the airship. The only thing in this mountain that matters is Thomas. He knows my plans, and he's equipped to carry them out alone if I'm stopped. Not just equipped . . ." Brunel leaned forward as if sharing a secret joke. "He's *built* to carry them out. Well, as are you, of course, Charlie. But you'll come with me, too. All of you."

What were Brunel's plans?

"Thanks." Ollie didn't sound very convinced.

Bob just beamed.

"But really, I won't leave it behind. I'm going to collapse it. The whole thing. Bury it."

Charlie's eyes widened. "Collapse the mountain? Do you mean that?"

"Well, I'm being a bit dramatic. I won't collapse Cader Idris, really. It'd be a shame to damage a good old mountain like this one. No, I'll just cave in all its tunnels. I've built all the main junctions in the passages on large, weight-bearing pistons, and I can trigger the collapse by ether wave from the airship, with a little creation I like to call my Final Device." He looked at Charlie and smiled. "Well, the name is so theatrical I couldn't resist it. So as soon as we're off the ground, us and the few dwarfs still here, I collapse all the tunnels with the Final Device and we're done."

Charlie's mind boggled. "And your plans? What are your plans?"

Brunel's eyes twinkled. "Hmm? Why, Thomas and I will defeat the Iron Cog, of course. What do you think Thomas is for? Why build Big Money as a prototype? I'm going to take the fight to them and poke them right where they live. You can't win any game playing defense the entire time."

BOOM!

The ground under Charlie's feet shook.

The sheyala cats that accompany dwarf caravans are not used to hunt food. They do not carry burdens, nor do they fight. Other than as watch animals, it's unclear that they serve any practical purpose at all.

—Smythson, *Almanack*, "Dwarf"

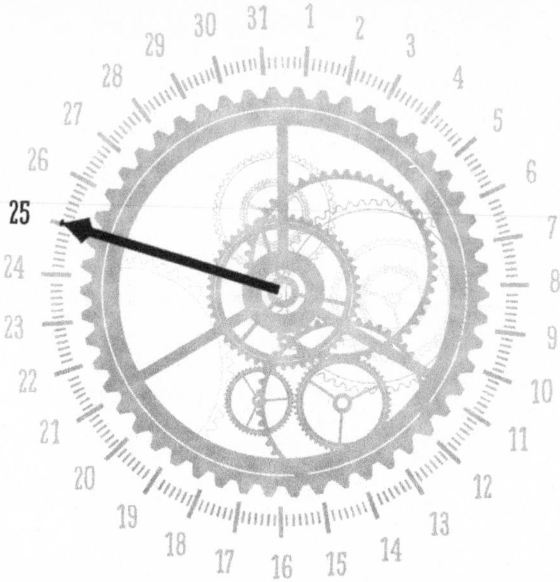

Brunel rushed to his control panels. He stepped sideways neatly from one viewer to the next, looking in each for only a moment or two. Occasionally he listened to the speaking tubes, and twice he shouted into the tubes' mouthpieces. Charlie didn't understand the words.

Bob rushed to the panels, too. She stayed out of Brunel's way, but she pressed her face to each viewer in turn, like a child examining an entire row of chocolates in the window of a sweetshop.

Charlie helped Ollie to his feet.

"Come with me!" Brunel marched out of the room at a brisk pace.

"The 'eck, lads," Bob whispered as they all trotted to try to keep up with the old man. "We're under attack."

As he stepped into the hall, Charlie hesitated—the air was thick with dust, and the passage by which they'd come into Mountain House was filled with rubble. In one hit, the attacking forces had taken away the only escape route Charlie knew.

He shook his head and followed Brunel deeper into the mountain.

"Napoleon!" Brunel shouted.

"Napoleon what . . . Napoleon Bonaparte?" Charlie was confused.

"Yes, Bonaparte! He started all this mess when he invaded Russia!" Brunel charged ahead at a pace that was almost running, then abruptly spun on his heel to face Charlie. "Of course, the Romanovs stopped him cold. But that's the problem!"

This story rang a bell. Charlie had never heard the details, but the *Almanack* said something about demonologists. "They used magic. They summoned something."

"By Jove, yes!" Brunel wheeled and barreled away again. "You see, all this"—he waved both arms above his head, vaguely taking in the entire mountain—"is magic!"

"The 'eck!" Bob cried. "No, it ain't! It's engineering!"

This time Brunel whirled to face Bob. "Very good, lad. And every engineer worth his salt has a bit of magic in him—don't you forget it!"

"Wait . . . Bap was a *magician*?"

"*You're* a magician?" Bob added.

Brunel snapped his fingers and shook his head. "How does

a magician work? She has a gift, doesn't she? But she still works, she still applies her will and thinks about what she's doing and says her incantations, doesn't she?"

"Something like that," Ollie said.

"What I do is no different!" Brunel pointed at Bob. "What your friend here does is no different! A special talent, hard work, focus, will. But where does that talent come from?"

Charlie's head hurt. "You're saying it's magic."

"And a bit of that magic is in every device I build." Brunel stopped and faced a blank wall, jabbing it with his finger. "Look, if you were to plot on a graph the number of significant inventions made in the world every year starting back at the beginning of time, it would go like this." He drew a flat horizontal line.

"Slow intimation."

"Innovation, Bob," Ollie said.

"A steady rate of new inventions," Brunel agreed. "Slow progress. Nothing much really changing, most of the time. Until eighteen hundred twelve."

"Napoleon invades Russia," Charlie said.

"You're a reader." Brunel's eyes twinkled. "And you're paying attention. Good. Napoleon invades Russia, the Romanovs summon a demon, and whether or not it was what they intended, the demon unleashes a new kind of magic on the world." He drew his finger up and to the right at a steep angle.

"Technology." There was horror in Bob's voice.

Brunel nodded solemnly. "A demon of frenetic invention. A demon of machinery. A creature whose power, leaking into the world and into certain people with just the right kind of talent, has led to the construction of amazing devices. Amazing, and also infernal."

"You're saying there's a bit of demon in me," Charlie said. Aunt Big Money had told him something similar. *A terrible knot of hell.*

"Yes!" Brunel was off again, waving his finger over his head. "And in Thomas, and in every airship you ever saw and every train you ever rode. That bit of demon is the power the Iron Cog wishes to use to rule the world. And *that* gives us our opportunity."

The engineer turned a corner into a hallway that had arrow slits in one wall. Charlie pressed his face into a slit.

On the lower slopes of the mountain—he thought this was the north side—trees burned. Mounted out in the forest and on hills across the valley, guns fired in long sequences, each shell slamming into Cader Idris and ripping out bushels of rock. The mountain trembled.

In the sky above, Charlie saw airships. Zeppelins, montgolfiers, and things that looked like Bob's flyer. Some held position and others circled, but all of them were firing on the mountain.

And the mountain was firing back. Charlie couldn't see the gunners, or the guns themselves, but gouts of flame and projectiles and rockets flashed back from the mountain side of the engagement. Forest in the valley burned. A zeppelin, struck through the middle by a shell, evaporated instantly and dropped its gondola from a height of thousands of feet.

Charlie raced to catch up to Brunel and Thomas, who led the pack.

"Who's shooting?" he asked.

"I am!" Brunel laughed. "That is to say, my devices are firing in accordance with my design. Though the enemy will believe they are being targeted by human gunners, because I've equipped each gun with a model. A simulacrum. A fake."

Charlie and Thomas looked at each other. Charlie grinned, but Thomas looked terrified.

Brunel moved on. Charlie ran to keep up.

"I still don't understand the plan."

"The plan! Isn't it obvious? The plan is to put the genie back in the bottle! I've collected the materials I'll need, Thomas will need. We fly to the scene of the original summoning—"

"Russia?" Ollie asked.

Brunel didn't miss a beat. "And Thomas takes away the Cog's power."

"That seems pointless," Ollie said. "You ain't going to stop people from being evil, mate. You ain't going to stop crazy people from wanting to rule the world."

Brunel laughed. "I won't stop anyone from being evil, and I won't even try. But what makes the Iron Cog dangerous is their machines! Without technology, that lot is nothing but a bunch of shopkeepers with funny handshakes and a few queer political connections. Ha!"

Charlie considered that. Without the fake Queen Victoria they had built, what would the Iron Cog's plan have been in London? Just assassination. It was the ersatz queen that would have put the conspiracy in charge of Great Britain. So maybe Ollie was wrong and Brunel's plan wasn't pointless.

Brunel led them down a staircase and opened another door—

and then flung himself back.

Whatever had once been on the other side of that door, now there yawned a chasm. Fire-scarred rock walls offered no purchase for hand or foot, for hundreds of feet both up and down.

Brunel slammed the door. He wiped sweat from his forehead with his sleeve, but then he saw Charlie looking at him and grinned. "There are other ways! No engineer worth his salt builds a system without redundancies!"

He backtracked for a minute, then climbed a ladder up through a circular shaft. The passage at the top led Charlie and his friends to a series of cisterns. Each cistern was a wide, deep shaft open to the sky, with catwalks circling it at several levels. As they crossed the pits, Charlie looked down and saw water that was reflecting the night's starlight, as well as the bright orange streaks of flame that filled the sky.

"But wait," he said. "If you . . . do that, if you carry out your plan, what happens to all the machines in the world. Do they just stop?"

"All of them? I doubt it. Some of them, certainly. Many of them. The most advanced, the things the Cog relies on, yes . . . I believe they stop."

"You're talking about a step backward, ain't you?" Ollie said. "I mean, no trains? No airships? Is that really a better world? All the things you ever built in your whole career, won't they all just stop?"

"The cost is great." Brunel stopped walking and bowed his head. "It is also necessary."

"And what happens to Thomas?" Charlie asked. "What happens to me?"

Brunel turned and met Charlie's gaze. "I have made horrible sacrifices before today, and I know that the sacrifices I have yet to make will be even more horrible. But I will make them, by Jove. Because I must."

"But my bap . . . did he . . . ?"

Brunel didn't answer. Slowly, he turned and led them on.

Beyond the cisterns, the engineer's path opened onto a single large chamber. Racks of mechanical tools stood around the perimeter of the hangar, along with coils of rope, pipes, folded sheets of fabric, wheels, and other airship parts.

Above them rose the airship. It was a zeppelin that had not one but three oblong chambers to contain gas. In addition to propellers, there were clusters of rockets at the hind end of the craft. The gondola hanging beneath it was the size of a small house. It hung fifty feet in the air above Charlie's head.

The airship was tethered to the hangar floor with half a dozen ropes. A wooden boarding tower rose from the floor to just below the gondola, and a gangplank ran from it to the gondola door. The tower hugged one wall, and beside it at the top was another control panel.

As Brunel and the others entered the hangar, a dwarf in a purple jacket and purple-and-white-striped trousers waved from the door of the gondola.

"Good," Brunel said. "We're almost ready to go."

"Well then, I *almost* feel relieved." Ollie was pale from the effort of walking so briskly on his injured leg. Bob limped, too, but her expression made Charlie think of a child at the carnival with unlimited money to spend.

"Wo-won't the Iron Cog just shoot us if we try to leave?" Thomas shook. His eyes were as wide as saucers.

Brunel put his arm around his clockwork son. "Yes, they will, by Jove. Hmm. Come with me."

The two climbed the boarding tower together, up the wooden steps to a flat space at the top. Charlie and his friends followed. As they arrived on the platform, Brunel pointed them toward a series of viewing scopes that ran straight up past the airship into the ceiling.

"Which one should we look in?" Charlie asked.

"All of them, preferably."

Charlie, Ollie, Gnat, and Bob each seized a scope and peered into it.

" 'Ey," Bob said. "I can see my flyer."

"What, has the Cog got it?" Ollie asked.

"Nah, it's just sitting there where I left it, next to the door we come in by."

"Thomas, my boy?" Brunel invited his son to look into another of the scopes, but Thomas shook his head and backed away.

Through his scope, Charlie didn't see Bob's flyer; he saw a cliff face. Above it drifted a pair of heavy montgolfiers. Men leaned over the edge of the airship baskets with long rifles and fired at the mountain below.

"On my count," Brunel said. "Three. Two. One. Now."

As the engineer said *now,* rockets fired from the hillside at the base of Charlie's cliff. One of the montgolfiers exploded. The other rocked back in the heat of the explosion, and the men in the basket redoubled their efforts with their rifles.

Then the cliff face opened; a sheet of rock fell away so fast Charlie realized it hadn't been a sheet of rock at all, but a painted canvas. As the canvas dropped, an airship launched. It was a zeppelin, and it looked just like the one that hung tethered over Charlie in the hangar, with three long gas-filled bags over its gondola and rockets at its rear.

"The 'eck!" Charlie heard behind him and guessed that the others were seeing similar sights through their scopes.

The airship's rockets fired. Under attack from the montgolfier men, the airship shot past the corner of the cliff face from which it had emerged and raced away toward the horizon. Scrambling, the montgolfier men tried to turn their craft and follow.

"My flyer!" Bob yelped.

Charlie staggered away from his scope. "I saw an airship!" he cried. "What about you?"

"Aye, so did I," Gnat agreed. "An airship that escaped and was fired upon."

"My flyer!" Bob shouted. "The rock opened, an' then there was explosions, an' I ain't got a flyer anymore!"

"Sorry, mate," Ollie said.

"You launched a decoy," Charlie said to Brunel.

"Hmm, not quite." Brunel shifted from foot to foot in a little dance of joy. "You were all looking at quite different parts of the mountain. I've just launched six decoys. In six different directions. And every decoy looks just like the real thing. That should clear the skies out somewhat."

"Wouldn't seven have been the luckier number?" Ollie suggested. He had his arm around Bob, whose face was pale as chalk.

Brunel swept his arm at the airship above them. "I've saved the lucky ship for us."

The gangplank to the gondola was attached to the tower platform by two large iron hinges. A handrail along one side of the gangplank was the only safety measure, but Thomas scooted up toward the gondola without holding on to it. Brunel followed with cautious steps and a hand constantly on the rail, beckoning Charlie and his friends to join them.

Charlie led the way, followed by Gnat and Ollie. Bob came last, a look of awe competing with one of shock on her face.

At the gondola door, the dwarf bowed to Thomas and let him in. Charlie saw flashes of purple and white through the gondola windows, suggesting the presence of more dwarfs. The dwarf at the door bowed again to Brunel, who entered.

And when the dwarf rose out of his second bow to face Charlie, he held a pistol in his hand.

Pointed at Brunel.

Charlie froze.

"Stop!" Brunel shouted.

The ceiling cracked open. It was made of canvas stretched over a framework of metal arms attached by hinges to a motor bolted to the wall. The motor whirred into action, the arms swung, and within seconds Charlie saw the night sky.

At the same time, the six ropes tethering the zeppelin swung free. Whatever clamps had held the ropes at the hangar end released, and the ropes dangled.

Then, as the airship started to rise, the dwarf at the gondola door kicked away the gangplank.

The gangplank swung to one side. It was still attached to the tower by its hinges, so it shifted and dropped, but not all the way to the floor. After striking the level of the platform, it snapped up twice and then settled, parallel to the floor, like the diving board at the swimming baths.

With the first bounce, Charlie lost his balance and fell. Grabbing blindly, he caught himself on the gangplank with one hand.

Through the gondola window he saw Brunel struggling. The old man managed to throw a dwarf to the floor and rush to the window.

Charlie dragged himself back up onto the gangplank. His friends fought to cling to the handrail, but he focused on Brunel and Thomas. He had time—he could climb up and then jump to the zeppelin—

Bang! Bang! Bang!

The dwarf in the gondola doorway shot Charlie. The force of the bullets knocked him off the gangplank. He fell hard, and landed on his back on the floor.

Above him he saw the zeppelin, framed against the night sky by the walls of the hangar. Fire and starlight lit the airship, and Brunel threw something out the window.

Charlie rolled to his feet and snatched the object out of the air as it fell.

It was a small, square object, the size of a snuffbox, and it had two switches on it. Each switch had two settings, labeled INERT and ACTIVATE, and both switches were set to INERT.

The Final Device. The ether-wave signal that would activate the piston supports in all the major passageways and collapse Mountain House.

" 'Elp!"

Charlie looked up. Bob clung to the gangplank with one hand and had one ankle up over its edge. Her other hand swung below her, holding Gnat by her tiny arm. Ollie, in the shape of a yellow snake, wrapped around Bob's other leg.

Charlie sprinted to a spot beneath his friends.

"Let go!" he yelled.

Bob did.

Charlie caught them. The force of their fall knocked him down, but they all rolled away from the collision and climbed to their feet.

Bamf! "You make a surprisingly good cushion, Charlie." Ollie limped to his feet and then helped Bob stand. She groaned and rubbed her arm. Gnat was already upright and pointing at the zeppelin.

The airship burned. It still rose, but it rose into the cross fire of several other airships. Dwarfs in purple and white slid down the tether ropes or jumped from the ship and disappeared from view onto the mountaintop.

"This ain't the way it was supposed to 'appen." Bob couldn't take her eyes off the disaster unfolding above. " 'E was betrayed by those dwarfs."

"What about Thomas?" Charlie looked at the Final Device and wondered when he should use it.

"Jump." Ollie fingered Thomas's scarf nervously. "Jump, mate, there's time."

Only Brunel wasn't jumping. He was struggling with someone inside the gondola, trying to drag that person to the gondola door.

Had one of the dwarfs stayed behind?

Then Charlie realized it was Thomas. Brunel was trying to make Thomas evacuate the aircraft.

Two of the flotation bags were already deflating when a hand grenade thrown from an Iron Cog montgolfier struck Brunel's airship right in its rockets.

BOOM!

The airship swung wildly. Flame engulfed most of the gondola.

Charlie saw Brunel one last time in the gondola doorway. He lurched forward and heaved—

and Thomas tumbled out.

But the zeppelin was passing the lip of the mountain. Thomas fell, but not back down into the hangar. He disappeared into the darkness outside, probably bouncing down the mountain and into enemy hands.

With the rocking of the zeppelin, Brunel fell backward into the gondola and disappeared.

KABOOM!

The airship exploded.

In the morning the young man called on his love. "Have you found a real name?" she asked him. "I will give you only three chances."

"Yes," he said. "I have spoken with many wise doctors in Wittenberg, and I have learned that my real name is *Homo sapiens*."

The maid looked sad and shook her head. "That is no name for a married man," she said.

"Well then," Hans said, "I have also spoken with many wise priests, and I have learned that in baptism I take upon me the name of the Lord. My real name is Christian."

The maid looked even sadder as she shook her head this time. "You have only one chance remaining," she said.

Hans was terribly afraid. He thought of the many other names he had learned and acquired, and, almost on a whim, he chose the last one. "I have also spoken with a cat in the forest," he said. "The cat gave me the name of Merry Merry Topkins."

The maid smiled. "That," she told her groom-to-be, "is the name of a married man."

—Grimm, *Tales*,
"Merry Merry Topkins"

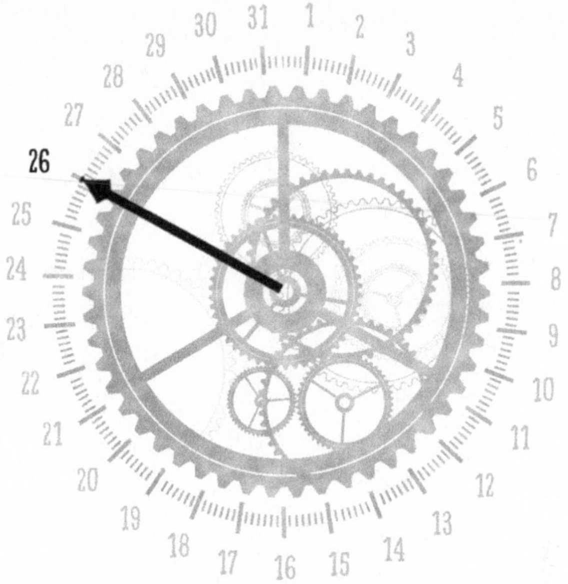

"Nooooooo!"

Charlie almost fell over.

He felt punched. He'd lost his bap to the murderous Iron Cog, then met this man, who was almost like his bap—well, like an uncle, like his bap's brother—and then Brunel had been killed as well.

But the shouting didn't come from Charlie. It came from Bob.

Chunks of airship rained down around them in the hangar, and Bob rushed toward the flame. She held her arms up, as if to catch each piece of wreckage as it drifted down.

Ollie grabbed her by the peacoat and tried to drag her away, but she wouldn't budge. "Charlie," he grunted. "A little help here."

Charlie scooped Bob up in his arms and dashed with her underneath the boarding tower. Ollie and Gnat followed close on his heels.

Fire crashed into the tower and struck the hangar around it.

"We have to go," Charlie said.

Bob crouched and buried her face in her hands.

"Really?" Ollie asked. "Where, if you don't mind my asking? Front door? Where's that? Back the way we came? Closed off, mate. Follow Thomas? We'd have to climb out of this pit first. Secret escape airship, crewed by dwarfs? Oh, sorry, that's already been blown up."

"Whoever told you life would be easy?" Gnat's face was fierce in the light of the burning hangar.

"No one," Ollie muttered. "But I keep hoping."

Bob emerged from behind her hands. Tears and soot streaked her face, but her mouth twitched in just a hint of a grin. "That's what I like about you, my china. Always full of 'ope."

Ollie elbowed Bob in the ribs. "I've got you to compete with, haven't I? I can't get *too* grumpy; I'll just look ridiculous."

Gnat looked to Charlie. "What d'you think, Charlie?"

Charlie stared at the device Brunel had thrown to him. "Down," he said. "I think the way out is down."

Ollie's eyes bugged from his face. "Down? And then what? Dig?"

Charlie thought about the trousers he'd found in the stream in Giantseat. "I know we didn't find an open door, but I think there must be one. I found a pair of trousers while we were hiding from the Hound. In the deserted fairy home. They were purple and white."

"Like the dwarfs around here," Bob said. "The trousers tell you there's some way to get through."

"That ain't much, Charlie." Ollie scowled. "A pair of trousers might slip through a pipe or a grate a human being could never fit into."

"It's the best we have." Charlie started walking.

They followed him. He broke into a slight trot, careful not to leave his friends behind.

They needed to head south. North lay the valley between Cader Idris and Snowdon, and it was full of the Iron Cog's men. This fact was helpful, because as they descended into the heart of the mountain and all the noise and fire was on one side of them, Charlie knew that way was most likely north.

He moved in the other direction.

All along, his path was lit by gas sconces set into the walls.

As they ran, the mountain fortress began to fall apart. Some hallways were full of water gushing from ruptured pipes—Charlie could cross them, but there wasn't time to explore passages and find distances short enough for the sweeps and Gnat to hold their breath. Some hallways began to fill with smoke. Some were already choked with rubble.

Charlie ran with the Final Device in his hand, looking for evidence of what Brunel had told him: that the fortress was built to collapse on order. Now that he knew what he was looking for, he saw it: at major intersections, and every hundred feet in the larger passages, the ceiling appeared to be supported by pistons taller than a hulder. Charlie couldn't be sure that the box he held in his hands would really push those devices into action, but if it did, the rock above would fall quickly and Mountain House would be buried.

They had to get out.

They ran past workshops, where Charlie saw devices including automata the size and shape of humans, creatures that turned their faces toward Charlie and cried out as he passed.

"Papa? Papa?" They reached for him with imploring fingers.

He ignored them.

They ran past furnaces venting hot steam through pipes in multiple directions. They ran past more viewing devices, and Charlie stopped to look into some of these, if only for a second.

He had his face pressed to one just in time to see the front gate of Mountain House fall.

It had to be the front gate, though Syzigon had said there was no such thing. Charlie saw two thick-paneled, ironbound doors closing off the throat of a wide cave. The slate paving stones of a highway led up to the doors.

Guns fired repeatedly from embrasures set in the stone around the doors, pounding a vehicle that resembled a brass log on six wheels and had an angled iron sheet with a slit for vision to protect the sole occupant of the cockpit. The front of the log came to a point like a sharpened stake.

Men behind trees fired back, with rifles and with mortars that sent shells high into the air and crashing down on the doors. Some lobbed hand grenades.

As Charlie watched, the guns fell silent.

The brass log cranked suddenly into gear. With a deep whine, it launched itself against the doors. Already battered, the doors splintered on contact.

Charlie heard the *CRACK!* as the doors imploded not far away.

He jumped back from the viewer and ran, his friends in tow. Behind them he heard the shouting of men and more gunfire.

When their path crossed a small stream, Charlie stopped. This wasn't water gushing from a burst pipe; it was water flowing through channels left or deliberately built for it.

"Charlie." Ollie leaned on Bob, and both panted heavily.

"I'm sorry." He had been so absorbed in finding a path out, he had thought too little of his friends.

"No worries, mate." Bob puffed. "Just tell us there's a way out of 'ere."

Charlie pointed at the stream. "This flows south, doesn't it?"

"Yes," Gnat said. "It probably runs through the old barony."

"There's no guarantee we can get through just because the water does, but it's my best plan." Charlie held up the box Brunel had thrown to him. "And I'm not sure, but I think this might destroy Mountain House behind us."

"Who says?" Ollie challenged him. "Maybe those switches launch another airship, and we're running away from our best chance to get out. And besides, a pair of trousers?" He shook his head.

"Brunel said he had some way to bring down Mountain

House." Charlie waved the Final Device, feeling less certain each second that he knew what it was.

"You 'eard him. Brunel said. Besides, look at it. It just says on an' off, basically. What you want us to do, Ollie? Turn it on an' just 'ope we don't get blasted to kingdom come?"

Ollie muttered.

"This stream goes down," Charlie said. "And south. That's no guarantee it's the stream that flows through Giantseat, but I think there's a good chance."

" 'Tis the right direction," Gnat confirmed.

"I reckon a good chance is all we 'ave. Let's take it."

Ollie shook his head, but he dropped the argument.

Charlie followed the stream. At every turn, he feared he would round the corner and see the stream sink into a hole in the wall. If that happened, what could he do? Even if he left his friends behind and dived into the water, the best case was that he wound up in Giantseat, on the other side of a wall he couldn't break through, with his friends still trapped inside.

But the stream didn't disappear into a hole. It crossed chambers; it ran along the edge of walls; it filled a sluice that descended more slowly than its parallel staircase, rising above Charlie's head before eventually spilling out in a waterfall into a dark pool.

Out of the pool rose a wall of steel.

"Giantseat," Gnat whispered.

"Maybe." Ollie staggered off Bob's shoulder to lean against the wall. "Or maybe there's whole big caverns we don't know nothing about that connect with Mountain House, and Brunel's walled 'em all off. For all we know, there's mountain lions on the other side of this wall, or ghouls, or lava."

"I reckon we'd feel the 'eat by now, if it was lava."

Ollie straightened his peacoat. "I'm just saying be ready."

"We've a bigger problem than that," Gnat pointed out.

"It's a blank wall," Charlie said. "No door."

"Aye, no door."

"I have a plan." Charlie turned to Ollie and Bob. "You two are hurt. Stay here."

"Well, now I'm 'urt more." Bob straightened and frowned. "Stay 'ere? Those are wounding words, Charlie."

"I don't have time to argue." Charlie pointed to a dark recess on the other side of the small pool. "Stay down, just in case."

Bob looked mortified, but she and Ollie stepped through the shallow pool and hid. When Ollie collapsed to the ground, he had a grateful expression on his face.

"I take it you've a mighty deed for me to do." Gnat grinned.

"Mostly I need you not to get shot."

Charlie retraced their steps.

Almost immediately there was a troubling development. Splashing down the steps by which they'd come, water began to flow over the floor. Water from Mountain House's broken pipes had caught up.

Charlie grunted.

"You're worried we'll drown," Gnat said.

"Well, I *was* worried this water would hide the stream and make it hard for us to find our way back. *Now* I'm also worried you'll drown."

Picking up a small pebble, Charlie used it to scratch marks

into each turn to remind himself of the way back. As they got nearer to the sounds of shooting, smoke filled the passage from the height of Charlie's waist. Fortunately, he didn't need to breathe, and Gnat walked beneath the smoke, sloshing in water that was up to Charlie's ankles.

Finally Charlie found a space that fit his plan. "Stay here," he told Gnat, setting her on a bulge in the rock wall that created a natural shelf. "All you need to do is be noticed."

"I'm the decoy," Gnat said.

"Or the bait."

Charlie hid himself in a sharp turn of the rock farther along the passage.

Three minutes later, two men with rifles stepped into the hall and saw Gnat.

"Who are you, then?" one of them barked. They both raised their rifles, and Charlie saw what he had hoped for: grenades hanging on one of their belts. Grenades such as he'd seen tossed at Mountain House's gate.

Gnat smiled. "Natalie de Minimis of Underthames."

"This stinking place," one rifleman complained. "Clockwork *fairies,* now? It's giving me the creeps."

"It wasn't giving me the creeps," the other said, "until you shot that metal boy with no arms or legs, and he kept talking."

Charlie almost jumped out at the mention of a metal boy. Could they mean Thomas? No, Thomas was somewhere outside, on the slopes of Cader Idris. It had to be one of the unfinished automata.

"Begging me to turn him off," said the first man. "The creeps, I tell you."

"And now fairies."

Charlie lunged from his hiding place. He snatched both guns from the men's hands and hurled them away into smoke and shadow.

One man punched at Charlie's head, but Charlie caught the fist with his hand.

"There are worse things than fairies," Charlie said. He grabbed the other man by the shirt, pulled him off balance, and threw him back. The man slid twenty feet, fell into the water, then lurched upright and ran.

The remaining man grabbed for a knife at his side with his free hand, so Charlie grabbed that wrist, too.

"You wouldn't dare." The man glared.

Curiosity made Charlie hesitate. "Why not?"

The man shook his head and snarled. "Revenge. As bad as you give it to me, you expect to get it coming back."

"I see. So if I took your trousers off, I should expect that someday you'd take off mine?"

Charlie's prisoner frowned. "What?"

Charlie yanked the man's belt from his body in a single pull. The grenades and the knife both came away with the belt, and the man's trousers fell around his ankles, into the water. "I expect I could live without my trousers." Charlie smiled.

Then he let go. The man yanked up his trousers and ran, showering drops of water all around him as he went.

Grenades in hand, Charlie grabbed Gnat and jogged to rejoin the sweeps.

It has been suggested that Britain's pixies are the descendants of the island's Brythonic kingdoms. Accordingly, the notions have been variously advanced that Rhodri the Great or Hywel the Good, the ancient kings and heroes of those realms that subsisted between the departure of the legions and the arrival of the Normans, were in fact pixies. Quite apart from the absence of any confirming archaeological data and the issues of stature and wingedness, though, there also persists the basic fact that every contemporary pixie realm is ruled by women.

—Smythson, *Almanack*, "Pixie"

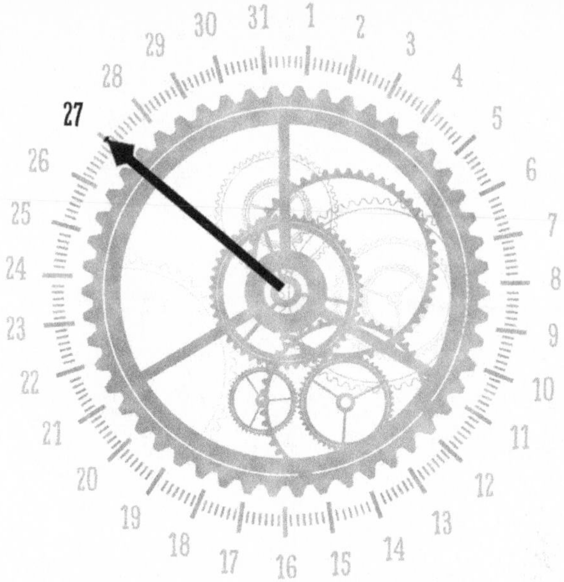

The water was knee-deep by the time Gnat and Charlie rejoined their friends. It was warm, being a confluence of hot water from Mountain House pipes and cold water from the stream.

Bob and Ollie leaned against the steel wall; they broke into relieved laughter at the sight of Charlie and Gnat.

"Mate," Ollie said, "now would be a good time to explain what you have in mind."

"I'm going to blow a hole in the wall." Charlie held up the belt of grenades.

"The water might make it 'arder," Bob said.

Charlie nodded. "I need a place where the grenades can be out of the water and against the wall. Help me find one."

After a few moments of searching, Ollie shouted that he'd located a good spot. An outcropping of rock created a tight space between itself and the steel wall. By rolling the belt up, Charlie found he could shove all the grenades down into the crack, with two of them angled up so he could pull their pins out and run.

By then, the water was flowing at waist height.

"This 'as to be it," Bob said. "We must be at the bottom of the place, if the water's starting to fill up on us. Giantseat's just on the other side of this 'ere plate, I know it."

"I don't know it, Bob." Ollie shook his head. "But I'm glad you do."

"The shock of the explosion will be huge in this passage," Gnat said. "And it will be even worse underwater."

Charlie nodded. "I'll pull the pins. I won't be able to run far, but I'll be okay."

"The rest of us should get as far away as possible," Gnat suggested.

Bob plucked Gnat from the rock where she perched and slogged down the passage. Ollie shambled at her side, and together they threw up a wave of water, now halfway up their bellies.

"Count to three," Bob called to Charlie as she sloshed out of sight around a corner. "Pull on three."

The stream was up to Charlie's armpits, and he held Brunel's Final Device above the water with one hand.

"Down this way!" he heard someone shout. "Has to be! And the little bleeder's got my grenadoes!"

No time to waste.

"One!" Charlie called. "Two!"

"That's him!"

Charlie turned and saw the two men whose rifles and grenades he'd snatched. With them were three others, and they all carried rifles. Seeing Charlie, they dropped the muzzles of their guns to point at him.

"Three!" Charlie pulled the pins.

He jumped. It was a leap made by springing forward, pushing himself slightly off the cavern wall with his feet, and diving. Like a fish, out of the water and back in a single motion.

He heard gunfire as he hit the water and then the *zip!* of bullets passing through the water around his head. Then the muffled, sloshing noise of submerged running feet.

KABOOM!

The grenades exploded. A wall of force battered Charlie and the water in which he was swimming. The blow knocked the air out of him and slammed him against the wall, but he pushed off the floor and emerged again.

The grenades had ripped the projecting rock out of place but hadn't blown through the steel.

Bob and Ollie rushed back into sight from around the corner. Gnat rode perched on Bob's shoulders, and Ollie clutched Thomas's scarf to his neck to keep it from shaking off. All three were dripping wet.

"DEAD END! AN' I CAN'T 'EAR, CHARLIE!" Bob yelled. "DEAF FROM THE GRENADOES!"

Charlie turned to see the riflemen floundering in the water.

Two of them covered their ears with their hands, and two had scorched faces and singed hair. The other held his breath and dived, trying to get at the rifles they had dropped.

Charlie roared and charged the men. It was a slow assault through deep water, but they still fled.

They didn't run far, though. He heard the splashing stop around the corner and then the shouting of more men. Then a bright orange light and a sudden increase in the air temperature suggested the igniting of some kind of flame.

Charlie turned to face his friends, shoulders slumping.

"I was wrong." He shoved Brunel's Final Device into the pocket of his peacoat, next to his father's broken pipe. He was going to apologize and then slosh around the corner to attack the Iron Cog's men.

"No, you weren't. Look!" Ollie pointed.

Charlie looked; water was now flowing around the steel wall. He swished closer.

The steel plate hadn't budged. But in ripping a chunk of stone from the cavern wall, the grenades had exposed a crack, along with a section of the steel plate that wasn't bolted to anything. Water was being sucked into the crack.

"Get back!" Charlie waded in. "Get on top of something. Breathe!"

His friends scrambled to climb the walls, anchoring their boots and their fingers into little irregularities in the stone and hoisting themselves precious inches higher into the air.

Charlie grabbed the steel and pulled. He could feel his mainspring unwinding to deliver force, but the steel was too strong.

The water passed his mouth. He kept working.

Charlie jammed his fingers into the crack. Digging with both hands, he scooped out fistfuls of pebbles and dirt. The water flowed faster through the hole.

But the level was still rising. He didn't dare risk a look at his friends—they didn't have the time—but he could hear them breathing.

He found a larger piece of the wall, a boulder he could get his fingers around. Gripping it with both hands, Charlie pulled.

Nothing happened.

He wished he'd asked Bob to wind his mainspring after they'd stolen back the flyer.

But it was too late now; he was underwater, and thrashing sounds from Bob's direction suggested that she might be, too.

Charlie braced his feet against the steel, dug both hands in as deep as he could behind the big chunk of rock, and threw his entire body into the effort. He hummed, he groaned, he felt himself beginning to slip away and shudder—

and then suddenly the rock was gone.

He ripped it away from the wall in a heave that launched it up and across the hall.

Charlie's body shook. He had no time.

Bob was trying to tread water but not doing a very good job of it. Despite Ollie's attempts to catch them from his perch on the wall, she and Gnat went under repeatedly, and Bob's feet kicked out in a random and useless pattern.

Charlie took her boot to the face twice before he was able

to grab Bob by the belt. Once he had the aeronaut, it was easy to snatch Gnat from the water with his other hand.

Turning, he shoved them both into the hole. He thrust Gnat first, because she was small. The flow of the water grabbed her pixie body and pulled her through the opening. As she slipped from his grasp, it occurred to Charlie for the first time that he didn't really know what was on the other side.

He hoped he hadn't just dropped his pixie friend into an abyss.

But there was no going back. He shoved Bob next.

She was drowning, and her flailing arms and legs prevented her from fitting into the hole. Charlie crawled around the front of her, took her face in both hands, and forced her to look into his eyes.

"You'll be fine!" he tried to shout.

She looked confused, but she stopped struggling, and Charlie pushed her through the opening.

He clambered back up the rock to get Ollie. But when Charlie pushed his head above water—the top of his head bumping against the ceiling—Ollie grinned at him.

"I got this one," the sweep said.

Bamf! Ollie the yellow water snake slithered past Charlie and dived.

Charlie followed. Once he had himself squarely in front of the opening, the rushing water pulled him through—

and he tumbled across hard stone.

He heard gasps for air. As soon as he could stand, Charlie counted his friends. They were all there and all breathing.

And they were in Giantseat. It wasn't the chamber they'd

been in before, but it must be part of the barony. Charlie saw nests and multicolored light scattered by colored stones in the walls and the ceiling. A thick stream of water burst from the steel wall and flowed away across the cavern, but Giantseat was vast, and it wouldn't fill up anytime soon.

"Charlie!" Ollie rose up from his snake form with a grin on his face. "Don't you ever stop being a hero, mate!"

Charlie wanted to answer, but when he opened his mouth and tried to talk, he spouted water instead.

"'IS LUNGS!" Bob shouted. "'E'S GOT WATER IN 'IS LUNGS!"

Stupidly, that made Charlie happy. He had lungs. Some kind of lungs, anyway.

But he couldn't wait for the Iron Cog's men to catch up. Charlie dug in his pocket and found Brunel's Final Device. He held it in his hand and looked at it. His plan had been to get out of Mountain House and immediately trigger its destruction, but now he hesitated.

If he triggered the device, would he kill the men in the tunnel behind them?

Were they dead already?

If he *didn't* kill them, would they catch Charlie and his friends?

"You ain't comfortable setting off that thing, are you?" Ollie looked intently at Charlie.

Charlie spat up more water trying to answer.

Bob threw a soaking wet arm over his shoulder and shouted right into Charlie's face. "I AIN'T EITHER, MATE. IT'S ONE THING TO STAB A MAN WHEN 'E WANTS TO STAB

YOU FIRST. IT'S ANOTHER THING TO DROP A MOUNTAIN ON 'IS 'EAD WHEN 'E MIGHT NOT EVEN BE FOLLOWING YOU."

Ollie gestured at the pixie barony around them. "Besides, who knows what'll happen to this place if you set off that device? Don't do us much good to squash them if we get squashed ourselves in the bargain."

Charlie finally managed to spit out enough water that he could talk again. "But what if they're right behind us? We're not armed."

"RIGHT AS ALWAYS, CHARLIE," Bob agreed. "SO I RECKON WE'D BETTER GET A MOVE ON. TIME TO 'IT THE OPEN ROAD, INNIT?"

Charlie shook his head. "Thomas needs us. And I have an idea how to find him."

Contrary to certain exaggerated initial reports, Cader Idris was not the site of a battle earlier this week.

"Some people always want to believe that secret societies are at war all about them," said Mr. William T. Bowen, president of the Machynlleth chapter of the Benevolent Society of Mechanicks, Engineers, and Friends of Industry. "But that's just bosh, isn't it? What we have here is a small earthquake and a fire. Fire reflected on a passing cloud can sometimes look very much like a zeppelin, but the society has a registry of all locally chartered airships, and I can assure the readers of the *Cambrian* that no craft is unaccounted for."

The only believed death in this week's fire is local resident Mr. Caradog Pritchard, who, Royal Mail officials inform the *Cambrian*, has not been in to pick up his letters.

—"Cader Idris Fires," *Cambrian News*, 1 July 1887

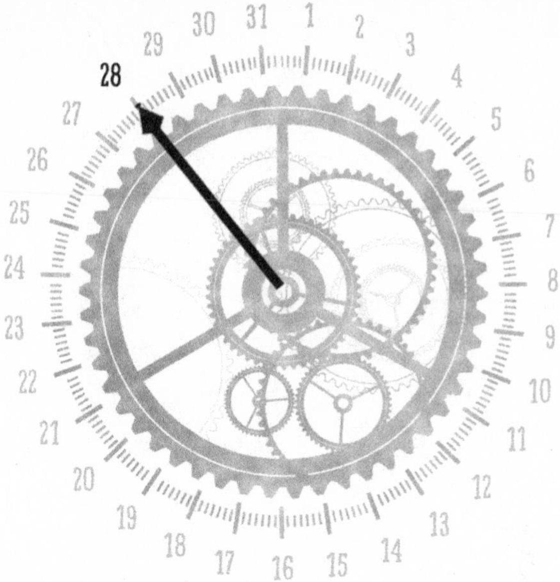

Bob gave Charlie's mainspring a few turns and they left.

The flood of water from Mountain House flowed into the brook splitting Giantseat in two and caused it to swell into a small river. Having found the brook, Charlie and his friends easily made their way to the big-folk gate they'd used before and exited into the high valley on Cader Idris.

The last stars were winking out in a field of indigo brightening into blue as they emerged.

" 'Elp me understand why you want to find Thomas, then," Bob said as she gave Charlie's mainspring a more thorough winding. Her shouting had lasted half an hour, but then her voice had returned to normal. They had seen no sign of pursuit, and Charlie wanted to have as much energy as he could for whatever he'd have to face that day.

"I understand it." Ollie looked at Charlie with piercing eyes. "He don't want to feel alone in this world."

"Charlie ain't alone." Bob finished and Charlie shrugged back into his peacoat. " 'E's got us."

"You're a mate, Bob," Ollie said. "You're a good mate. You ain't a brother."

Charlie felt embarrassed. "Yeah, but also, Brunel said that Thomas was part of his plans. And he said a good engineer always built redundancies into his devices. That means—"

"I know what it means," Bob said sharply.

"I don't," Ollie said.

"Having redemptories means there's a backup plan," Bob explained impatiently.

No one corrected her vocabulary.

"I think *I'm* the redundancy," Charlie said. "So whatever it was Brunel was doing to defeat the Iron Cog, Thomas knows about it. Thomas knows how to *do* it, and if he fails, I'm supposed to do it instead."

"That's a bit of a leap, mate," Bob said. "Your dad ever tell you about 'ow you were part of a plan to defeat an evil organization?"

Charlie wasn't so sure. Hadn't Brunel said that Charlie had also been built to carry out Brunel's plans? That left Charlie very uncertain how to feel about himself, about his bap, and about Brunel.

Also, he had only recently learned he was not a boy of flesh and blood. Now, on top of that, he struggled with the idea that there was a demon in him. Or some kind of demonic power.

Charlie was a mechanical boy. And in some way he didn't quite understand, he was a creature of magic.

It was a lot to deal with.

"I'm with Bob," Ollie said. "Don't go jumping to conclusions. What is it you think Thomas is supposed to do, anyway?"

Charlie hesitated. "I think maybe it's a spell Thomas is supposed to cast."

"You know 'ow to cast any spells?"

Charlie shook his head.

"There you are, then," Ollie said. "Brunel had a plan, and Thomas was part of it. You don't figure into it."

Charlie nodded slowly. "But I still want to help. Brunel is gone and so is his airship full of supplies, but if we can find Thomas, maybe we can defeat the Iron Cog. And I know someone who can help us find Thomas."

He pulled Thassia's compass from his pocket, the one that always pointed to Syzigon's wagon. Its needle swung around and indicated east.

Bob stuck her hands in her pockets. "Sorry we ain't got the flyer no more." Her lip trembled. "This would be a quick little jaunt."

Charlie shook his head. "Even if we had it, I think we'd be better off walking. We'll attract less attention on foot."

They hiked down Cader Idris.

Charlie deliberately kept them away from the trail, instead cutting across sheep pastures and heading east when the trail would have taken them south to Machine-Town. He skirted

Aunt Big Money's burrow by a wide margin, but Ollie still stopped on a high knoll and looked in the direction of the witch rabbit's mound.

He stood a long time with his hands in his pockets, peacoat slowly drying in the morning sun. "Thing is," he eventually said, "all my life, all I've wanted to be is an Englishman. And because I'm a shape-changer, a loup-garou, all my life I've known I'm really French."

"Easy, Ollie," Bob said.

Ollie shrugged. "Each folk has got its magic, doesn't it? The Dutch have got fish wizards."

"Ichthyosaurs."

"I don't think that's quite right, but yeah. And Russians have demon summoners. And the English can muck about with the weather. And the French change shape."

"And dwarfs have finding and not-finding spells, and trolls have blood magic." Charlie wondered about pixies.

"Yeah." Ollie looked at him keenly. "But what magic has a clockwork rabbit got?"

Charlie considered that.

"See?" Ollie's face brightened. "Got you thinking, hasn't it? Because she had something. And it wasn't magic that came from being of a folk. Because a clockwork creation doesn't have a folk."

Ollie didn't mean that in a hurtful way, but the truth of it still stung. A clockwork creation didn't have a folk.

Except maybe Thomas. He had Thomas, if he could find him.

"And you," Ollie continued. "You and Thomas, Charlie.

Turns out maybe you've got magic, too, if I'm understanding that right. You've got magic in you. And Thomas, you think he can *do* magic. And if old Brunel was right about engineering being magic, well . . . he and your dad had the same kind of magic, even though one was from England and the other was from India."

"What are you saying, Ollie?" Bob asked.

"I'm saying maybe people have got it all wrong."

" 'Twouldn't be the first time," Gnat said.

"Maybe magic talent has nothing to do with your folk at all. Maybe it's just a gift, like being tall, or fast, or clever."

"Or ambivalent."

"What?"

"You know. Able to use both 'ands just as well."

"Ambidextrous, Bob."

"You're saying maybe you're not French?" Charlie asked.

"Maybe I ain't French." Ollie folded his arms across his chest. "And maybe . . . I don't know. If Aunt Big Money could learn to do that thing she did with eggs and rocks, maybe I could learn to do a little weather magic. Or whatever."

"Yeah." Bob clapped Ollie across his shoulders. "I reckon you could."

"There's another possibility." No one asked Gnat what she meant, but she pressed on anyway. "Perhaps clockwork creatures are indeed a folk." She pointed at Charlie. "Charlie here is clearly more than a machine."

"I have feelings," Charlie said.

They all nodded their agreement at that.

"And I'd say the same of Thomas and the witch rabbit. So

who really knows? Maybe clockwork folk have a magic and it has to do with scrying, or maybe it has to do with stones or eggs or fire. Or maybe Charlie and Thomas and the rabbit and the two inventors all together make some kind of folk, in a way we don't understand."

Ollie cursed. "That's why I wanted to talk to Big Money."

"Aye, I know," Gnat said. "And I'm sorry. But since we can't do that, maybe we should go find Thomas instead. Maybe he can help us understand more about clockwork folk."

Ollie nodded firmly and led the way.

Bob lingered after the others had marched on, looking down the hill at Aunt Big Money's warren with her hands in her pockets. Charlie stopped and waited for her to catch up; when she did, she whistled, winked at him, and passed him on the trail.

* * *

As before, the compass led Charlie and his friends to the crimson-and-gold dwarf wagons off the highway and hidden in a stand of trees. The wagons abruptly appeared from nowhere once Charlie got within the circle of Thassia's Wards of Distraction.

But this time the wagons weren't a wreck. Three sheyala heads peered from the backs of three wagons as Charlie and his friends approached.

"A certain friend is back!"

Aldrix ran to Charlie and threw himself around Charlie's knees in a tight embrace. Charlie tousled the little dwarf's hair.

The adult dwarfs all came out of their wagons or from the woods. Their faces were deeply lined and their eyes sleepless. Syzigon carried little Yezi in a sling around his chest. "Praise earth and sky," he said.

Lloyd Shankin crawled out from under one of the wagons, brushing dirt and grass from the elbows of his black coat.

"We saw the fire," Yellario said. Syzigon leaned on her as if he might fall over if she stepped away.

"The Old Man is dead." Charlie couldn't think of a better way to say it.

Atzick burst into a long wail. Syzigon and Calphor joined him. They sounded like three wounded wolves, howling at the sky.

"So your warning . . ." Yellario trailed off.

"It got to him too late," Charlie said. "It was too late, even before I set out from London."

"My condolences." Lloyd Shankin made a small, solemn bow.

Yellario nodded. She took little Yezi, shrugging into the sling.

The male dwarfs began unplaiting their beards. They did it while wailing, and Charlie had a hard time focusing on his conversation.

"But worse . . ." Charlie forced himself to continue. "I'm not sure how to say this, but I think you need to know. . . ."

Yellario raised her eyebrows.

"It was dwarfs. Dwarfs betrayed him. Dwarfs working for the Cog."

Yellario pursed her lips. "What colors?"

"Purple," Charlie said. "Purple and white."

Yellario nodded. "Will you come with us, then? You can share our road, wherever we go." She pointed at her husband, whose wailing continued to grow louder. "It's not ordinarily my place to offer, but a certain dwarf who can get things done must mourn now. I'm sure the invitation will be approved."

"Isn't he worried about being heard?" Charlie asked. Syzigon had been so emphatic about secrecy.

Yellario nodded. "This is a sacrifice certain dwarfs make to honor their friend the Old Man."

"The Wards are still in place," Thassia said. "They'll be as loud as they're able, and I'll do what I can to keep anyone from noticing their lament."

"Naught so queer as folk," Ollie muttered.

"Are you not going to mourn, then?" Gnat asked the dowser. "Did you not also know the Old Man of Mountain House?"

Thassia watched Atzick fall to the ground and pound the earth with both fists. "There are other ways of mourning than men's ways."

"Will you come with us?" Yellario repeated.

"Maybe afterward," Charlie said. "It's a generous invitation. But now I must find . . . I must find, and maybe rescue, a certain boy who is my brother."

Yellario, Thassia, and Patali all stared.

"I didn't know you had a brother," Thassia said. "Do you mean . . . ?"

"He is the Old Man's son. Like me, he is a created boy."

Comprehension spread across the women's faces. Patali and Yellario nodded, but Thassia frowned.

"It might be easier to help you if you were more . . . *traditional* brothers. Are you made from the same materials? Maybe from the same design?"

" 'Ere now, no need to be *rude.*"

Charlie raised a hand to wave off Bob's indignation. He knew what Thassia wanted.

"Ollie," he said. "Can I have the scarf?"

Ollie's face showed he was puzzled, but he handed the scarf right over. Charlie passed it to Thassia. "This belongs to a certain boy who is my brother. Will it serve? Can you help me find him?"

Thassia nodded. "Only make sure a certain lad who is your friend"—she nodded in Ollie's direction—"doesn't stand too close to the dowsing rod. The scarf may want to find him instead, since he's been wearing it recently." She looked closely at Charlie. "You say this boy is a made boy, as you are?"

"Yes."

"Only 'e ain't 'alf so brave as Charlie."

Ollie laughed. "Ain't none of us half so brave as Charlie."

"Wait here." Thassia climbed into her wagon.

Yezi was beginning to fuss, probably from the wailing sound her father and uncle and grandfather were making. She pulled at her own tiny beard and whimpered, and Yellario sang a droning tune in guttural words.

Thassia emerged from the wagon with a long piece of copper wire and a pair of pincers in her hand. "You'll be the one using this?" she asked Charlie.

Charlie nodded. Thassia took his hand and guided it to grasp the wire. She nodded her approval.

Then, as Charlie stared, Thassia bent the end of the wire, twisting it back along its own length and then out again to create a Y-shaped fork. She knotted Thomas's scarf around the joint and wrapped it tautly along the wire's length.

She grinned at Charlie. "This will do the trick. Now keep your grip tight."

Rubbing the pincers up and down along the length of the wire, she began to chant.

In traditional story, the Cantre'r Gwaelod existed in the land now covered by Cardigan Bay. There are two principal accounts describing how the Cantre'r Gwaelod flooded. In one, a young woman named Mererid assigned to continue emptying a prodigious well neglected her duties, and the overflowing of the well drowned the land. In the other, an officer named Seithenyn failed to maintain the county's seawall, which ruptured, leading to a deluge. Both stories are tales of negligence and resulting loss, but in each one the church bells of Cantre'r Gwaelod are still diligent: in times of danger, they ring out a warning from beneath the waters of the bay.

—Royal Geographical Society, *Gazetteer,* "Drowned Hundred"

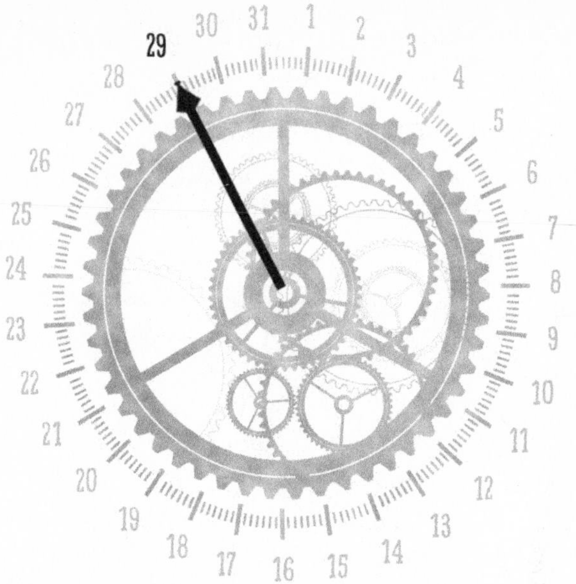

Charlie looked about him for watching eyes and saw none.

The metal dowsing rod with Thomas's scarf wrapped around it was dipping down, toward the lake.

The sliver of moon coming up over the mountains in the east and turning the angel in the center of the lake into a dark-eyed gargoyle told Charlie it was late. He stood again with his friends on the shore of the lake in the park adjacent to Plas Machynlleth.

And under the dark waters, Charlie again saw lights.

"I know what you're thinking, mate," Ollie said. "Don't do it. You don't know what's under there."

"Yeah," Bob agreed. "Could be photogenic sharks."

"Photogenic?"

"You know. Sharks as glow in the dark."

"Phosphorescent, Bob." Ollie scratched himself. "Yeah, that wouldn't be the strangest thing I've seen since I left London, not by long odds."

"Or 'ave Lloyd 'ere sing 'em all to sleep again first."

Lloyd Shankin had insisted on coming along because he wanted to be useful. Now that he had his chance, he shook his head. "I don't think that would work, not unless I could see them."

"Even then," Ollie agreed, "those Cog gents didn't all fall asleep the first time, did they?"

Lloyd nodded glumly and looked at his feet.

" 'Ere now," Bob said. "Lots of 'em did fall asleep, an' that's the key thing, innit?"

Charlie pointed. "The lights aren't moving, and I read in *Flora and Fauna of the Mediterranean Sea* that sharks can't stop swimming, or they die."

"Dead sharks aren't less 'orrible. After all, you got to wonder what killed 'em."

"It's not sharks. This is a lake. Sharks don't live in lakes." Charlie considered. "I'll take a look and then I'll come right back."

"Yeah." Ollie hefted a short length of heavy wood. "You come right back, or we come in after you."

"You can't swim, mate," Bob told her friend.

"I don't have to swim. I just have to sink and be able to hit with this club."

Lloyd scratched his chin and looked thoughtful.

The chimney sweeps' bluster made Charlie feel good. "Wait right here."

He handed the dowsing rod to Lloyd Shankin and waded into the lake.

The water was cold, though it was summertime. The lake must have been fed by the melting ice packs on Cader Idris.

Three steps in and the ground disappeared beneath Charlie's feet—he sank.

Charlie tried to kick, which did no good—he was too heavy to swim—and he stared up. Through the lake's surface all he could see was a shaking silvery band that was the stars, rippled by the water, and shadows where his four friends stood. As he fell, a stray root caught at his ankle and threatened to turn him upside down. He wobbled, bumped his knuckles against the steep slope, and nearly pitched over.

But he kept his head, and after a few seconds he turned to examine the lake beneath the surface of the water.

There were no sharks.

Instead there was a glass dome. The monument in the center of the lake, he saw, didn't rest on an island, but on the height of the dome. It stood like the cross on the cupola of a church, or the weather vane on the peak of a house.

The dome was built of curved panes fitted into iron frames and sunk at their base into the floor of the lake. The panes were taller than Charlie and almost as wide. The floor, Charlie now saw, was not a natural lake bottom covered with sediment and weeds, but was paved with large slabs of stone. The lake was artificial. It was a stone bowl, steep-walled and filled with water, the purpose of which seemed to be to hide this dome.

From one side of the dome, a tunnel of glass extended and connected into the wall of the lake. The passageway was peaked, with a curve to its surface that reminded Charlie of minarets he'd seen in books. It ran in the direction of the Plas Machynlleth—if a person in the palace basement knew which door to open, he could probably walk right through the tunnel and into the dome.

Opposite the glass tunnel, a steel box the size of Pondicherry's Clockwork Invention & Repair clung to the side of the dome. It reminded Charlie of a steel carriage house attached to the side of a glass house.

Beyond the structure lay dark space—Charlie stared, and he thought he saw the opening of a cavern in the wall of the lake.

There were people inside the dome, and one of them looked like Thomas.

Charlie plodded forward. He wished he *could* swim—swimming was fast. Instead he walked, and the water resisted, and he worried he might not have enough power to rescue Thomas when he finally got to him.

Inside the dome, light came from six globes sparking with blue fire atop tall brass poles. Similar glowing spheres hung on thick cables running along the minaret-arched ceiling of the tunnel.

Charlie crept up to the base of the dome.

He could see into the steel box now. There was a pool of

water, and it ran right up to the far wall, and in the water floated a vessel. The steel box wasn't a carriage house—it was a boathouse! The vessel looked like a canal boat—long and thin and pointed. Only this canal boat didn't seem to have windows; it was made of steel, and it had a large circular blade attached to the hind end.

But how could the canal boat go anywhere? The pool didn't have any visible exits.

Three men Charlie knew stood in the center of the dome: the heavyset speculator William T. Bowen, wearing a green frock coat; the Frenchman Gaston St. Jacques, in his long black cape; and the kobold Heinrich Zahnkrieger, wearing a waistcoat and rolled shirtsleeves such as Charlie had seen him wear many days in Pondicherry's Clockwork Invention & Repair. It didn't surprise Charlie to see the Iron Cog's men down under the lake, but he did stumble backward for fear of being seen . . . until he realized that the lights inside the dome probably meant he could see in but the Cog's men couldn't see out.

What hurt him—what felt as if a nail the length of his forearm had been driven through his chest—was the sight of Thomas.

Thomas was unmoving. He held still, frozen, immobile. He might as well have been a statue. And he was being carried by two men into the steel box.

A flicker of movement inside the dome caught Charlie's eye. The tiling of the dome's floor was interrupted by a band of glass running across the middle. Something was moving under the glass.

As it moved, it churned the water and generated a cloud of sand and dirt, but Charlie saw flashes of metal and teeth. He wasn't sure whether he was seeing the champing teeth of a huge mouth or the threshing teeth of a gear wheel.

Or both.

Whatever the thing was, it was emerging from under the glass dome into the lake.

Charlie heard a whine behind him. He grabbed the iron frame of the pane in front of him and turned himself around—

BANG!

Something slammed into him. Because he was turning, Charlie caught the blow at an angle. Instead of being pinned against the dome, he bounced and skidded up it.

His chest *hurt* where he'd been hit.

Charlie looked at what had hit him and almost froze.

It looked like an enormous wild boar. A huge gearwheel circled on each side of its small body, driving its motion. Two long spikes protruded from the front of the device like tusks, and two arms with pincer hands sprouted from its top. India rubber tyres dragged it around the ground, but they were in a strange pattern, four to a side, with the front and rear tyres raised. Charlie wondered why the tyres were arranged so oddly, until the machine charged the dome—

and the front tyres dragged it neatly up onto the glass and straight at Charlie.

Charlie jumped.

He couldn't swim, but with the strength of his legs he

could kick away from the surface of the dome, and he did, slowly somersaulting through the water. The charging device whined as it turned after him again.

Charlie landed—

and a second machine lanced him in the side.

Charlie fell, and the eight heavy tyres of the second machine ground over him like stampeding cattle. He cried out, felt his chest fill with water.

He clapped a hand to his side. The fabric of his skin had torn. So had the metal underneath. Charlie felt a whir of cogs within himself.

The machine growled and reversed direction to run over Charlie again.

Charlie rolled, reached up—

and dug his fingers into the axle connecting two of the wheels. He picked himself off the floor, hugging the underside of the machine, and found he was being carried along for the ride.

Toward the dome.

He looked past his feet and saw Thomas being loaded into the canal boat.

And a wall, a sheet of steel, was slowly dropping from the ceiling where the box and the dome joined. The steel box, with its pool and its vessel and Thomas inside, was being sealed off from the dome and from Charlie.

The machine groaned in complaint and reversed direction again.

The first machine rumbled past. Its pincer hands scratched

at the stone about it, churning up more dirt and sand and obscuring Charlie's view of Thomas.

The machines couldn't find Charlie. Even the one he was clinging to didn't realize he was there.

He waited until he had a clear line of sight, then straightened his arms, extending himself as far from the dome as he could—

and snapped himself forward, feetfirst, like a rocket.

His aim wasn't perfect. His heels and back banged along on the stone, and it was a good thing it was smooth slate. He skipped, and eventually his trajectory turned into a bouncing roll, but when he came to rest, Charlie was leaning against the glass dome.

The boar stopped and turned toward him. Charlie didn't see eyes, but with the spikes coming out of the end of each machine, he felt as if two wild animals were staring at him and pawing the earth. He had come into the thicket as a hunter, but the animals had cornered him.

The boars charged.

Charlie scrambled to his feet and lunged sideways.

His legs didn't push him fast enough through the water, so he grabbed the frame of the dome with both hands and pulled. Charlie rocketed forward, rushing as fast as he could toward the hole he knew had to be there.

He heard the rumble and rattle grow louder behind him as the boars gave chase.

And there it was.

The hole the boars must have come out of.

The hole opening into a tunnel underneath the dome, under the band of glass in the dome's floor.

The dome's frame created an iron lintel running over the top of the tunnel. Grabbing it, Charlie dragged himself into the tunnel.

He bent at the waist and yanked his feet up after him—

KA-CHANG!

The nearer of the two boars rammed against the tunnel opening. It was too big to fit into the passage coming at it from an oblique angle, so it jammed its tusks in, narrowly missed Charlie, and ground at the floor with all its tyres.

Charlie ignored it and dragged himself onward.

There had to be a way up. A hatch. For maintenance, or to lower a boar from the dome down into the tunnel.

But he didn't see one.

Behind him, he heard grinding and clawing as the boar repositioned itself. Then, with a whine, it charged him.

He risked a glance in its direction. The boar almost entirely filled the tunnel, and as it raced toward Charlie, it held its pincer hands low on the ground.

There was no room to go over or under. Charlie would be trampled, grabbed, or impaled.

Then he heard a whine from the other direction. Feeling a heavy sinking in his chest, Charlie looked, and he saw that the tunnel opened into the lake at the opposite end, too—

and that *that* exit was now blocked by the second boar, also charging in his direction.

There had to be a hatch. There just had to be.

Charlie dragged himself as fast as he could with both arms and kicked with both legs.

The boars came closer.

There had to be a hatch.

Only there wasn't.

The growling and whining of the boars was so loud Charlie could barely think.

He stopped, stood, braced his feet against the floor and his shoulders against the glass and then hurled himself up.

The glass didn't shatter—

but, as Charlie pushed, a long plate of it bumped up and slid aside.

Charlie dragged himself out of the water.

With a muffled thud, the boars collided. Water sloshed up out of the hole, but Charlie didn't wait to see what happened to the machines that had been trying to destroy him.

The steel wall sliding down from the ceiling was only a few feet from the floor. Thomas was on the other side.

Charlie tumbled to his feet and ran.

Of all Britain's folk, dwarfs are surely the least hospitable and the most mistrusting of outsiders.

—Smythson, *Almanack*, "Dwarf"

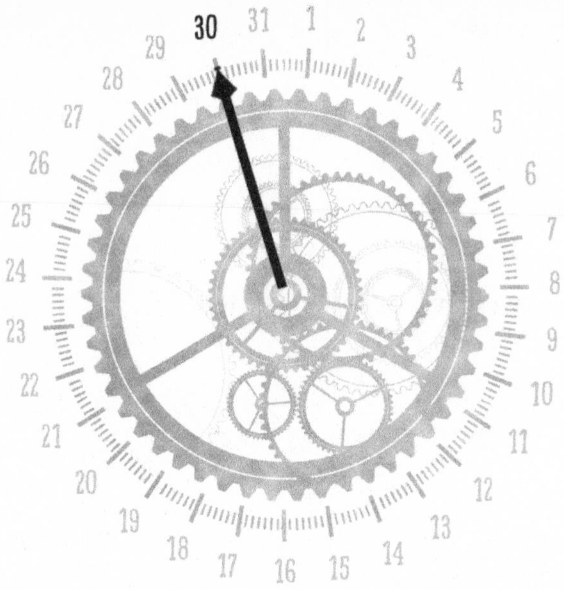

Charlie threw himself onto his belly and slid.

It hurt. The skin of his chest felt as if it were being scraped right off, and his shoulder caught on a lip of upraised slate, turning his slide into a violent tumble that sent him rolling headfirst into the metal box.

WHAM!

The steel wall slammed down behind him, shutting him in.

Charlie staggered to his feet. Water poured from the hole in his side. He coughed and spat water up from his lungs. But he didn't stop his ragged run.

The thing he'd been thinking of as a canal boat was airtight, top and bottom, and made of sheets of metal riveted together. Closer up, it looked more like a cigar than a canal boat.

The strange craft bobbed in a long pool, and as Charlie

rushed toward it, the Frenchman Gaston St. Jacques stepped into a hatch on top of the vessel.

In his mind's eye, Charlie saw the same Gaston St. Jacques, just a few days earlier, hurling Charlie's bap to his death out of a leisure-wheel carriage.

Charlie erupted into a sprint. The Frenchman was gripping the hatch cover and about to shut it behind him when Charlie's foot hit the top of the boat.

St. Jacques looked up. His mustachioed face twisted into the same disdainful curl Charlie had seen when the man had murdered his bap.

"Bowen!" The Frenchman pulled a pistol from his belt.

Charlie ran faster. As he pushed his gears to extend themselves beyond their ordinary range, he felt his insides warm and tremble—and he saw St. Jacques's sneer evaporate.

Before the Frenchman could bring the pistol up to bear, Charlie slammed into him. Gaston St. Jacques grunted as he tumbled backward. Charlie pounded him to the boat's deck, knocking all the air from the man's lungs.

Then he noticed the burbling sound.

Charlie looked up. A second steel wall, this one on the opposite side of the chamber, began to rise. The floor surrounding the boat's pool was already submerged, and as the wall rose, air bubbled out of the room and water flooded in.

Charlie looked back down at the vessel he was standing on. It was airtight, and the blade at the back was a propeller.

The craft was built to travel underwater. It was a submarine vessel.

Bob would have been fascinated.

BONG!

Something struck Charlie in the back of the head.

Bells. Maybe it was because of the blow to his head, but Charlie could have sworn he heard bells ringing, over and over. They sounded like church bells. And they seemed to surround him.

He fell forward. His head butted Gaston St. Jacques in the belly, and Charlie felt a moment of satisfaction to hear the man lose all the air in his torso again. Then Charlie bounced off the Frenchman, slipped, and fell into the water.

He hit the slates beneath the submarine boat and scrambled to his feet. The vessel was rising steadily and was now beyond his fingertips.

Charlie crouched, aimed, and jumped.

Whoosh!

He hurtled out of the water so fast he cleared the submarine boat's deck and launched a few feet into the air.

William T. Bowen turned to stare, a length of lead pipe in his hand, so Charlie crashed down on top of him. Bowen dropped the pipe into the water and tumbled in after it.

Charlie climbed to his feet—

and found himself looking down the open barrel of St. Jacques's gun.

"Help! Help!" William T. Bowen thrashed in the water, keeping his head from being submerged, but only barely.

The ceiling was only a few feet over St. Jacques's head and getting closer.

"Again?" The Frenchman sighed. He pulled back the hammer of his pistol with a loud click.

Then he fell sideways.

Charlie looked down to see four arms emerging from the water and grabbing Gaston St. Jacques by both his ankles.

Heaven-Bound Bob surged out of the water. With one hand she pulled herself up, and with the other she yanked one of the Frenchman's feet left. Ollie, meanwhile, dragged St. Jacques's other leg in the opposite direction.

Bang!

The gun went off, but missed.

Bob and Ollie heaved, and Gaston St. Jacques yelled. Then the Frenchman did the splits and somersaulted backward off the deck of the ship—

"No!" Bowen cried in the water below—

St. Jacques crashed on top of him.

Ollie shifted immediately into his snake form and came aboard. Charlie grabbed Bob by the forearm and yanked her up. Behind Bob, singing, was the dewin Lloyd Shankin. Charlie seized the Welshman's high black collar and dragged him up, too. He still held the metal dowsing rod with the scarf wrapped around it.

None of Charlie's friends were out of breath, even though they must have dived to get to the bottom of the lake.

Bowen and St. Jacques were in the water, but he had no time to think about them. He didn't even have time to talk—he shoved Bob and Lloyd down the hatch. Ollie slithered in along with them, and then Charlie dropped in after.

He found himself standing in a short vertical shaft, pressed shoulder to shoulder against Bob. At the bottom, a horizontal passage stretched through the ship. Glass bulbs set into the walls and containing tiny humanoid figures, just like those within Bowen's steam-truck, gave light.

The hatch cover scraped the top of the steel box.

Bob kept her head. She grabbed the cover and yanked it shut, elbowing Charlie aside in the process. The inside of the hatch had a latching mechanism shaped like a ship's wheel; Bob spun it tight with quick and confident motions.

Bamf! Ollie the boy appeared in the horizontal passage. In the closed space, the rotten-egg smell was worse than usual.

"Like you been a sailor in this getup for years," Ollie said.

"Me an' machines." Bob shrugged. "Natural friends, I guess."

"Where's Gnat?" Charlie squeezed past Ollie and started down the passage. It was narrow for Lloyd, but for Charlie and the two chimney sweeps the hallway was wide enough to be comfortable. There were tanks and levers set into the walls of the passage, all of them labeled and most of them attached to gauges. Charlie didn't take the time to look closely.

"I came after you," Ollie said, "once I saw those metal things trying to grind you up. Bob jumped in after me."

"I didn't see 'er," Bob added. "I reckon she's up on the shore, ain't she?"

"You couldn't have cut that any closer," Charlie said. It wasn't a complaint.

Lloyd Shankin grinned. He looked huge in the tight space. "It was the Drowned Hundred that got us here."

"You sang an englyn?" Charlie asked. "A song about the Drowned Hundred let you come down?"

"No hero should have to fight alone." Lloyd nodded. "So I brought you your folk!"

"But not Gnat?" Charlie did worry about her.

Lloyd Shankin said, "I cast the spell on her, too. Maybe she just didn't follow us."

"I breathed water like it was air," Ollie said.

"It wasn't swimming, Charlie!" Bob laughed. "It was . . . running in water, an' you got reason to know I ain't much of a swimmer."

Charlie came to a shut door. "Who's operating the ship?"

The door was a solid metal sheet, with a round glass panel set at eye level. Charlie pressed his face against the glass sheet and had his answer.

Through the glass he saw the craft's control room. At a central seat, with a viewing scope to one side of him, charts to the other, and a steering wheel in front, sat the kobold Heinrich Zahnkrieger.

Thomas, still frozen, leaned against the corner of the chamber.

Zahnkrieger met Charlie's gaze.

He chuckled and then picked up a speaking tube from the console in front of him. His voice boomed out of a metal cone set into the wall near Charlie's head. "Charlie Pondicherry, welcome aboard!"

Charlie grabbed the door and shook it. It wouldn't open.

"Don't waste your time," the kobold said. "You're a powerful little machine, but not that powerful. And if you are, any force that would rip the door open would likely damage the hull and sink us. You would survive, of course. But your friends might have trouble. Indeed, since we are at this moment traveling through an underground river, your friends would almost certainly die."

"He doesn't know about the Drowned Hundred," Lloyd whispered. "Don't you worry about us, Charlie. If the ship sinks, we'll breathe just fine as long as we need to."

Ollie and the dewin crowded Charlie to peer over his shoulder.

Bob stroked her chin, looking at the locked door. Then she turned to the side, pried open a panel with several gauges mounted on it, and began digging in the pipes and wires behind it with both hands.

"You don't need my brother!" Charlie shouted.

The kobold cupped a hand to his ear and shook his head. "Sorry, my little automaton, I can't hear you! But don't worry, soon we'll be able to have all the conversations you like."

Bob crept forward next to Charlie, on her knees. "Keep 'im talking." She started probing the door's lock with a pair of stiff wires.

"Put him to sleep!" Ollie hissed to Lloyd Shankin.

"And then who'll pilot the ship?" The dewin moved his lips and furrowed his brow as if he were making a great effort to think of something. "We're locked out."

Charlie cast about and found a speaking tube on his side of the door. He pulled it to his mouth. "You don't need the other automaton." The word *automaton* felt like ashes and salt on his tongue.

"It's not any affair of yours what I need!" Zahnkrieger snapped.

Charlie remembered then that, although his father had finished the automaton Queen Victoria for the Iron Cog that ersatz queen had been captured by the police—by honest police—in Big Ben. So maybe the Cog did still need whatever technology was built into him and Thomas.

Or maybe they knew Brunel's plan. Perhaps they knew that Thomas—and Charlie, too?—was designed to put an end to their schemes.

"You could let us go," Charlie said softly. "You and my father were partners. Do you really hate him so much?"

"I didn't hate Joban Singh," Zahnkrieger said. "This isn't personal at all. And I *will* let you go." He chuckled. "In not very many minutes, we'll surface in the southern Irish Sea. We'll be met there by friends of mine. They will be very happy to see you."

Click. "Got it." Bob dropped the bits of wire. "Give 'er a try."

Charlie pushed the door—nothing.

"It's barred!" The kobold laughed. "You know, if you opened the hatch right now, you, at least, could probably escape."

"What if you took me instead?" Charlie said.

Heinrich Zahnkrieger laughed.

Bob grabbed the speaking tube from Charlie and covered it with her hand. " 'Ave you lost your mind?" she whispered.

"Thomas knows more than I do," Charlie said. "About Brunel's plan, I mean. Maybe I am the redundancy in the plan and maybe I'm not, but either way I don't know what to do next. We need Thomas to defeat the Iron Cog. That makes him more important than me."

Ollie spat on the floor. "No offense, mate, but no. You're my friend. Thomas is . . . I dunno, he's something to you, but to me he's nothing."

"We're not going to trade you, Charlie," Bob agreed.

Lloyd nodded vigorously.

The kobold's laughter continued to boom over the amplifying cone in the wall. Charlie took up the speaking tube again.

"What's so funny?" he asked.

"Don't you see, Charlie?" The kobold stopped laughing and beamed at Charlie, his pointy little nose and ears looking devilish in the dim light of the control room. "I have you and the other automaton both. I also have your friends. You have *nothing in the world* to offer me!"

Bonk!

Heinrich Zahnkrieger suddenly slumped forward, unconscious.

Behind him, on top of a control panel, stood Gnat. She was wet and bedraggled, but she was smiling.

She dropped the bottle of water she held in both hands and leaped over to the kobold's panel to take the speaking tube. It looked gigantic with the pixie's arms wrapped around it and its open mouth pressed to her face.

"Sorry for the delay," she said. "It took me a few minutes to find something to hit him with."

These are certainly not all the cities, towns, rivers, mountains, moors, forests, and counties of Britain. This island contains many places too small to describe in a single volume such as this. And this world yet holds many secret spots, unknown to the general traveler or indeed unknown to all.

—Royal Geographical Society, *Gazetteer,* "Other Places"

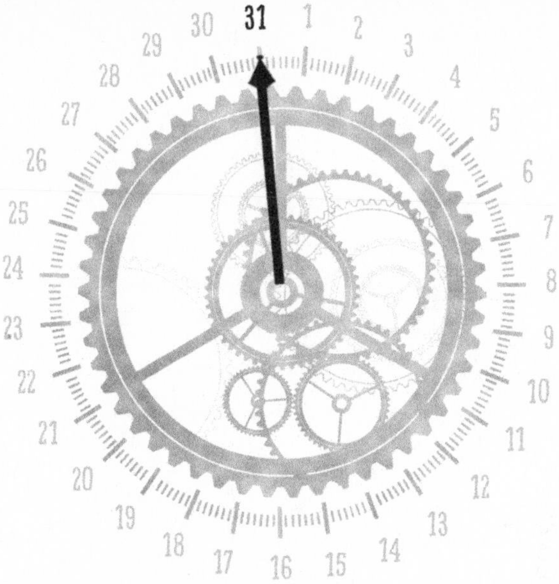

It took Bob an hour to figure out how to operate the submarine vessel, by which time Heinrich Zahnkrieger was awake, as well as tied up and gagged. Charlie would have liked to ask the kobold questions, but Zahnkrieger was a redcap, a wizard whose magic could interfere with machinery. It would be bad enough if he targeted Charlie—if he cast his spells on the boat, he could kill them all.

All the while they were underwater, Lloyd Shankin sat with his ear pressed to the wall of the ship. "There are no windows to see out this vessel," he explained when asked. "So I'm *listening* for *sounds* of the Drowned Hundred."

"Your englyn worked," Charlie said, "whether or not there really is a Drowned Hundred."

Lloyd only nodded.

If he ever heard what he was hoping to, he didn't tell the others.

Once Bob brought the submarine boat to the surface, Charlie and Ollie were able to row the kobold to shore in an India rubber raft. They left him there, tied to a tree far above the waterline and gnawing fiercely at his gag. He'd escape sooner or later, but not before they were long gone, and he wouldn't be casting any spells in the meantime.

Charlie would have liked to take the submarine craft, but he was afraid the Cog might have some device aboard that would let them find it, or even destroy it remotely. So Bob gleefully sailed the craft a few miles north along the coast and then, somewhat less gleefully, ran it aground on a stretch of rocky beach.

"A waste of good machinery, that is," she sniffed, marching up into the trees on the western slopes of Cader Idris toward a sky beginning to brighten in the east.

Lloyd and the chimney sweeps all took knapsacks stuffed full of provisions from the submarine boat. Bob's knapsack included a belt of tools. Each of the sweeps also had a straight, sharp machete at the belt, but Lloyd declined one when Ollie suggested it. At Charlie's belt hung the dowsing rod Thassia had prepared, the metal one that would find Thomas . . . just in case. Gnat walked leaning on a spear she'd fashioned from a long rod yanked from one of the craft's control assemblies.

Charlie had planned to say good-bye to Lloyd Shankin on the beach. Lloyd had other ideas. "I'm still condemned for trying to help your friends, and probably for escaping from gaol now, too. I'm a criminal, Charlie. I think if I stay in Wales, I'll end up hanged. And after all, I can as easily find good deeds to do wherever you lot are bound."

"Maybe we're more to each other than just the guardian of the fairy gate," Charlie said.

"I'm glad you'll be coming along, Mr. Shankin," Gnat added. "I'll have need of someone with your storytelling gifts once I've done two more deeds."

Lloyd Shankin patted the knapsack where he'd stowed two new journals, both taken from the submarine boat, and laughed.

Charlie carried Thomas.

He didn't want to wake his brother up until they were safe. He knew Thomas was skittish—*shy* had been Brunel's word—and he didn't want Thomas to run away. It was easy enough to stop every twenty minutes and ask Bob to wind his mainspring, and that let him march rapidly with the other boy slung across his shoulder.

The other boy. Charlie needed better words to use when talking and thinking about Thomas, but in their march up to Giantseat he wasn't able to come up with any. *Brother* it would have to be.

Gnat found another big-folk gate into the abandoned barony. They lay in the narrow crack leading into the cave until past noon, watching to be certain no one followed them.

They found the nests again, and the steel wall Charlie had ruptured with hand grenades. The waters unleashed in the destruction of Mountain House had mostly dried up, leaving only a few puddles, and the gap in the wall was plugged with debris. Charlie threw Brunel's Final Device onto the rubble and sat as the sweeps ate.

The fairy barony was entirely new to Lloyd Shankin. He stared at everything and barely managed to get down a couple of bites.

"Charlie," Gnat said, wiping crumbs of ship's biscuit from her tiny mouth, "will we be staying here long?"

"We came here for you," Charlie said. "We'll stay as long as it takes."

"I, for one," Bob added cheerfully, "am quite interested to see the metempsychosis of the thing." She settled in, leaning against her knapsack like the back of a seat, munching on a strip of dried beef.

"Metamorphosis." Gnat laughed. "Well, that isn't quite right, but I'll do my best to entertain you."

Charlie never saw where Gnat's webbing came from. After situating herself into the low center of a convenient nest, the pixie proceeded to weave her arms about her in a complicated pattern that seemed never exactly symmetrical in the execution, even though it looked entirely symmetrical in the result. She might have been pulling silk from the palms of her hands, or her mouth, or from the nest itself, but a ball of silk built up around her and she slowly crouched forward into her sleeping position, until all that remained was a puffy white ball that filled the nest.

Lloyd wrote the entire time, transfixed.

Ollie whistled low when Gnat had finished. Then he

yawned, pulled his bowler hat over his face, and began to snore.

Charlie gently eased Thomas over onto his belly. "Can you help me find his mainspring, Bob?"

It turned out to be quite easy to locate, once they'd rucked Thomas's shirt up under his arms. It looked like twin crescent-shaped depressions, right between Thomas's shoulder blades. Once they'd gone that far, though, Charlie had to stop and stare.

"Do I look like that?"

"You're 'andsomer. But yeah."

Bob had opened Charlie up once, and Charlie had a sudden impulse to open Thomas up, too. If he looked inside his brother, wouldn't it give him an idea of how he himself was built, inside? And maybe Bob could tell him what differences there might be.

But Charlie resisted.

It felt wrong to think about opening Thomas. Not that Thomas wasn't a machine—Charlie knew that he was. But Thomas had a right to privacy. Machine and magical creation, yes, but Thomas was a person. It was bad enough that they were pulling his shirt up while he was unconscious; looking inside his chest without his permission would be much worse.

Maybe later he would ask Thomas's permission.

He turned Thomas's mainspring, cranking it all the way to fully wound.

"Interesting that old Pondicherry and Brunel didn't put those things on your bellies," Bob said. "I reckon you could

’ave ’ad just as much power with the spring tightener on the other side, an’ then you could ’ave done the tightening yourselves.”

Charlie had a dark thought. “Maybe they didn’t want us to run away.”

Lloyd Shankin stopped writing. “Or maybe they didn’t want you to realize you weren’t flesh and blood. Maybe they did it out of love.”

“Maybe,” Charlie said. “Though Thomas knew he was a made boy. I think he always knew.” So had Brunel put the mainspring on Thomas’s back to control Thomas, as Syzigon had once controlled Charlie?

And what did that say about Charlie’s bap?

Charlie found he had many dark questions about his bap. With Bap dead, could he possibly ever get answers?

He probed his side with his fingers and found the hole left there by the mechanical boar. He resisted an impulse to stick his finger inside and feel his own gears.

Thomas rolled over and sat up, then scooted away on his hands. “What happened?” His eyes shot back and forth between Charlie and Bob.

Bob laughed. “An ’eck of a lot, mate. You fell, the mountain exploded, we all ’ad to ’old our breath a couple of times, an’ then there was this submarine ship.” She looked sad. “I kind of liked the ship.”

Charlie patted Bob on the shoulder. “I liked the submarine boat, too. But I like Thomas here quite a bit more.”

“Yeah.” Bob nodded. “I reckon Thomas is all right.”

Thomas didn't look consoled. "Is my father safe? What happened?"

Charlie didn't have the heart to tell him. The dwarfs' weeping had been bad enough. He tried, but found he could only shut his mouth and stare at his own shoes.

"Look," Bob said, "there ain't a good way to say this. You was sold out. Betrayed, by those dwarfs in purple. They done for your dad."

"You should know," Charlie jumped in, "your father saved your life."

"Yeah," Bob agreed. "That's right. 'E threw you right out of the airship, an' you lived."

"But the airship exploded." Thomas's eyes looked enormous. "I remember. And then . . . men with guns, and machines."

"Yeah." Bob and Charlie both looked at the ground.

Thomas slowly climbed to his feet. "You saved me?"

Charlie stood, too. "We're brothers." He took a step toward Thomas.

Thomas took a step back. "Not really."

"You're as much a brother as I'm ever going to have. Also, your father said you knew his plans. You knew what he was going to do to stop the Iron Cog."

Thomas was quiet for a long time, looking off into the dark corners of the cavern. "Yes," he said at last. "And more than that. I know his spell."

"His spell?" Ollie sat up abruptly. "So it's true, is it? You're a magician? You and Charlie here?"

"Not so fast asleep after all, eh?" Bob elbowed her friend. He ignored her.

"You know a spell?" Ollie asked again.

Thomas nodded. "Only one. But my father thinks it will defeat the Iron Cog."

Ollie squirmed, but Bob held him back.

"What does it do?" Charlie asked. Would it destroy him and Thomas? And was Charlie also built to be able to cast the same spell?

And what had his bap intended for Charlie?

And how had his bap felt about Charlie, really?

Thomas shrugged. Did that mean he didn't know what the spell did, or did it just mean he wouldn't say? "It's the reason I was made."

"That can't be the only reason your father made you," Charlie said. "I saw the way he held you. You're his son."

Thomas looked down at his feet, and his shoulders slumped.

"But that sounds like a spell worth knowing," Lloyd Shankin said.

Thomas nodded, and he looked again into the darkness. "If you will excuse me, I'd like to have a little time to myself. To mourn my father."

Charlie nodded.

"Of course," Bob said. After gritting his teeth, Ollie managed a nod as well.

Thomas shuffled slowly away. He was a tiny figure, frail and alone. He looked over his shoulder several times, and then the shadows swallowed him.

"'Ow long do we let 'im stay out there?"

Charlie patted the dowsing rod. "As long as he likes."

Ollie lay back again, but he left the hat off his face this time.

"You're thinking about Aunt Big Money again, ain't you?" Bob asked him.

"And Thomas. And Charlie."

Charlie was thinking about the witch rabbit, too, but he doubted his thoughts were much like Ollie's. He remembered the vision in three parts the witch had shown him. The grave in the pit. The river on fire. The monster on the peak.

What did it mean? Did it have to do with the spell Thomas thought he was made to cast? And what was Charlie's role? Was he just Isambard Kingdom Brunel's backup plan?

And what would happen to him after the spell was cast?

William T. Bowen had described Charlie's father's death as a sacrifice. And Isambard Kingdom Brunel had used almost exactly the same language about Thomas.

What, really, was the difference between them? *Was* there a difference?

"Aunt Big Money showed me a vision," he said.

"I remember," Ollie said. "It ended with you falling on the floor and screaming."

"Part of the vision was a boy standing beside a grave. The boy knew a secret, and I thought it might be me. But Aunt Big Money said no vision was that simple."

"You reckon it was Thomas?" Bob asked.

"I think it was *at least* Thomas." Charlie thought a moment. "Maybe it was more than that, too."

He slipped a hand into his coat pocket and cupped his

father's broken pipe. He would get it mended as soon as he had a chance.

Thomas didn't come back.

Ollie, Bob, and Lloyd ate several times and slept twice. When they were awake, they talked, but Charlie wasn't in the mood to chat, so mostly they waited. Charlie thought about his vision, about Brunel and his bap, and about Thomas. Lloyd wrote many pages. When asked if he was working on a song, all he would say was "Mmm."

A few hours after Gnat spun herself into her spherical cocoon, her wings began to show. They poked straight up from the silk, and at first they looked like glossy leaves. Charlie stared hard at them and thought he could almost *see* them getting bigger as he watched.

When they were half-sized, they started to flutter. Slowly. They looked wet, but none of the four ventured to touch them.

"You know, we left the flyer up on top of this 'ere rock when we went into Mountain 'Ouse," Bob said, "an' I saw it wrecked."

"You can't be sure, Bob," Ollie said gently. "Maybe the flyer's all right."

"Nah," Bob said, "it's burned to nothing, mate. Along with the spare bits for Charlie, I reckon." She looked down at the submarine tools. "So these will have to do."

Ollie nodded. "Sorry about the flyer."

"I'm more sorry about those spare parts." Bob nodded at the pixie's budding wings, which took a deep flap as if acknowledging her interest. "I suppose the baroness could go 'ave a butcher's."

"Butcher's hook, look," Charlie reminded himself. "Gnat's not the baroness yet."

"Nah, but she will be. You see the way she killed that 'Ound?" Bob scratched her chin. "I wonder if she can count the kobold as one of 'er three . . . what is it, three deeds?"

Ollie snorted. "You're dreaming, mate. Three mighty beasts. If that fussy little midget counts, she might as well come pick a louse off my neck and call it number three."

"You 'ave lice, Ollie?"

"Nah." He shrugged. "A louse never sticks around once I change into a snake."

"Nice flange benefit, that."

"Fringe, Bob."

There was a soft, wet tearing sound, and Natalie de Minimis rose. Strands of silk fell off her like a gown, and she stood in the torn remnants of her cocoon. She smiled broadly and flapped her beautiful, full-sized, iridescent green wings.

"I'm ready," she said.

ACKNOWLEDGMENTS

Thanks to Michelle Frey, Stephen Brown, and the rest of the team at Knopf, for shaping my stories into things of greatness.

Thanks to Deborah Warren, for connecting me with editors and cheering me on.

And thanks to Kevin J. Anderson, Rebecca Moesta, Alexi Vandenberg, Quincy J. Allen, Aaron Michael Ritchey, Ramón Terrell, Michelle Corsillo, Cat Rambo, Barbara Buffington, and my other fellow laborers in the WordFire shop, for helping Charlie Pondicherry find friends all across the nation.